j.h. white

Azygos

a novella

Azygos ā-ˈzī-gəs

(n) a vein that receives blood from the right half of the thoracic and abdominal walls, ascends along the right side of the spinal column, and empties into the superior vena cava

(adj) not being one of a pair: single

1

...Ever since that day, it haunted her. Like dull blades sawing through flesh, that one memory grated through her mind, and sometimes she could feel herself slipping away. But it was only recently that her resolve began to falter. Others were starting to see her weakness through the tiny cracks that etched their way into her visage. They would stare or ask questions and she would plaster the cracks with excuses or ignore them altogether, but those cracks began to build upon themselves, shifting her foundation and crippling her resolve. Each night was either labeled as good or bad. This night happened to be the latter.

The wet air licked at Marlowe's hands and face while the amber light of a lamppost receded behind her as she walked beside the narrow street. Gravel crunched beneath her footsteps while insects hummed and clicked in the trees along the lane. A light summer shower fell in cool droplets, forcing her to pull her jacket up over her hair causing little brown wisps to dance out from underneath the hood. Marlowe's lips tightly pursed together in annoyance, but a small part of her was happy she didn't have to trudge down the street alone. She looked over her shoulder and watched as her lone companion Lydia fought against the shower and gathered her red curls onto the back of her head with a clip. They bickered softly in the night.

"I don't see why he thought it necessary to make us get out of the car," Marlowe curtly stated, kicking a twig out of her path.

Lydia nudged Marlowe with her shoulder. "Maybe because you and Evangeline wouldn't stop arguing the entire way."

"Dorian could easily have made her get out of the car instead," Marlowe laughed.

"Evangeline? Walk?" She paused to stare blankly at Marlowe. "I think you *are* losing it," Lydia chuckled to herself.

Marlowe gritted her teeth and looked away from Lydia's smiling face. She decided to walk a little faster, her boots landing a tad bit harder on the gravel than they had before. It was the same reaction every time. Whenever someone would point out Marlowe's obvious instability or crack a joke on her behalf, she would be forced to confront her own demons, and Marlowe hated confrontation. Lydia stopped in her tracks and looked up toward the sky in irritation.

"Fuck," she said under her breath as she trotted up to Marlowe. "I'm sorry. I didn't mean it like that."

"No. It's fine," she replied as she pulled the hood closer around her face. They walked in silence for a few minutes.

"Do you want to talk about it?" Lydia quietly asked.

"No." Pressing her tension to the side, Marlowe decided to change the subject. She fished in her thoughts before catching a topic that Lydia was sure to stick to. "Do *you* want to talk about last night?"

Lydia blushed and attempted not to smile. "There's nothing to talk about."

"That's not what it looked like. You totally liked him!" Marlowe teased as she skipped forward a few steps.

"I guess I did," Lydia confided.

Marlowe couldn't help but pry. "But…"

"But it takes a lot to make it work out. I mean…the long distance, the different schedules, not to mention that we are two totally different kinds of people, if you forgot that little obstacle."

Marlowe placed her arm around Lydia and hugged her as they walked. "Yeah. I see what you mean," she sighed.

Lydia smirked, "You know what this reminds me of? The two of us, alone on the side of the road?"

Marlowe playfully nudged Lydia out from under her arm, "If this is your attempt at humor, it's not working."

The rain began to lighten until all that could be heard were a few drops falling from the trees into muddy puddles along the street. Marlowe would occasionally glance at her watch but was more annoyed than relieved when the passage of only a few minutes goaded up at her. Another lamppost beamed at them from further up the road, and a light wind curled its way around their faces. Marlowe and Lydia inhaled, turned to each other, and smiled. They quickened their pace.

As they rounded a bend, they noticed a small sedan parked off to the side of the road. Its hazard lights were flashing into the darkness and the hood was perched open. Marlowe bit at her lip in anticipation. Her fingers began to twitch as if all of the nerve-endings in her body spurred her forward toward the broken-down car. The pressure was relentless, and they had to keep themselves from sprinting to the sedan in excitement.

"I thought men were supposed to be good at the car thing," Marlowe yelled out to the car with a smile.

A young man poked his head from around the hood and wiped his hands on his jeans. "I thought I was," he said.

Marlowe walked to the front of the car and bent curiously over the engine. He motioned to the innards of the car with his cellphone's flashlight. "I think it's the battery."

"But your hazards are on." Marlowe cocked her head to the side and smiled.

His bright eyes locked onto hers and sighed, "Yeah…I have no idea what I'm doing."

Marlowe bit at the inside of her cheek when he smiled. The man couldn't have been more than twenty. His jeans were frayed around the pockets and cuffs and his skin was slightly sunburned. Marlowe noticed him toying with the loose gravel on the side of the road with his sandal and sheepishly looked at his car. She offered her hand in reassurance.

"I'm Marlowe," she said.

"Bryce," he replied as he shook her hand. Another man walked gingerly from around the side of the car. "And this is my brother Chad. Well, not my real brother. My friend."

Lydia took a few steps out from behind Marlowe. "I'm Lydia," she said with a wave as she gawked awkwardly at Chad. After a few seconds of self-conscious silence, Marlowe leaned in between their stares.

"It's nice to meet you guys, but I'm sad to say that batteries are the extent of my car knowledge," she explained with a regretful sigh, "and Lydia here doesn't know much about them either."

Lydia's intense concentration broke at the mention of her name. "What? Oh yeah, I don't know anything," she quickly trailed.

Bryce's eyes shifted between Marlowe and Lydia. Finding their behavior amusing, if not a little odd, he answered, "It's okay. We called a tow truck and they should be here in an hour." He held up his phone.

Lydia playfully shoved Marlowe's shoulder with one hand, "You hear that? One hour until they get here."

"Can we borrow your phone?" Marlowe asked, "Because ours are dead and our car broke down not too far from here."

"Yeah. You can use mine," Chad answered. His eager voice rang through the cool air and Lydia practically tripped over herself to follow him around the hood of the car to the passenger door where his phone awaited.

Marlowe and Bryce continued to lightly converse. He relaxed into their banter and leaned up against the bumper of the car. Marlowe pulled her hood down from around her face and tied her hair into a neat ponytail. Every now and again, she would lean over to inspect the mechanics under the hood or lightly touch him as they laughed, but after a few minutes Lydia and Chad's soft chatter from the side of the car became silent and was replaced by the briefest sound of scuffling against gravel.

"Chad?" Bryce called from the front.

Marlowe followed him around to the side of the car, a tinge of excitement hidden beneath her worried face. He stumbled on the gravel and froze. Chad was slumped onto the ground next to the open passenger door. His blood-soaked t-shirt was torn open, and his empty eyes focused past his friend into the distance. Blood dripped down from Lydia's face and onto her chest as she struggled to wipe herself clean. Marlowe pointed and burst into laughter.

"Shit. Did I miss a spot?" Lydia smeared blood to the clean side of her face, not helping in the least.

"Stop. Stop," Marlowe chuckled, "You're making it worse!"

Bryce doubled forward and moved to touch Chad's forehead, but his hands couldn't even make it halfway. He looked up at Marlowe, her laughter cutting into his paralyzed body like a knife. He rose to his feet and tackled her. After a quick grapple, Marlowe spun on top of him and rammed his shoulders into the ground.

"Don't you ever," she threatened him as she slid his phone from his hand. He struggled against her, but she effortlessly held him. His face sunk to a gray pallor as the fine points of her teeth glinted in the night. Lydia began to whine.

"I can't get it off!" she whimpered.

"Here. Give me your sweater," Marlowe sighed as she stood and moved to help her.

Lydia removed her green cardigan and helplessly handed it to Marlowe. Wadding the cardigan up into a bundle, Marlowe dabbed at Lydia's ears, neck, and chin. She smeared the beads and rivulets of blood across her skin but couldn't soak all of it up with the expensive cashmere, so Lydia flailed her arms and groaned against the slow progress. Amidst their low laughter and amusement, Bryce struggled to find his footing as he attempted to back into the woods. Marlowe and Lydia paused just long enough to hear his slow, stumbling footsteps and they turned to him as a predator might regard its wounded quarry.

"Aren't you going to get that?" Lydia asked. She became worried as she glanced at Marlowe's inaction, and feared for a sudden repeat in dangerous behavior. "You can't just let him go...you know that Marlowe."

Marlowe focused onto the man with an unblinking stare before she flicked her hand, shooing him into the woods behind them. He cut behind the brush and began to run as quickly as his legs could carry him.

Lydia grabbed Marlowe's arm. "What are you doing?" she yelled.

As if Lydia's doubt had pulled her from a trance, Marlowe ripped from her hold and bolted after him, tearing past bushes and over fallen trees. She hesitated at every intersection of foliage to inhale the scent or study the ground. The mix of perspiration and cologne was barely concealed by the smells of cedar and birch. It was incredibly teasing to Marlowe. Every time she brushed past the leaves on a branch where he had rushed by it left that teasing scent. It lingered on her skin and propelled her forward toward its source. The closer she stalked that intoxicating scent, the more she could taste it. Marlowe could even feel the blood pulsating through her target's veins, the capillaries contracting as he ran. The top of her mouth began to water as she resisted the pain in her jaw and the emptiness in her stomach.

Suddenly, she stopped and grazed the contours of her teeth with her tongue. Marlowe slowly turned on her heel, making sure to be quiet around the crunching leaves. She released a soundless breath as she listened. And then she heard it. The thrumming of a frightened heart against a cage of bones. The sound was exhilarating. She leisurely crossed to the terrorized noise emanating from behind a large oak tree. Leaves shuffled and quickly stopped. He was trying his best to hide, but not succeeding. She waited, unmoving, for as long as it took for him to feel secure. His fluttering heart slowed, and she could smell the conviction in his will to survive.

As he stood to creep out from behind the tree and run, Marlowe grabbed him by the collar and threw him to the ground. His fear overtook him for the last time forcing his pupils to dilate, his brow to furrow, and his fists to clench. She could feel the inescapable pressure on her canines. It was as if every part of Marlowe's body wanted what was just below his skin. Her posture tensed. Her eyes narrowed. Even her teeth ached. In one quick motion, she clutched his arm with one hand and pushed her other against his face, stretching his neck. She inhaled his scent through her nose, opened her mouth, extended her canines, and tore into his throat.

*   *   *

Marlowe wiped her mouth on the edge of her sleeve as she

gracefully walked back to the stranded car. She didn't mind the blood on her coat. It was black, the better to disguise stains from a successful meal, and she could always acquire another. Her long, dark hair bounced over her shoulders, a full stomach giving her that extra skip in her step, but her uplifted mood didn't last long after she had passed the tree line onto the street.

A red SUV was parked in front of the sedan and a man was talking in hushed tones with Lydia. He had piercing, steel eyes and deep, brown hair that almost appeared black in the night. He towered over Lydia, which made his frustration look even more formidable. Marlowe coughed slightly as she walked up to them. They immediately separated from their conversation. His face relaxed as he attempted a look of pleasantry. He was about to speak when Marlowe cut him off.

"I know, Dorian. It was reckless," she tried her best to appear apologetic and regretful, but Lydia and Dorian could see through it, and instead of bickering they both decided to leave it alone.

A petite blond exited the car followed by another man. She had not been able to acquire a meal, and it left her face in a hungry sneer. "What took you so long?" she inquired.

"Nothing. I was just having some fun." Marlowe fought to control a smirk adding, "And how was your night?" She knew perfectly well from Evangeline's tone she had not eaten.

"It was brilliant. I *watched* Oliver eat, and then, after he was through…I helped him clean his mess." Oliver suppressed a smile as he leaned monotonously against the vehicle. He wasn't as tall as Dorian, but his broad shoulders and soft features contrasted nicely with his brother.

"How was your night, Oliver? You look as though you might have had more fun than me," commented Marlowe.

They all looked Oliver over, noticing that his hair was unkempt and his button-down shirt was missing a few too many buttons. His blue eyes happily met Marlowe's. "Oh, as a matter of fact I *was* having a bit of fun before I fed. Actually, come to think of it, I was allowing *them* to have a bit of fun."

Evangeline turned and glowered at him from under her

eyebrows as her wavy blonde hair fell from her fingertips. Her sneer was expected in these situations like the nervously awaited buzzer on a kitchen timer, and her narrow eyes and pursed lips were just as obnoxious. Marlowe and Lydia looked amusedly over at Oliver for the punch line of his story, but Evangeline's cold gaze made him decide to keep his mouth shut this time.

Dorian decided to answer, "Well, we managed to arrive at the house and these two women were immediately smitten with Oliver here, so he obliged them. Granted, it probably didn't end the way they were expecting."

Evangeline took Oliver's hand in her own, a slightly possessive reminder to him. Oliver quickly changed the subject, "And how about you Dorian? That girl couldn't have looked more than twenty-two."

"Twenty-one actually, and she was lovely. She actually called me 'tall, dark, and handsome.'" Dorian looked more than pleased with himself as he puffed his chest out like a peacock.

Marlowe beamed up at him, "I would have to argue with the 'handsome' part."

He looked at her questioningly while he opened the passenger door for her. "I'm hurt," he played, touching his hand to his heart. She smiled and grazed a finger alongside his cheekbone as she stepped into the car.

Lydia moved to the sedan and looked helplessly down at the stiff body lying next to the car. "Hey Oliver, want to help me with this one?"

Oliver grabbed Chad's body by the shoulders, leaving the feet for Lydia.

"Really? I always get the feet!" she whined as she wrapped her hands around the ankles.

"The head is the heaviest part of the body. I'm doing you a favor by taking this end," Oliver argued with a wink. They carried the body with ease, but they had little care for Chad's dangling appendages that haphazardly knocked on branches and pushed through brambles. Evangeline followed behind to gather the flip-flops that had fallen off of the dangling feet and cover their tracks as they disappeared into the woods.

Marlowe looked at Dorian as he watched them leave. His voice softly broke the silence, "Marlowe. You're growing more reckless." He was unable to look her in the eye.

She spoke slowly and under her breath. "What do you mean?"

"You let him run; and from what Lydia said, *encouraged* it. What if he had found help or escaped you? I'm beginning to think you want to relocate again." He was treading carefully, but his rage began to seep through his calm exterior. "Someone could have easily found him."

"But *I* found him," Marlowe interrupted.

"We don't need another incident like the one in Boston."

"I know." Marlowe was hard. Quiet. Her mind was distant. Dorian paused and surveyed her face for any indication of an impending argument. He couldn't find any. The tension lifted.

"All right," he said, "Move over." Marlowe slid to the middle seat as Dorian slipped into the SUV.

Lydia came skipping out of the woods. Humming a familiar tune, she slammed the car hood of the empty sedan down and locked the doors. She scribbled a quick "Ran out of gas. Walking to a station" on a piece of paper and placed it under the windshield wipers of the car before checking the area for any evidence. After a thorough inspection, she made her way to the car and jumped in beside Marlowe and Dorian.

Oliver and Evangeline slowly broke through the bushes. His arm was wrapped around her shoulders, and he delicately played with the tips of Evangeline's hair as they walked. In the process of concealing the body all had been forgiven, like usual, and they lovingly peered into each other's eyes like delusional newlyweds, every flaw and annoyance being covered with adoration and amusement. They were in love. The kind of love that made Marlowe jealous, but nauseas at the same time, and if the saying "opposites attract" had a marketing campaign they would be plastered across billboards and smiling up from brochures.

Evangeline was high maintenance yet beautiful with a voice that sounded put-on and bubbly. She could make an insult sound like high-praise, and she was very used to getting her way, especially with Oliver. His debonair looks and mischievous smile always appeased Evangeline, but, like a double-edged blade, that same laid-back charm and easygoing attitude caused much of their relationship strife.

They giggled and quickly lowered their affection in front of their family's gazes. Oliver moved behind the wheel and Evangeline perched next to him in the passenger seat. With a start of the engine, they headed out toward the city. The car wove down the street and an occasional lamppost would illuminate the inside of the car to reveal Lydia flipping through a map or Evangeline fiddling in her purse.

Marlowe looked up through the open moon-roof into the night sky. The wind lightly howled over them as clouds rolled in the distance. Welcoming the fresh air, she inhaled the aroma of the passing trees. Clean. There was something invigorating about it. The air restored her from the sensory overload of the night's hunting. The muscles in her face relaxed around her eyes and while searching the stars she felt that familiar burn of someone watching her. She turned to see Dorian looking at her, just as she expected.

"What are you thinking?" He placed her chin between his forefinger and thumb.

She lied. "Nothing."

normal circumstance. Something was very wrong. The three of them retrieved their flashlights revealing new pools of light around the basement. Sloan couldn't keep his breathing steady. His heart raced and his stomach was beginning to tighten. His insides grew hard and heavy as if they had suddenly turned to stone. Something else had heard the loud noises, too.

They weren't alone.

Across the room, they could hear rustling and fluttering, but their flashlights were always one step behind the sound. Sloan's light fell upon an old rocking chair. Its seat was falling through, and it creaked as it rocked back and forth. He swallowed hard. Jess's beam of light darted around the room as she placed her gun over her flashlight. Sloan followed suit, but his hands couldn't help but shake. The barrel of his gun rattled next to his light.

Suddenly, a massive figure lunged out of the darkness and into his father's path. The imposing attack amidst snarling teeth and grasping limbs was lightning fast, but Sloan's father was quicker. He fired two silent shots into his chest, and as quickly as the male had appeared from the darkness he faltered on the bullets and dropped to the floor. Sloan glanced pleadingly up to the basement window covered in aluminum foil.

Get me out of here, he thought to himself, wishing he hadn't been forced to come on this expedition, and an idea was born.

Sloan turned his gun and light to the window, relaxed his shoulders, and fired into the panes of glass. They shattered to the floor. Light poured into the room uncovering a geography of haphazard antiques and garbage. A mattress surrounded by photos and books lay in the far corner, exactly where Sloan had heard the breathing. The noise settled just like the dust that found its way back down to the furniture where it had been disturbed. In a matter of seconds, the frantic attack had ended. The chaos of moments earlier was eerily contradictory to the silence now flowing through the basement, so quiet that Sloan felt as if he might have gone deaf. He walked toward the mattress, his gun by his side, his face tired.

Jess moved about the room looking under tables and behind

shelves and paused next to a nearby desk. She lifted her gun and fired one quick shot into a cowering female hiding from the penetrating sunlight.

"That didn't go as planned," Jess curtly stated as she turned toward Sloan. "Did it?"

Just then, Patrick quickly rushed into the room followed by his father, holding David's body. Jess's eyes fell and a white pallor overtook her face. Sloan couldn't move. His feet planted to the hard ground beneath him as if cement had dried around his boots. They laid David's body onto a tattered sofa crumbling in the center of the room, and spoke quickly, lower than Sloan could hear. Even if he could understand them, he wouldn't be focused on their words. It was the situation unfolding before him on the matted, brown couch cushions that held his gaze.

His father looked blankly at Sloan. His throat was hoarse and, even though he was holding back his emotions, he kept his voice calm and collected. "You do it," he said as he held a gun in Sloan's direction.

"What?" Sloan could barely get the words out of his mouth. His father couldn't be asking what Sloan thought he was asking.

"Hurry up. There's not much time," hissed his father.

Sloan walked to the sofa. Each step landing loudly in the silence of the room. He trudged toward his father as if he was being led to a slaughterhouse. His mind raced.

It's fine. They're just overreacting.

As he reached the rotting sofa he swallowed uneasily. There, huddled on the cushions, was his brother David. Blood was rolling out of his neck and right arm, pooling beneath his body and soaking into the tattered cushions, but David wasn't dying. He was sweating in waves and his hair was matted into wet clumps against his forehead. Instead of slowing with every passing second, his pulse was racing. Sloan could see the veins on his arms, neck, and face thudding under his pale skin. He was losing so much blood, but his body was not reacting the way it should under normal circumstances. Sloan felt a hand on his shoulder. He suddenly realized that tears were beginning to sting his eyes and his throat was stiff and dry. He tried to swallow the intruding lump in his throat, but he couldn't.

"You have to know what it's like." His father's voice was soft but troubled. "It's painful – both options are. But you have no other choice."

Sloan turned and looked into his eyes. He searched for a choice, an option, any alternative but this. He couldn't find one. "You want me to kill him?" He could barely ask the question.

"David would have had the courage to pull the trigger if it was you." His father said the words with a hidden menace that Sloan hadn't heard in years. It was barely noticeable, but it was still present in his deep voice. His father wished that David, his first born - his prodigal son - wasn't the one on the floor. He wished that it were Sloan instead.

Sloan took the gun from his father's hands and held it loosely in his own. He didn't want to look at David's body again and decided that his attention would best be served concentrating on the weapon in his hands. He flipped it over and over. His eyes penetrated into each crevice of the gun's smooth shape. David's body began to convulse slightly, shaking the sofa beneath him. Sloan hesitantly pointed the gun toward his brother's trembling body. His mind fought back and forth between pulling the trigger and dropping the gun to the floor.

You have to know what it's like, Sloan repeated to himself.

He took a sharp breath in, placed his finger on the trigger, and took one final look at David. The bleeding had stopped and his body no longer seized, but Sloan could hear his brother's heartbeat. It was louder and more pronounced than his own, conflicted pulse. Sloan looked toward the open gashes that now appeared cauterized. David was still very much alive.

"I can't!" Sloan struggled between gritted teeth. He was unable to drop the gun to his side, frozen in place staring at the face of his fallen brother.

Patrick took the gun violently from Sloan's hands, stepped to David's body, cocked the gun, and quickly fired two shots into his brother's head. David went limp.

The room was still.

No one moved until a passing car horn was heard from the street outside of the condemned house. It was hard to believe that the world still existed, still moved forward.

Sloan's head hung in shame as his sister and father left the cold, unwelcome basement to retrieve the gallons of gasoline waiting on the back step. Whatever remorse, sadness, or anger they were feeling wasn't visible to the outside world. It was just another heaviness that they had to force into themselves to carry for the rest of their lives. Their footsteps receded until Patrick and Sloan could no longer hear them on the stairs. Patrick turned toward Sloan and paused, staring at his face. Moments passed before Patrick broke his stare to pick up his bag and move toward the door. A few feet after passing Sloan he stopped and turned. Sloan did not reciprocate and continued looking blankly down at David's limp body. He felt as though every emotion and thought within him was about to overflow like boiling water tipping over the brim into the fire beneath.

Patrick's words cut into Sloan. "You know...David wanted to stay home for this trip. He wanted one week of peace..." He had more to say but couldn't get the words out.

*   *   *

The car ride back to their hotel was filled with an impenetrable silence. It was as if the world around them had been put on mute and nothing could tear them away. The four of them sat motionless in their seats as Jess drove steadily up and down the rolling streets of San Francisco. Their father stared emotionless out the passenger window, sunlight hard against his stone face.

Glancing across his left shoulder, Sloan could see that Patrick was leaning his forehead against the window. His breath was controlled against the glass, too controlled. As Sloan watched him, he noticed that Patrick was not only controlling his breathing, but also his thoughts. His face was torn between rage and sorrow underneath the barest mask of restraint.

Taking his eyes from the agony of his brother, he moved his gaze toward his own hands. They seemed inadequate in comparison to Patrick's, or even David's. He turned his palms over one by one and surveyed their smooth surfaces. They lacked the scars and calluses that the rest of his family had developed. His hands were unaccustomed to the cold steel of guns, and although he had learned to shoot when he was a child, he still never felt truly comfortable with one in his hands. Sloan suddenly felt an overwhelming surge of guilt wash over himself. His open palms turned closed and hidden, and he looked out of his own window to keep from looking at the occupants of the car. His mind was spinning. Every part of him was a disappointment to his father, right down to his unscarred hands.

He forced his racing thoughts back into their cages. *They can't blame me.*

As if she had felt the air in the car change with his mind, Jess sighed, "It's okay. David would have wanted us to." She paused and considered. "He would have done it to any of us if we had been bitten."

That was true. David would have pulled the trigger, but Sloan wasn't David. Sloan didn't want that ultimatum. He knew the consequences of inaction. Their father had told them of the process, but it was different for Sloan to actually see it up close, even more difficult because the change was taking place in his own brother. He knew that once the bite had taken hold, David wouldn't have just died. He was an ideal candidate, one who was physically able to withstand the change. His heart was strong, and his arteries were clean. Instead of bleeding out, the toxins would have changed his brother. He would have writhed and trembled. It would course through his veins like a snakebite. His heart would have sped up to incredible speeds to either sputter to a quick finish and die or withstand the strain of the venom and grow stronger, every cell in his body absorbing it and evolving. Sloan wished that David would have just died, but he wouldn't have. His brother would have stayed on that tattered couch until he woke up, heart beating at an unwaveringly rapid rate for the rest of his life. And

David would have stood up and been different; he would have tried to live normally, but that would prove impossible. So, while Sloan stood over his brother's body aiming the gun, he knew this, he knew the path David would have taken and the darkness that he would have receded into, and he still couldn't go through with it.

Nearing their hotel on the outskirts of the city, the car travelled down the road; and as the electric current of anxiety was absorbed into the stained gray fabric of the seats, Sloan could sense a change in the air. Anger and sorrow were replaced by weariness. He was encouraged by this shift in the mood and hoped that the rest of his family was edging out of their rage as well. Patrick sighed and turned toward the window, but this time his face was more relaxed. His sister's knuckles relaxed on the steering wheel, and his father was preoccupied with something. His head looked toward the floor and his shoulders were slumped over in concentration as he looked down into his wallet at a small photo. The corners were worn and there were deep creases around the edges. His father traced the image lightly with his thumb. Sloan had seen him do this many times before, but it was a ritual that he couldn't take his eyes away from - the tender caressing of a small photograph of his mother. Her hair was loose and wavy around her shoulders as a soft wind caught under the strands. She looked into the distance rather than at the camera and it was obvious that she was laughing at the precise moment the camera captured her.

Sloan's eyes darted down again at his hands. He felt like he had temporarily intruded upon a private moment of his father's, and he chose not to think of the members of his family being ticked off of a list. Their hobby had always been a job to him, a burdensome thing that they were thrown into, and he couldn't wait until it was finished. He wanted nothing more than to move on. But now, after all he had experienced, all he had witnessed that day, he was resolved with newfound commitment. He vowed never to be the one looking nostalgically at worn photos in his wallet.

Marlowe snapped up in bed. Her body was drenched in a warm sweat causing the hotel sheets to cling to her legs. She shook slightly as she grasped her hands together in order to calm her rattled nerves. Peering around the room, she noticed that the others were still fast asleep. Dorian lay unmoving beside her. He hadn't been woken up by her turning dreams as she had been. The digital clock on the bedside table glowed a red "5:05 PM" into the darkness, and sunlight still peeked around the corners of the heavy curtains, only managing to creep a few inches into the room. She had about an hour before her family would begin to wake and pack for the final leg of their trip home. Refusing to fall back asleep, Marlowe quietly crept from the bed.

She grabbed a set of clean clothes from her suitcase and snuck into the bathroom. Clicking the door closed, she flicked on the light and laid her clothes upon the toilet seat before turning the hot and cold faucets in the shower. Warm water shot out of the spigot and flowed into the tub. She grasped the edge of the sink as she peered into the mirror. Marlowe was still shaken by the images that had burned into her nightmares. Her face brought her nightmares to the surface and worried crevices dug into the small space between her eyes. She rubbed them away and tried to relax her muscles, forcing her dreams into the back of her mind.

Studying the reflection, she criticized her features. Little had changed in the many years she had looked into mirrors, and every time she gazed upon her face it was as if a memory was brought forward to implant itself upon this time. Everything around her continued to change and morph, but her face always stayed the same. The same expressions. The same intent. The mirror became a self-portrait, lost in time, continuously moving into each new decade with every passing tick of the clock.

Getting closer to the mirror, she leaned forward over the sink. There was a difference in this portrait that she hadn't seen before. Her eyes held a slight age about them. The lids were a fraction heavier, and microscopic crevices played near their edges. No one would ever notice these infinitesimal changes, but Marlowe could. In the past ninety years, she had aged about one in comparison. Immortality was a myth, but her unchanging reflection had always caused Marlowe to consider herself devoid of that necessary conclusion of life. It made her feel invincible, until this singular moment in front of the mirror in a hotel just off I-80 West in middle-of-nowhere Nebraska.

A small knock tapped on the bathroom door. Marlowe jumped. The bathroom was filled with steam and her reflection was barely visible. She had lost herself in the mirror. Realizing she had been staring past her own image for longer than she meant, Marlowe quickly undressed and jumped into the shower.

"Yes?" she called as she began to wash her face.

"The sun just went down. We're going to leave in about thirty minutes," Lydia explained through the door. When she opened it a crack, steam poured into the bedroom. She cocked her head down and whispered, "You alright?"

Marlowe paused in the shower. "I'm great. Just wanted to get an early start." She attempted to sound buoyant amidst the clamoring sounds of water hitting porcelain, "I'll be right out so you can get in here."

"It's like a sauna in here." Lydia reached in and turned the bathroom fan on to disperse the steam before she shut the door.

Marlowe quickly finished washing her hair and turned the faucets off. She dried, dressed, and brushed her teeth. Upon opening the door, Evangeline bustled by with her toiletry bag and closed the door behind her.

"Really? She needs makeup on a road trip?" Lydia jibed as she clicked through the images in her camera.

"There is no harm in looking your best," Oliver quietly countered as he brushed and styled his hair in a mirror.

Lydia flung herself on the bed in boredom. "In my day, we would have had a name for those kinds of people."

"In your day, you believed mud and flowers made everything better." Oliver winked over his shoulder at Lydia and sat down on his bed to tie his tan leather shoes.

Lydia laughed, "In my day? Oliver, the 1960's weren't that long ago. And for your information, mud baths and essential oils are now fashionable."

Marlowe sat across from Dorian. He carefully folded his map and placed it on top of Marlowe's bag as he looked across the table and smiled. The same worried crevices had once again formed between her eyebrows.

"If you don't stop that you're going to get wrinkles," he joked. Dorian leaned over and playfully rubbed at them with his thumb.

"Do you want to go check-out with me?" Marlowe replied as she took a long breath to relax her face. Dorian nodded as he grabbed his and Marlowe's bags and flung them over his shoulder.

"When Evangeline gets out, bring the car around front for us?" he asked Oliver. He nodded as Marlowe and Dorian exited the hotel room. They removed the *Do Not Disturb* sign from the doorknob and flipped it over to *Please Clean*.

Nebraska's night air meandered by as they walked to the front lobby. Marlowe sighed, "I found a wrinkle."

"A wrinkle?" Dorian laughed.

"Well, not really a wrinkle. More of a heaviness around the eyes." Even as Marlowe said the words she began to laugh at her own worry.

Dorian offered his arm to her. "The first time I noticed that I was aging I was actually relieved."

Marlowe took his arm and looked curiously up at him.

He looked down and smiled as he continued, "To know that you are a part of the world is a comforting thing. Looking back now, it amuses me that the smallest fraction of a wrinkle on my brow could cause me to think so much more about my place, that I am moving with time, not outside of it. I wasn't a nightmare or a monster anymore." He paused at this thought. "To die is to live, and I became alive. Everyone dies, Marlowe."

The conversation fell silent. Nothing more had to be said. She considered all that he had shared and imagined what Dorian would look like in another two-hundred years, if he would appear more to be thirty-five than thirty and if, like human aging, they would eventually lose their strength and, with it, their minds. It was as if life had set up a track and each species had its own lane. Insects ran their tracks at an incredible speed, and so they came to the finish line all too quickly. Humans ran it at a steady pace, giant tortoises at an even slower pace, and then there were those like Marlowe, who had been given a lane of tar. Moving slowly and steadily through life but moving none-the-less.

They reached the hotel lobby and smiled as they came up to the waiting receptionist.

"Hello! How may I help you?" she warmly said with a grin.

Marlowe looked down at her nametag. "Hi Melanie. We wanted to check out."

Melanie took their room keys and began to close out their account while Marlowe watched from the counter as Dorian went to the front doors to help an elderly couple with their luggage. The cumbersome old-fashioned luggage struggled to fit through the door, and Dorian smiled politely as he dislodged it. He held a small conversation with the couple about their trip, their family, and the possibility that they should find some new luggage with wheels. They laughed and argued that travelling with luggage you were forced to carry reminded you of where you had been. Dorian nodded his head and held out his hand in farewell before walking back to the counter.

"Excuse me, ma'am?" Melanie was looking intently at her.

"I'm sorry. What?" Marlowe stammered. She had become lost in Dorian's encounter.

"Did you find your stay comfortable?" she cordially asked.

"Oh," Marlowe replied, "Yes."

"You know, most people travel during the day, so you don't have to pay for two nights."

"Less traffic," Marlowe shortly answered.

"And it would probably be safer while you drive, so you're not all alone on the highway," prodded Melanie.

"There's always truckers." Marlowe's stomach growled.

"It would beat checking in at dawn and leaving after dusk." She couldn't help but pester Marlowe with the point.

"But then I probably wouldn't have met you." Marlowe gave a wry smile. The tips of her canines were a fraction more extended.

It caught Melanie by surprise, and she averted her eyes to the computer screen. "All right. That's a two-night stay, no phone calls or movie rentals. Would you like me to put it on the card?"

"No. Cash, please." Marlowe handed her five crisp twenty-dollar bills and some change.

"Here's your receipt." Melanie handed her the receipt and quickly hustled away from Marlowe's hungry glare into the back office.

As Dorian and Marlowe exited the lobby, he softly asked, "What was that about?" Dorian looked accusingly down at her.

"What? She was being nosy." Marlowe pulled her hair into a ponytail and hopped into the waiting car.

"What did the couple have to say?" Marlowe asked Dorian.

He took an old, leather-bound book from his bag and opened it to a cloth, ribbon bookmark. "They were heading across country on what they called a 'third honeymoon'. It sounded nice, especially at their age."

Marlowe grinned as his eyes lit up. She had always enjoyed how Dorian shared a certain amount of compassion for humans.

Lydia turned in the front seat and stared back at Marlowe and Dorian. "Does anyone else think it's strange that you converse with your food so much?"

"It's not much different than humans who accommodate their chickens or can find a calf amusing or sweet," Dorian quietly replied as he began to read.

"Maybe, but I think it's kind of masochistic." She continued to look through her camera, deleting inadequate photos from the last leg of their journey.

Marlowe put her feet up on the center console. "I think it's an endearing quality."

"Thank you. I happen to enjoy learning about a person's history as well as their future." Dorian flipped to the next page.

"Where are we stopping to eat?" Evangeline leaned forward

and wrapped her arms around the driver's seat to Oliver.

"A rest-stop about twenty miles from here."

"Sounds wonderful," Evangeline sung as she leaned back and began to pick at her fingernails.

Oliver glanced over to Lydia. "Are you looking forward to it...being back home?" he asked.

"I'm looking forward to the mountains and the Pacific. The mid-west doesn't really impress me much," Lydia announced.

"Personally, I just want to make it back to Portland alive," Evangeline huffed. "After what's been happening recently, we'll be lucky if we can ever return to the east coast...especially Massachusetts."

Marlowe could feel Evangeline's head turn ever so slightly to face her. It was as if everyone's eyes were crowding around her, waiting for some response, some outburst at Evangeline's pointed remark, but Marlowe wouldn't give in to her jabs and ignored their glares. Staring blankly through the windshield from the middle seat, she had nothing to say. Marlowe sat firmly planted like a statue. Underneath her placid exterior Dorian knew she was struggling. He clutched her hand in his and sat silently beside her while the others talked.

Lydia and Evangeline chatted about the concerts they couldn't wait to see, while Oliver intermittently chuckled or professed his disapproval in their eclectic tastes. Marlowe leaned upon Dorian's arm and rested against his shoulder as he read to himself. Her head felt incredibly heavy and all she wanted to do was fall into a deep slumber, but distant memories snuck back into her mind causing her heart to race at an even quicker speed. Rumbling trains carrying all of her thoughts and emotions barreled down her consciousness and filled her head with noise. She felt as if her mind was being filled with clouds of steam and dust...the heaviness of the moment pulling her down into a fruitless respite...

Marlowe lurched awake to Dorian's pensive stare.

Rubbing her hair from her forehead and adjusting in the cramped confines of the middle seat, she redirected his eyes away from herself and onto his book by asking, "What are you reading?"

He flipped it over to reveal the spine. "Just a collection of plays. I just started rereading *Doctor Faustus*. You have more in common with the playwright than you know."

"*Doctor Faustus* sounds wonderful." She rested her head against the seat and shut her eyes to avoid his curious stares.

Dorian chuckled at Marlowe as he turned the page. He lightly cleared his throat before he read, "If we say that we have no sin, we deceive ourselves, and there's no truth in us. Why then belike we must sin, and so consequently die…"

4

As Sloan unloaded their creaking car, he looked up at the worn siding of a dilapidated cabin. Its red trim ached for some long-needed touch-ups and its lonely wooden shingles clung precariously onto the sides of the house, leaving a few patches bare. The ones that had fallen quietly decayed in overgrown beds of weeds and grass and, although the exterior withered away, the cabin still had potential. The roof and foundation gently sloped with the rolling of the hill and the bones of the home still stood tall and sturdy, but no one could deny that its maintenance and care was sacrificed for the tending of familial wounds as if a cancer had spread into the home and the cabin's once charming façade had worn weary in its recovery. *Welcome home*, Sloan thought to himself.

He grasped the strap of his gray duffle bag and trudged up the stone pathway, but Jess cut him off for the door. As she flew past him with her backpack and suitcase, she couldn't help but explode with happiness by rushing into the house with a smiling sigh. Sloan stepped into the overgrown weeds to let her pass, her strawberry blonde hair zipping by him. He had hoped for a relaxing return home after weeks of travel, but everything in the world seemed to be pushing its way around him. Even the wind in the trees rushed by in a hurry, but everything inside of him moved slowly as the ache of the trip dug into his stomach. Just as he was about to brave the path once more, his father exited the house with a slam of the screen door. As he brushed by Sloan, he flinched at the touch. Evidently, his father hadn't remedied the ache in his stomach either.

"Lots to do," his father called from the car. "I was thinking that you and Patrick could work on the house. Jess and I were going to head to Mag's and work on some paperwork, maybe stop by the restaurant and see if things are still going."

Mag was the family lawyer. She was constantly helping them in and out of tight situations by dealing with their money and arranging for falsified documents. Being the closest thing they had to a mother, she often acted as general advice giver and there weren't many things they couldn't talk about with her. She was aware of their present objectives and travels, and, although levelheaded, she had a vested interest in the outcomes of their hunts because Sloan's mother was her sister. Aunt Mag felt an obligation to help her sister's family.

"No problem. We'll get started on the house today," Sloan replied.

He opened the rickety screen door and stepped inside. The cabin's interior was muggy. Light dust sifted on the air hitting sunlight spilling in from the windows. The living room was exactly as they had left it a few months ago. A few magazines lay open on the wooden coffee table in front of a sinking, blue sofa. An area rug curled up at the edges under the table, and crooked slats of light patterned the floor from the horizontal blinds that were left slanted in a haphazard fashion. Sloan crossed the living room, dropping his bag near a high-backed chair. Its cushions were perky and unused in comparison to the lumpy, worn-in bulges of the sofa, and Sloan subconsciously brushed the top of the pristine antique chair as he walked by it on his way to the kitchen.

Crossing the threshold of carpet to linoleum, he noticed Patrick leaning over the kitchen table scribbling on a scrap of paper. The white cupboards were open revealing lonely inhabitants: a can of pears, box of pasta, and a container of breadcrumbs. Sloan looked sideways at his brother while he hung from the empty cabinets.

"Grocery list?" he asked.

"Yep, and things-to-do." Patrick ripped off the bottom portion of the paper and handed it to Sloan. "I'm going to hitch a ride with dad. I'll get a cab home from the grocery store." Sloan looked at his paper of chores, none of which looked particularly appealing, and Patrick left the room without a goodbye or wave. Sloan took his seat and slid the paper around on the table with his finger. He was beginning to feel as if he was the only one moving at a normal pace and it made him feel less than adequate.

"You want anything special from the store?" Patrick unexpectedly craned his head into the kitchen.

Sloan looked up from his list, surprise tinting his expression. "Um, no. I'm fine with whatever you get." *Thanks*, Sloan thought with a smile.

"I'll get a case of something cheap. Then we can work on the shingles," Patrick said, lifting his eyebrows with sarcastic excitement.

Sloan laughed, "Sounds like a plan. It'll be like Ernest Hemmingway and his stone wall."

Patrick hesitated and replied with a long, unaware "Yeah" before turning and walking to the front door. His brother hadn't heard of the stone wall - beginning straight and, after an afternoon of drinking, finishing the property line with a weave and a curve. Sloan could hear the sound of the screen door creaking to a close and the car leaving the driveway. Alone.

He held his breath at the silence. Mounds of tension pulled away from his body and fell to the floor of the house like snake's skin. Feeling lighter and more at ease in his glacially paced world, he moved to the kitchen window over the sink and slid it open. The paint peeled and the wood creaked. He could hear sounds of water coming from behind the house as a creek wove through the tall trees of the national forest. Fresh air intruded into the kitchen, and Sloan breathed a sigh of relief. Just like his breathing, the house seemed to stretch and expand as if it had been suffocating while they were gone. It felt unbending to be there. His thoughts loosened in his head and their knots untangled and unwound as he moved about his home.

Grabbing his bag from next to the high-backed chair, he walked down the hall to his bedroom. It had been a small home office that his mother had turned into a nursery for him. The dainty white curtains had been taken down and the crib had been removed, but it still held the childish quality that Sloan loathed because faint buttercup yellow paint peaked out from underneath the paintings, posters, and papers strewn over the walls. Ever since Sloan was a small child his father had always promised that he would help him paint it some other color. Now, whenever Sloan would come home, the worn walls of yellow served as yet another reminder of their faded relationship. He took the paper of chores out of his pocket and scribbled "Paint Bedroom" at the bottom.

Sloan tossed his bag onto his unmade bed. He unzipped it and removed its wrinkled occupants. Sorting through the clothes, he stopped on one of Patrick's shirts that managed to wriggle its way into his belongings. After shoving his emptied bag under his bed, he threw his own clothing into a whicker hamper in the corner and went across the hall to Patrick and David's room.

David's room. His hand paused on the doorknob, the cold brass uninviting.

Sloan reluctantly turned the knob and edged into the room. He didn't look up from the hardwood floors creaking below his feet and kept his eyes plastered to the seams and notches. With each step that he took toward Patrick's bed, he wanted to turn and run out of the room. As he laid the shirt on the mattress and turned to exit, his eyes betrayed him. They strayed from the grain of the slats of wood and came to rest on David's bed in the far corner. He stood stationary while his shoes gripped the floor, unable to move from the gaze of his traitor eyes. The comforter was pulled back into a heap as if David had just woken up seconds ago and would walk through the door from the bathroom, and Sloan thought that if he reached his hand out to touch the sheets by David's pillow they might even be warm. It was as if all of the memories of his brother ran from his mind, through his heart, and down to his feet like cement. They oozed out of his body until Sloan felt like a stone.

And literally, just as they had flowed down to the floor, they retreated back into his head and released his feet from their captivity. As he left Patrick's room, he shut the door behind him.

*   *   *

The final hours of daylight slowly waned away leaving Sloan and Patrick to hammer in the glow of electric work lights. Little by little, they had made progress on the siding of the house, replacing wooden shingle after wooden shingle. They were almost to the bottom of their to-do list only leaving the removal of a broken-down vintage car that sat dead and lonely next to their garage, but they were proud of everything else they had accomplished. The lawn had been mowed, the garage repacked, and the gutters gutted, and Sloan and Patrick definitely looked worse for the wear. Bits of grass and clumps of dirt clung to their shirts and jeans, and Patrick routinely bent backwards and forwards cracking his spine and neck.

"We probably should have started with this job," Patrick commented after a particularly refreshing pop in his back.

"You think?" Sloan sarcastically retorted while missing a nail, almost putting a hole in the wall. "I don't understand why dad wants us to do all this shit right when we get home anyways. It's not like it's going anywhere tomorrow."

Patrick laughed and took another swig of his beer. "Just think, tomorrow we can lay around all day and do nothing." He held up a shingle next to Sloan's and began hammering it into place.

"We better do nothing. Cause let me tell you, my ass is not moving from that couch." Sloan was beginning to lackadaisically hammer each nail, and he couldn't think of anything except taking a shower and falling into bed.

His father's voice boomed from the kitchen, "If by do nothing you mean go into the restaurant and clean the fryers than yes...you guys aren't doing anything tomorrow."

"Thanks for the clarification," Sloan called back with a sigh.

Patrick let out a whine much too prepubescent for his twenty-five-year-old body. "The fucking fryers?! Don't we have employees for that kind of garbage?"

Their father laughed from within the warm confines of the house. "Yeah, but it'll give the locals a chance to see you both before you 'Go back to college'." They could just imagine their dad using air quotes from inside the house.

"One of these days that excuse is not going to work...and then what are you going to say?" Sloan finished off his beer before packing his hammer in the toolbox.

"Easy. You came back to help your old man with the house."

Patrick mumbled under his breath, "If I keep working on this siding in the middle of the night with a handful of beers in me there won't be a house."

Sloan bent over and laughed as he placed the leftover nails in the toolbox.

"Sounds like you're about done. Come in for dinner," their father called. Patrick carried the toolbox to the front door and left it waiting by the stoop for after dinner. They came into the kitchen and Patrick went straight to the kitchen sink to wash his hands, but Sloan stood awkwardly in the doorway. The table was set for five. Five plates. Five forks. Five napkins. Five glasses. Before he took his seat, Sloan gathered up the extra place setting and snuck the items back into the cabinets and drawers. His father caught a glimpse of Sloan's actions as he took the casserole out of the oven but paused only briefly to acknowledge his own miscount. After Sloan had placed the extra fork back into the drawer, he took his seat near the door. Jess walked in from the living room, dark soot smeared across her face and arms. Patrick caught a glimpse of her face and stifled a laugh.

"Don't." She grabbed a towel from a kitchen drawer, ran the tap over it, and attempted to wipe it off. "That is the last time I clean the flue."

Patrick poured a glass of water from the fridge and sat next to Sloan. "Great. Next time *you* can mow the lawn. I would be happy to clean the fireplace." A smirk spread over his expression.

Sloan's father heaped piles of casserole on to each plate and took his seat near the fridge. "Eat up. We have to talk about tomorrow."

"I know, Patrick and I get to clean the fryers," Sloan murmured between forkfuls of rice and chicken.

"After a thought, I decided that Jess and I would go clean the fryers." His eyes tried to dodge Jess's stare, but to no avail.

"What? Why? I thought we were going to go stake out a nest in the city!" Jess hunched back into her seat and tossed her fork onto her plate.

Patrick perked up with an obstinate glare, "Wait! You were

going to go hunting without me?"

A brief yelling match broke out over the kitchen table. Sloan sat over his food and continued to eat as if they were arguing about a sporting event, and every now and then he would laugh to himself. They whined and argued, trying every tactic in the book to convince their father why they wanted - no, *needed* - to go on another hunt. But Sloan really couldn't care less what was happening tomorrow.

As long as I don't have to clean the fryers, he thought to himself.

Sloan's father halted the conversation with a loud, "Shut it!" Patrick and Jess quieted around the table and picked at their food. "I decided that Jess and I would go to the restaurant and clean out the kitchen…" He ignored a stare from Jess before continuing, "While Patrick and Sloan go to the nest." Patrick looked pleased at this decision, but Sloan slouched back in his chair. His father noticed his shift in posture and finished, "You need more experience."

Sloan robotically ate his food in silence as his family morphed into excitement. Jess and Patrick threw questions across the table about location, number, approach, and strategy. Jess whined every now and then about how she wanted to go along instead of cleaning fryers, and Patrick beamed at the thought that tomorrow would bring about, in his perspective, a new adventure. Their father joyfully looked at each one regaling them with how Aunt Mag had mustered up the courage to investigate some local disappearances that had made the news and eventually tracked the guilty couple to a shoddy apartment in the middle of the night. Amidst their amusement by the image of Aunt Mag tracking across town, hiding behind dumpsters and attempting to look inconspicuous, Sloan caught glimpses of his father's pain.

Between all of the excitement, joy, and eagerness, was a stagnant pool of suffering, and no matter how hard their father tried to fill in this pool with vengeance and justification there would always be this placid despair lingering beneath it all. Sloan focused on his father as the conversation wore down and his siblings began to eat their meals again, and there it was. His father's face adjusted into a grim, empty expression as soon as he thought no one was looking, the photo in his pocket burning into his leg.

Patrick broke his father's hollow concentration. "Is it in the city? Like downtown?"

His father jumped at the sudden question. "What? No. It's near Grant Park, a little west of Portland."

Sloan became tired and he couldn't decide whether it was the conversation wearing on his nerves or the day's work stressing on his muscles. He excused himself from the table, placed his dish in the sink, and walked to his bedroom. He didn't turn on the light as he entered his room; it would have been glaring to his heavy eyes. Taking off his pants and shirt, he decided to leave the shower for morning and fell into bed. As he drifted into his sheets, Sloan hoped that the comfort of his own bed would console his restless sleep. He pulled the covers around him and breathed in deeply. The months on the road had taken their toll on his mind, and with every passing year of life his sleep grew heavier with nightmares and restlessness. He wished that his own bed would relieve him of his nightly suffering, but, in the back of his mind, he knew that his home would bring him no peace.

5

They arrived just after one in the morning. Marlowe stretched as she exited the car and looked warmly up at her house. It had been more than ten years since they had left. Time's slow passage and the inevitable boredom that tagged along with it forced them to leave and return in steady intervals. The two-story house sat squarely on a gently sloping hill. A stacked stone wall graced the edge of the property and a lane of steady steps rose from the street up to the front porch. The clean, painted wood of the house shown with a light green hue, and quaint gable windows looked out under the eaves near a brick chimney. All in all, it was a rather stately house, and Marlowe found herself immensely exhilarated at the sight of it.

They carried their suitcases up the steps, and when Dorian reached the front door he had to push a little harder than usual to open it, the wood clinging to the frame from lack of use. Sheets covered each piece of furniture. Ten years should have proven dustier, but the hardwood still gleamed up at them and the walls and corners were cobweb free. Marlowe dropped her bag on the tile of the front foyer and bounced to a sheet in the corner. She removed it revealing a small blue chair and gracefully lounged in it.

"It feels more than good to be home," Marlowe exhaled.

"If you hadn't have made it a point to ruin every trip, you might feel differently," Evangeline belittled.

Oliver cast her a warning look, and Evangeline shrugged up at him like she didn't know what he was implying.

Dorian crossed to a sheet covering a table and picked up a small envelope. "Looks like Grace left a note with her keys." Grace was a feisty yet polite woman in her fifties that had been contracted to look after and take care of the house in their absence. She cleaned, made sure the exterior of the house looked up to par, and arranged the property taxes; in return, she was paid quite generously. Even better, she never asked any questions. For the past ten years, she had made a substantial living on only working once a month.

"She says that she enjoyed working for us and if we ever go out of town again she would love to be considered. She also says that she tested the shutters to our specifications last Thursday." On the interior of the house, each window had storm shutters that moved like accordions to the sides. It was difficult to convince the contractor who installed them that they were for security purposes, and even more difficult to get hurricane shutters in Oregon, but they proved to be perfect additions.

Dorian folded the note, placed it and the keys in his pocket, and began to help Oliver remove the sheets from the rest of the furniture in the house. They moved from room to room, casually talking and laughing. As Dorian uncovered the plush chairs in his study, he glanced pensively across the far wall. He moved to the large sheet hanging from end to end and carefully removed it revealing rows upon rows of shelves. Sweeping his hands across the heavy oak trim, a smile spread across his face as his fingers catalogued past the shelves' inhabitants as if he were playing the piano. His collection sat quietly and respectfully in their places. Various trinkets stared out at him from every nook of shelving and hidden within every one of them was a reservoir of memories.

Each decade and event of his life encapsulated in an antique. Dorian held his life as the equivalent of these objects, but he never had more than his shelves could hold. Just as the brain would remove old, dusted memories to be replaced with newer ones, his shelves would ebb and flow with objects, some tokens remaining since the beginning, and some coming and going within the quick span of years. The constant movement of objects resembled a breath but, after an object would serve its purpose, it would be restored and sold, sent out into the world to become a part of someone else's collection. A few wouldn't even make it to the shelves and would be boxed up for a different owner who had eagerly placed the winning bid for the prized piece, but there were those that never left, the ones that had become permanent staples of his study: a broken clock, a jeweled brooch, an ivory doorknob, and a small unassuming wooden box. Marlowe had sometimes asked about those pieces. He would respond with a simple "I'll tell you some other time" and occasionally he would remove one and gently brush across its finish. A longing nostalgia or pained recollection would swell over his eyes, for each was attached to a memory and every memory a lesson. They never left his shelves.

Marlowe watched as he removed a cloth from his desk drawer and began to gently dust a small tin.

"Do you need help?" she asked.

"Sure. You can start at one end, I'll start at the other, and we'll work our way to the middle," Dorian replied with a smile.

Marlowe found another soft, cotton cloth and sat upon a short wooden stool near the bottom shelf. She picked up a small china teacup. A few slight flowers gestured up at her from the porcelain, and she imagined they were grateful for some attention. Dorian laughed.

"Would you like to know the story?" he asked as he referenced the tiny cup in Marlowe's hands.

Marlowe nodded as she set the teacup back onto the shelf.

"That reminds me of *The Scarlet Letter*. When that novel came out almost everyone wanted to read it, and a few months after it was first sold Oliver and I were the guests at a young man's house. I was interested in him, and his sister intrigued Oliver. We were waiting in the sitting room and their mother was being hospitable, offering us tea. Obviously, we didn't drink it…however, we pretended to, as not to offend anyone, and an old grandmother was reading quietly by the window. Oliver and I were talking to the mother about the weather and the news from California, when all of a sudden, a crash came from the window. We looked over and the old woman had dropped her tea to the floor while reading *The Scarlet Letter*. She tossed the book across the room, raised her hands in protest, and proceeded to scuttle out of the room never to open that book again! Well, Oliver and I laughed and laughed, causing the mother much offense so she kicked us out of the house…teacups and all." Dorian laughed to himself and sat next to Marlowe on the wooden stool. They both looked admiringly at the little cup.

"Whenever I look at that teacup it makes me laugh," Dorian moved to his desk to make a note on a sheet of paper, "I should sell it."

"Sell it? You just said that looking at it made you happy," Marlowe smiled as she moved on to another trinket.

"I have other things to make me laugh, and I have new objects to take its place. Besides, its value has increased and now I can feel comfortable with the price." He moved to his bag and removed two new additions for the shelves.

Oliver peeked his head into the room. "Anyone hungry?" he asked with a smirk.

"Starving," Dorian replied. He ran his hands through his hair and his steel eyes twinkled at the thought of a meal. Marlowe could see his canines extend ever so slightly into his mouth as he spoke. He held his hand out to her. "Shall we?"

"I'm not too hungry." Marlowe finished dusting a pewter bowl and set it back into its place.

"Great, then there will be no one to ruin it," Evangeline loudly sneered from the living room. She knew that everyone could hear her whisper, making the comment even more insulting.

Marlowe's stomach growled hungrily up at her, but she had no intention of going with them when each time felt like a test. She was exhausted from walking on eggshells at every meal, and she found herself constantly hesitating at the thought of feeding. Slow, creeping guilt always peered in at her from her peripheral. She brushed by them to go upstairs to her room. "I'll stay home."

"Just come, Marlowe. I want you to. We'll get back to the normal rhythm of things." Dorian attempted to remain pleasant, but his face began to show signs of annoyance.

"I need to unpack," she called from the stairs.

Dorian couldn't keep himself from prodding, "Marlowe, you need to eat."

Evangeline huffed her contempt at his show of concern.

Eyes blazing, Marlowe stormed from the stairs into the living room. She grabbed the magazine out of Evangeline's hands and tossed it to the coffee table.

Evangeline snapped, "What is your fucking problem, Marlowe?"

"I have had to listen to you for the entire trip, not to mention the past seventy-six years, and my problem is that you just can't keep your mouth shut!" Marlowe's eyes narrowed as she leaned over Evangeline.

"Keep my mouth shut? That's the problem? What about you? You don't have any issues you want to air out for the group! I am so sick of you just sulking off to go and talk to Dorian."

Marlowe glared contemptuously down at her, "What is that supposed to mean?"

"You have daddy issues you don't even know about," Evangeline sneered.

Marlowe stepped closer to Evangeline as her fists rolled up. The air siphoned from the room. Dorian and Oliver sat upon the bottom stair and unenthusiastically watched from the sidelines. Lydia's eyebrows rose as she looked from Dorian to Oliver.

"You have got to be kidding me," Lydia scolded them from under her breath. She crossed in front of Marlowe just before their tension exploded into fists and teeth. "Evangeline, keep it to the point."

"Fine, Lydia," Evangeline spoke slowly through her teeth, "I am shocked with what Marlowe can get away with. I mean, the woods? You let a man go, just so you could chase after him! What were you thinking? You need to keep your 'urges' on a shorter leash and stop acting like you are smarter than everyone else."

Marlowe had nothing to say. She was right, but she couldn't help but give a juvenile retort when Evangeline looked so content in her rationality, "In your case...I am smarter."

"Then how in God's name do you explain Boston! Huh? Answer me...or was what you did just a slip of the mind or an accident, because from where I was standing it looked pretty intentional to me!"

Marlowe stared at Evangeline. "Do not bring up Boston!" she yelled. The air in the room began to heat as their arguing came to a crescendo.

"Why not? We can't all talk about it cause poor Marlowe doesn't want to? You put all of us in danger! It's inexcusable!" Evangeline turned to Oliver, "I am tired of the hierarchy in this family. Someone needs to address her actions now before one of us gets hurt."

"Why did you have to turn *her*, Oliver? There were…what…fifty other women there. You had to pick this one!"

"At least Oliver *wanted* me!" Evangeline's words cut into Marlowe with a fierceness she had not anticipated. Marlowe quickly turned to Dorian and scanned his expression, but his eyes were downcast. He could neither argue with Evangeline nor comfort Marlowe, and as the silence covered the room like a thick blanket Dorian left to the study and into the sanctuary of his collection.

6

The day after his first kill he felt a different heaviness in his step. Sloan took no particular pride in what he had to do with his brother in Grant Park, but he was filled with immense relief that the event was over. His father looked at him differently, patting him on the back and sighing as if he now held his youngest son in a higher regard. Breakfast went by without incident or off-hand remark, and Sloan found that he could now join in on the incessant conversations of hunting. He knew that he had passed into a new level of belonging with his family, but in the back of his mind he wished that he never had to hunt again. Not wanting to lose his new sense of acceptance, Sloan retained his false smile until he was able to slip into his bedroom out-of-sight.

Every moment of the prior day replayed in his mind. With each recollection came the smells, the touch, and the anxiety. He tried to distract himself with a book, but the memory refused to unhook itself.

Upon the turn of a page, he would catapult into the parking lot of the peach apartment complex, a lump in his throat and gun in his backpack. At the close of a paragraph, he found himself looking over his shoulder as Patrick shattered a window to reach in and open the adjacent door. He would read the same word over and over, its meaning lost within the sounds of crunching glass beneath his boots as they crept into the apartment. Boards covered the windows blocking out any sunlight, but doilies and worn seventies furniture dotted the room. A photo of an elderly couple smiled happily from the wall and Patrick motioned to the far bathroom where blood pooled upon the floor and limbs dangled from the tub…

Sloan shut his book and tossed it across the room onto an empty chair. He ran his fingers through his hair as he placed his head in his hands. Struggling to commit the images back into their locked drawers, he went to find Patrick. Sloan wanted desperately to force the pride and happiness back upon himself, and he couldn't do that when he was alone. He found Patrick in the garage sifting through old boxes.

"Need any help?" Sloan called from the driveway.

Patrick looked up as he placed a lid upon a bin and hoisted it up to the shelf. "Sure, grab a box. Just going through stuff, reorganizing it all."

Sloan opened a box and began to trifle through some of his old high school belongings. With each touch, an avalanche of yesterday's memories burst into his thoughts. Unzipping an old backpack, he found himself kneeling upon the linoleum floor of the apartment removing his gun and silencer...His heart started to race as he shut his eyes and tossed the backpack into a nearby bin.

Stop thinking about it, Sloan told himself, but his memories would not permit him to rest. They kept intruding upon his actions.

Sloan felt the gun in his hands while Patrick turned the doorknob to the bedroom where *they* slept. He couldn't stop himself from shaking as he and his brother slowly entered the bedroom. Gentle light seeped into the edges of the room from a far window. A couple was lying in a bed, and Sloan suddenly felt a surge of doubt. He knew that these beings were killers; that they had boarded up this apartment. That they had slaughtered the happy inhabitants that once called this place home, drained their blood, and left them rotting in their own bathtub. But even so, they looked so calm, so tranquil, and so normal sleeping under quilted sheets, their chests rising and falling as they slept. Patrick lifted his gun, Sloan lifted his, and they fired. Even after Patrick had stopped and lowered his gun, Sloan continued to fire his. Round after silent round emptying into the bed, the faces of the guilty dead staring up at the ceiling.

"Sloan. Sloan!"

Startled, he looked over at Patrick. A blank stare plastered on his face.

"Um. I don't think you'll be needing a pencil case or chemistry book any time soon. I say toss 'em." Patrick pointed at Sloan's hands. Sloan had been staring blankly into his memory, not realizing that he had been holding an old textbook and plastic box.

"Yeah. Tough decision. I was weighing all my options," Sloan joked as he placed the items into a donation bin.

Patrick walked over to him and looked into the box. He began to shuffle through its contents, looking for something that couldn't be found tucked away in the recesses of the garage.

"What happened to David?" Sloan quietly asked.

Patrick mumbled as he latched onto the side of the box, "He hesitated."

"Why would David hesitate?" Sloan felt like he was pulling sharp knives from Patrick's stomach, and Patrick felt each one.

"He didn't want to do it anymore. He was sick of our life. Every day he would talk about how he wanted to tell dad that he just wanted to move out, do something different, actually have a life. Believe it or not, he started out just like you...the nerves and all. But once he started, it slowly chipped away at him bit by bit. He would scream in his sleep, told me every day that he didn't want to go through with it, the hunt, but in the end he would, and it would start all over again for him. And then, a week before he died...he stopped talking about it all, the screaming stopped...but now he's gone." Patrick moved to another box and resumed sorting; however, he now moved quickly and thoughtlessly.

"You think he wanted it to end like that?" Sloan asked, his chest beginning to tighten.

Patrick turned to him and considered his words. The air in the garage seemed to suffocate around them. "I think he hesitated."

They stared blankly at each other and when Patrick spoke again the words cracked in his throat, "You know, I can sort all this if you're not too attached to anything. Don't worry about it. Go get some air."

Sloan looked into his brothers' eyes and knew that he knew. His brother was able to see what no one else in the family could observe, and he was grateful. As he left the garage, he looked up at the cloudless sky. It reflected the deepest, clearest blue and a slight wind blew ripples through the leaves on the trees. With a sigh, Sloan made up his mind, took a few strides from the house, and pulled his keys from his pocket. His truck rumbled to life as he made his way to Mag's.

*   *   *

The leather of the chair squeaked and groaned as Sloan fidgeted. The office was quiet except for the soft ticking of a pendulum as it swung back and forth inside the chest of a small clock on the wall. Wooden shelves lined the back of the office behind the desk; each one housing rows upon rows of hard, leather-bound books, their contents an array of law and history, with the exception of an occasional self-help book on the bottom row. Sloan toyed with his car keys. Clinking in his hands, he spun them on the ring, the keys rolling over themselves. The calm gave him the opportunity to simply sit and unwind while he waited for his Aunt Margaret to get out of a meeting down the hall.

The door clicked open and a tall woman with upswept brown hair entered. Gray wisps fluttered around her warm, round face. Sloan smiled at her genial expression. A look of enjoyed stress played across her eyes while crow's feet and smile lines deepened in their furrows.

"Hey Aunt Mag." Sloan got up from the leather chair and helped her unload the large volumes of files and notepads from her arms onto the desk.

"If I had known that you were coming, I would have rescheduled the meeting," Mag said as she gave him a hug. She sat behind her desk and began to toil over a scattering of papers. Sloan looked into her eyes. A part of him always hoped that her eyes resembled the eyes of his mother, that each time he caught a glimpse of himself in their reflection that the image of his mother would reside in them as well. But this time, like all the rest, his mother was not to be found, and he looked away.

Mag quietly spoke from her papers, "I'm sorry about David."

"Me too," Sloan whispered as his voice cracked. He cleared his throat. A few silent minutes passed between them.

"How was the trip…for you?" she asked.

"Same as all the others. I just hung back," Sloan rubbed his hands on the leather arms of the chair.

Mag opened a few folders and began marking them with a highlighter. "Did you like San Francisco? I haven't been there in ages."

"I didn't really pay any attention to it. I guess it was nice." He fidgeted uncomfortably in his chair.

She looked up at him and nodded, "I suppose it would be hard for you to focus on the city."

He felt like ropes were being coiled around his body, and he needed to talk about anything but San Francisco. "Last night Patrick and I went to that apartment complex you told dad about," he blurted. It wasn't the change in subject he had hoped his mind would produce.

"How'd that go?" Mag's voice grew soft and calm as she cocked her head to the side and surveyed her nephew.

"Everything according to plan. No mess-ups this time." He stopped. Sloan couldn't believe that he had just referred to his brother's death as a mess-up. "I mean...I didn't mess anything up, but..." He could feel knots forming in his stomach and he chose to remain silent and uncomfortable.

The highlighter squeaked back and forth across the paper. As Sloan looked down at his hands, he heard the dragging of the neon ink, the paper shuffling, and the creaking of her rolling office chair as it leaned back and forth. His nerves scattered in frantic sprints down his arms and up his back.

He whispered, "I can't get their faces out of my head. Every time I try to do something else, they just appear. I keep freezing up today, like my brain is on a loop."

The noises stopped. Aunt Mag peered over her papers at her nephew, slumped with exhaustion on the chair. She rolled over to him and placed her hands over his as she nodded her head in understanding, "The faces of their victims."

Sloan looked up at her. Confusion melted around his eyes. "The victims? No. The ones I killed. The ones that were sleeping." He grew silent and knew that he shouldn't have said anything.

Mag looked him over and sighed. "It takes a strong person to do what you and your family do. I'd be lying if I told you those faces will disappear. You'll carry them with you for the rest of your life. Your dad knows a lot about this, more than anyone. You know I don't usually say this, but you really should talk to him about it."

Sloan stood up from the chair, dejected and alone. He wasn't about to go ask his father for advice on coping.

"Do you want to talk about David?" she asked from her chair as she wheeled back behind her desk.

Sloan hesitated at the door mumbling, "No."

"Do you know how it happened?" she dug.

Yes. "No. I have no idea." He could feel his insides stretch as the knots toppled over on top of each other. As he left her office, a highlighter could be heard squeaking across paper. He had never left before without feeling reassured or comforted. However, her office was colder - and she had found a new attitude to match. He felt betrayed. Instead of the solace their conversations usually brought him, he was reeling with an abandonment he never thought he had to feel again. The responsibility was beginning to feel more and more like liability. This new skill catapulted him into a world of quiet suffering with every action leaving him to spin with mounting guilt, and their faces surrounded him.

He had to find a way out. A release. A distraction. A way to erase those faces before he fell even further into his nightmares, eventually turning into his father...or David.

7

The last fleeting traces of sunlight dipped just below the horizon as Marlowe walked the paths of the nearby park a few blocks from her home. The evening around her was filled with a cool breeze accompanied by a soft rhythm. The murmur of conversation hummed by her, and as she moved closer to her usual spot on her usual bench the murmuring developed into discernable speech. Tonight was Portland's annual *Classical in the Park* event and, instead of going out with her family, Marlowe decided to relax for the evening while enjoying some music and people-watching.

She took a seat on her lonely, metal bench on the far edge of the park. A stage of musicians played far from where she sat, but the music still reached her curious ears. The maestro waved his hands delicately through the air while the steady bows of violins ran across taut strings. The despair of the orchestra calmed Marlowe. Against its intricate backdrop, her mind reorganized itself, gathering like a deck of chaotic playing cards. Evangeline's words faded from her memory as if it were a splinter being pulled from her skin. For Marlowe, nothing mattered at this moment except for the music, and in that resolve she was happy.

With a smile lightly turning up the corners of her mouth, Marlowe scanned the audience that peppered the park before her. Families and lovers alike were strewn across the grassy lawn. Some sat in camping chairs while some lay on blankets, and all of them seemed to rotate between attentive listening and low chatter throughout the evening. Marlowe observed as a young man fumbled for the hand of his date and, once grasped, was put at ease when the young woman reciprocated his affection with a gentle squeeze. The young woman's grin was enough to make Marlowe grin as well. Marlowe's own subconscious smile caught her off-guard, so she directed her attention elsewhere. Farther down the grass, she watched as a small child ran up to its mother, its tiny hand clutching a collection of flowers and weeds. They couldn't have been in worse condition, petals falling off and leaves wilting from their stems, but the mother joyfully thanked the child for the gift with an affectionate embrace. Marlowe felt a tinge of tenderness and exhaled. Her pensive stare shifted to other groups before her.

Some people chose to move their seats as they attempted to sit closer to the stage. Some people ate dinners on their blankets, their meals ranging from greasy food trucks to homemade, romantic dinners. A few pulled beers and cocktails from small coolers. Marlowe observed each person with the same curious regard, eyes watching tenderly like an elderly woman feeding birds on an early Sunday morning. She was enthralled by each action of hunger or necessity or impulse, and occasionally she would come across a gesture befitting a rare gem of human nature - an attentive listener completely moved by the music, or a gaze between two people where nothing had to be said but in that moment every thought of affection was exchanged. Marlowe had sometimes thought that becoming what she was, what some called a monster, removed her from humanity, but recently she had realized that it had done just the opposite.

She crossed her legs and focused her eyes on the distant stage. Her foot moved in concentric circles to the music as she lightly hummed along. It was nice to enjoy a night of solitude. On this cold, lonely bench, Marlowe didn't have to plaster a false guise of happiness upon her face or suppress some deep-seeded sorrow. She could simply sit with a genuinely peaceful blank expression. Sleep couldn't even offer this kind of requiem.

The air was a cacophony of music and conversation. As Marlowe listened to the movement of the noise, people would pass behind her on the nearby sidewalk and hesitate for a second to observe the orchestra before moving on their way. An occasional jogger would trample by, hacking and huffing as they plodded along the concrete path. It was easy to distinguish between the stumbling footsteps of the out-of-shape and the steady rhythms of the prime. Marlowe would hone her senses in on the runners as they moved by and she would guess at their build and age based on their heartbeats, the muscle laboring over the quivering of violins to hit her ears. Marlowe would input the weight of their footsteps and the length of their strides into her equation before she would turn her head to see if her predictions were correct. Middle-aged men with hearts skipping to keep up with their over-zealous steps. A couple of young women with hearts steadily thumping along as they chattered between themselves. She reveled in her success at the game.

A runner approached from her right side, so she focused in on the sound of the shoes hitting the sidewalk with every stride. *Too heavy to be a small build. Wide difference in step means longer legs; six foot one.* She tried to focus in on his heartbeat as it neared the bench, but its cadence surprised her. Instead of the rapid palpitations she had expected, the muscle kept its pace with the rhythm of his long strides. And as she focused in on the heartbeat emanating from his chest, a man slowed to a stop behind the bench, placed his hand beside her on the back of the bench, and leaned down to tie his shoe.

She cocked her head to the side as she looked over the back of the bench down at his messy, brown hair, and just managed to flick her eyes back to the stage before he stood up and stretched.

"Can I sit here?" Sloan questioned.

Marlowe looked up at him and before she could think of her actions, she complimented him. "You're in shape."

"What?" Sloan asked with a tint of embarrassment and flattery on his face. He laughed uncomfortably and attempted to fix the sweaty mass of his hair.

"Um...yeah. You can sit if you want." Marlowe motioned beside her as she crossed her legs away from him and attempted to refocus on the music. Kicking herself from the inside, she couldn't believe that she had just let the game beat her and then proceeded to compliment the man on his ability to have a slow heartbeat while sprinting. She rolled her eyes, all abilities to listen to the music floating away in her embarrassment.

They both sat in silence, their pause filled with the awkward tension of new acquaintances. A million static shocks jumped between them, each jolt containing the impulse to move or stay or speak. Five hundred different topics coursed through each of their minds, some about the weather, some about introductions, but each with the faint hope that the other would speak first. The urge to laugh was creeping up Marlowe's sides as her foot fidgeted in the air, and Sloan felt the need to cough and fought against its harsh sound on the silent noise flowing between them. Instead, he decided to speak.

"I love Hummell," he mumbled.

"What?" Marlowe asked, partly because she was so preoccupied with what she was going to say first that she didn't even hear his comment.

"The music." He pointed to the orchestra across the park and smiled hopefully across at her.

"Oh! Yeah. The cellos are great," Marlowe replied. Relief spread across her face as the unsteady anxiety of a first encounter subsided. They both relaxed into the bench and listened to the heavy sounds of instruments before Sloan spoke again.

"It's been a long time since I was last here for this," Sloan said with a miniscule amount of sadness. Most people would never have picked up on it, but it was something Marlowe could easily sense.

"Why?" she asked as she turned toward him.

He sighed, "My family and I travel a lot and we've been out of town for every concert since I was twelve. My dad used to take me to each one. What about you? Is it your first time?"

"Yes." *If you don't count the one I went to in the early seventies.* She decided to lie in order to keep the conversation simple.

"It's really nice. Tomorrow, they'll have vendors and artists all around in this area," he explained, motioning to the grass in front of them as he leaned back in the bench.

"Is this your hometown?" Marlowe cocked her head to the side.

"Pretty much – we live just outside of town. We have a family restaurant, and it's the place we always come back to."

"That's nice." Marlowe responded with genuine sincerity, "I'm from all over." She was shocked at how easily this conversation was coming, and even more so at her own divulgences.

"Well, you must have a hometown. Where were you born?" Sloan asked.

She thought a few seconds more than any normal person would ever have to as she sifted through her recollections of cities, roads, and faces. She answered with a melancholy, lost breathiness, "Barnstable, Massachusetts...near Cape Cod." Her mind was miles away.

"We don't have to talk about your hometown. I promise." Sloan forced a smile. He could sense her quiet despair and decided to change the subject. "The restaurant is horrible though. Some crummy diner that my mom and dad opened to feed our side of town, the usual greasy fries and burgers. Epitome of the little hole-in-the-wall on the outskirts of town. Kind of predictable, if you ask me."

Marlowe was glad for the shift in conversation. "Does your family want to be predictable though?"

Sloan looked around the park as he rolled over her question in his mind, eyes stopping on a couple feverishly kissing on a blanket. He awkwardly shifted his eyes to the cuff of his shorts and tried to swallow his discomfort as the couple rolled off the blanket. "Um, not predictable - just normal, I guess. A diner seemed like the right fit, and it's helped a lot with money while we move around."

Marlowe stared with an unwavering curiosity at the couple, bits of grass sticking to their clothes while they shifted back to their crumpled blanket. "Even though things may seem like the practical choice at the time, it doesn't mean you should keep doing it when it loses its purpose."

Her words dug into his ribs, and he fidgeted nervously in his seat. Now he was the one avoiding the conversation, and Marlowe was quick on the uptake.

"I guess you really don't need air to survive," she laughed as she gestured toward the grinding couple.

Sloan laughed in return. They sat smiling and looking out into the crowd as the concert came to a close. Marlowe stretched as she stood. Exchanging a furtive glance with Sloan, they looked at each other in awkward silence before she walked from the bench.

Sloan struggled with his confidence. He looked at his hands. He looked at his tennis shoes. He looked everywhere but at Marlowe as she walked away, and with one final push from his conscience, he blurted, "Do you want to get a drink?" It came out much louder than he meant.

She slowly turned on her heel and looked at him, considering. After a few pensive moments she argued, "You don't even know my name."

"Well, a drink will give me a whole other hour to figure that out, and if I don't get it by then I've got bigger things to worry about." Sloan scratched nervously at his arm. He hoped his line would work.

Marlowe grinned, and for some unknown reason she nodded. She couldn't understand it, but he made her feel comfortable, like she already knew him. As they walked away, she looked at his sweatshirt and asked, "You're going out like that?"

"What? You don't like sweat as an accessory?" he teased, "I promise we won't go anywhere nice."

"Every girl's dream," Marlowe responded sarcastically.

She laughed without effort. It rang out from her chest and made Sloan grin.

*   *   *

"So, this is going to sound corny, but…what do you do?" Sloan asked, an innocent smirk spreading across his face.

Marlowe kept her face steady and smiling before she uttered the first thing that was a lie. "I'm a phlebotomist." *That…that is what you came up with? Great, Marlowe, might as well have told him the truth*, she thought.

"Isn't that a blood lab tech or something?" He looked amused.

"Yeah. I work at a blood bank," Marlowe responded. She had to keep herself from giggling, and she hoped that he wouldn't see through her lie.

"So, you're good around that kind of stuff? It doesn't make you sick?" Sloan shifted in the padded booth. Curiosity and mild discomfort peeked across his face.

"Yeah, it's nothing…just a little blood." Her thoughts became distracted as she mentioned the warm, dark liquid. Her eyes darted around the room in slight hunger as she tried to focus on anything but the man sitting across from her. She had to change the subject quick before she allowed her thoughts to gain control of her. "What about you? What do you do?"

Shit. What do I say? Think of anything…something, Sloan's mind raced for the first thing that was a lie. "I'm a refinisher…" He paused after hearing the words that uttered from his lips and leaned back, slightly slumping over as embarrassment tinted his face.

"You make furniture?" she asked.

"Yeah. I…um…track down antiques and"…*kill them…*"refurbish them" *You suck at this*, he thought to himself.

"You know…you kind of suck at this. Lying." Marlowe stared at him, but instead of being angry at his fib, she was intrigued. She scanned his face, noticing his features. Something about him seemed so familiar to her, but she couldn't quite decide what it was. However, she could be sure that Sloan was hiding something from her, and it sparked her interest.

"I'm not lying." Sloan awkwardly toyed with his silverware, dropping his knife to the floor in the process.

"Okay," Marlowe grinned.

They paused and inspected each other's expressions. Suddenly they both burst into laughter. Each occupant of the restaurant turned toward the din. Sloan shied away at the unwanted attention. It caused him to divert his gaze back to Marlowe's deep, smiling eyes.

Very slowly, invisible strings were cast off across the table and tied down upon one another. With every adjustment, the other longed to counter their movement, putting the twitching strings back to rights. And with every millisecond that passed between them, they became aware of those microscopic strings, tugging upon their eyes and hands, eagerly stretching for a glance or touch.

Sloan hadn't even noticed the man standing idly by the table waiting for his response. "Sir?"

He snapped to and stammered, "What?"

"He wants to know if you want another drink," Marlowe answered for the server, "I ordered a sidecar."

"Oh...I'll just have another beer." Sloan thought that the night had been over with their one drink but was pleased that they could continue the evening and their conversation. It was pleasant talking to someone about something other than tracking, moving, or hunting.

The server quickly wrote down their orders and headed for the bar.

Marlowe chuckled to herself. "In all my years, nothing has changed. The phrase 'I'll just have another beer' is as popular today as it was yesterday."

"All your years? What are you twenty-five?" Sloan laughed.

Marlowe slightly tensed and diverted her gaze to the empty table. "Actually, I'm twenty-four."

"Well, I'm twenty-three, so don't feel too old." Sloan tried to recover from his first conversational flub.

Marlowe met his gaze. "I don't feel old."

The strings wilted at the first sign of disconnect and dropped to the table, a few snapping with the weight of tension flowing between them. Sloan's mind backtracked as he tried to figure out where he had gone wrong, and Marlowe barely noticed Sloan, preoccupied with her own mortality, even though it was longer and more drawn out than those around her.

The server set down their drinks, their unseasonable silence causing him to stiffen as he stood shyly by the table. "Do you want me to start you each a tab?" he coughed.

Marlowe quickly retrieved a stolen credit card from her pocket for the bar to hold onto. She would pay in cash at the end of the night; she always paid in cash. Sliding it toward the server, she grinned as Sloan rummaged for the wallet in his shorts, twisting his body as he struggled to fumble it out from its back pocket.

"That would be great," Sloan smiled as he gave his credit card and picked up his drink, tilting it toward Marlowe. "Salud."

Marlowe clinked her glass to his and responded with a simple "Prost."

Forty-five minutes and a few more drinks later, Sloan leaned comfortably against his booth grinning like a Cheshire cat while Marlowe leaned over the table, her head resting in one of her hands.

"Favorite book." She pointed at him with her other hand. Her eyes were narrow as she attempted a look of seriousness.

With a disgruntled sigh and a smirk Sloan replied, "It's a play. Not a book. *Doctor Faustus*, by Christopher Marlowe."

"I'm reading that right now! And I know you won't forget my name now." Marlowe shrieked in laughter. She contorted her face in a subdued look of contemplation, barely masked by intermittent slips of giggling. She put on her best British accent.

"'What are thou, Faustus, but a man condemned to die? Thy fatal time draws to an end.'"

Sloan drank from his beer as he listened in awe. "Wow, so there is a bigger fan."

"A lot of time on my hands."

"I can see that," Sloan nodded.

Marlowe's mouth fell open at his backhanded comment. "Hey! I don't have *that* much time on my hands! I do things!" They laughed at each other as Marlowe took a coy sip of her drink.

Sloan pointed at her. "This is a tough one. Favorite color."

Weighing all her options, Marlowe paused and considered.

"No thinking! Just answer!" Sloan argued. She was obviously disobeying the rules of the game.

"Brown," she blurted. It was the first color that had come to her mind.

Sloan looked at her in disbelief, obvious disgust clouding his face.

"It's a nice color! It's soil, trees – natural."

"Brown?"

"Yes, brown."

"*Brown?*"

Marlowe laughed, "Okay, gray."

Sloan choked on his beer. "That's even worse!"

"Then I'll stick with brown," she conceded. "Favorite movie."

"*Nas Veratu.*" Sloan had grown up with this movie his entire life. It was a classic and he couldn't help but vomit it out in his tipsy stupor.

"What?!" Marlowe moaned in protest throwing her head back against her booth. "You like that piece of garbage?"

He stared questioningly at her in disbelief. "What?" Sloan questioned, "How could you not like it?"

"The entire thing is dated. Not to mention their impersonation of a vampire, and the cowering, and the non-stop fainting by what's-her-face! It's comical! Give me a monster story that is realistic, or at least an accurate portrayal of a vampire!"

Sloan stared hesitantly at her. "What…you like the whole Vlad the Impaler notion?"

"No. I'm just saying it could be possible that there might be a species that has naturally evolved. Look… there's a food chain, right? And man is at the top of the food chain. Maybe nature just decided that the playing field had to be evened out. The only reason vampires got a bad rep was because that was the only way for man to justify their existence, to say that they are an abomination and that they're evil, but it's just the circle of life. Everything dies and everything eats." She stopped short in her rant and bit her tongue. She had said too much and immediately tried to backtrack. She took a drink and reconsidered, "I mean…I'm just not a fan of the monster genre. The whole brooding internally conflicted vampire thing. I'm more of a…romantic comedy?" *Fuck my life.* Marlowe gave up and downed the remainder of her drink.

Sloan paused and considered all that she had explained. He had the feeling that she knew more than she was letting on, or at least was extremely lucky at being right.

"I see what you mean. I guess it is a little far-fetched...the whole undead thing. But the *whole* thing is, right? Their existence is laughable," he chuckled half-heartedly and sloshed the last inch of beer around in his glass.

Marlowe was suddenly very eager to finish the conversation and leave. She motioned to the server, signing an invisible pen in the air.

"It's terrible that we had to end a night of great conversation on fairy tales and monsters," Sloan mumbled. No matter how hard he tried his life always went back to the same subject.

"It's okay. I don't mind. This was a great night...really." Marlowe loosened the tension in her shoulders and looked into his eyes. She desperately wanted to stay and continue talking until the sun came up but feared that too much of a connection with the human species would cause her to feel guilt. That was an emotion she believed to be a handicap for her particular species; an identity crisis left to other literary genres.

Marlowe slid a wad of cash into the billfold as Sloan signed his tab. They quietly slid out of the booth. "I'll see you around," Sloan said with a wave.

"Sure. Have a good night." She smiled politely and rounded the corner to exit the restaurant, leaving Sloan next to their empty booth. The night had ended as abruptly as it had started. Their cold, separate departure from the restaurant was as if they had never met, but they had. And the smallest spark of exhilaration told each of them that they had begun something within each other, although they thought that they would never see each other again.

Sloan gathered his sweatshirt, and briefly hesitated before crossing the street. He couldn't decide whether another run, or a light snack at a food vendor, or a possible stroll downtown suited him best. Anything but go home. He refused to tell himself that he had to go home.

8

Sloan crept by the living room, sweatshirt dangling from his hand by his side. Shoeboxes of old photos lay open on the coffee table and albums littered the couch cushions. His father lay slumped in an old high back chair, shirt stained with booze. Empty bottles gathered around their family photos and an unopened case of beer sat next to the chair waiting to be inhaled. As Sloan tiptoed past, his father grumbled to consciousness.

"Sloan? That you?" He slurred. His father's eyelids barely parted and bottles clattered to the floor as he stood.

Sloan didn't even try to be courteous; his answer was short and to the point. He didn't want this conversation to last longer than it had to. "Yeah, dad. Just went for a run. I'm taking a shower and then going to bed."

"You should have been in bed hours ago…if your mother were here," he mumbled while ambling to the case of beer, footsteps landing loudly in his wake.

Sloan stood defiantly still and stared across the room at his father. He knew that his father wasn't thinking clearly and wouldn't even remember anything past beer number thirteen, but in the back of his head he couldn't help but wonder if his father was saying things he couldn't say when sober. Sloan turned and walked to his bedroom, locking the door behind him. After the deadbolt clicked, he scanned his sanctuary. Even his own room was unappealing to him. And there were the walls - four walls of that yellow buttercup paint. Four walls to constantly remind him of his father's resentment. Every night he had to fall asleep looking at those walls.

A sudden surge of productivity overcame him. Sloan ripped his posters off of the walls and tossed his photos onto his desk. He tore down a corkboard littered with notes and papers, and as he cleared off those four walls he could hear his father gaining his own destructive momentum in the living room. The sound of glass smashed against his bedroom door. Sloan listened as the noises turned into fists pounding heavily upon Patrick's door, and the pounding moved to his sister's door before finally landing heavily upon Sloan's.

"Get out here!" his father roared in the hallway.

Patrick exited his room and commenced with the usual routine of disaster aversion, talking slowly, empathetically, and quietly. Jess didn't even bother to come out. Her contribution would be to make their father his "morning-after" breakfast. Being careful to not open the door more than an inch, Sloan peered into the living room that had turned into a landslide of angering memories and whimpering emotions. Between bursts of "that bitch" and "I promised I'd kill her", his father pulled stacks of papers outlining patterns of disappearances and unsolved homicides from the corner cabinet. Hectically looking past each one, he tossed the papers throughout the room. His father swayed and swung around the room. Rolls of maps were knocked from shelves, his father falling to his knees to toil over them as he spilled beer and swore when the ink ran. Sloan stared emptily at his father. He wanted to go and comfort him, to be able to sit patiently beside Patrick as they waited for the night to run its course and be there when his father would eventually break down, but he felt nothing for this man who had made his life into a hell of repetition and blame.

His father looked up from his circled and crossed maps to take a swig. He saw Sloan peering out from behind the door, and he flew into an erratic rage.

"You're *pathetic*! You know that?" his father yelled down the hall, "You can't do anything. *You* should have died!"

Patrick stood from the couch and gave Sloan a mixed look of apology and the "you-know-dad" stare. He attempted to intervene, "It's no one's fault, dad. What happened to David was an accident."

"Not David. Your mother!" His father gave Sloan one last stare of contempt and grabbed another bottle.

Sloan clicked the door shut and slid the locks back into place. His father continued to chide him from the other room and those yellow walls seemed to laugh along with him. Immediately regretting his curiosity, he rushed to the radio and found the most raucous station he could find to drown out the fury. Sloan began to move his furniture away from the walls, but even with his efforts the belligerence continued to seep under his door. Amidst the scratching of furniture as he moved his desk to the center of the room and the blaring radio, he could hear his father banging around in the kitchen as Patrick struggled to herd him into bed. Sloan fought hard against the hatred spewing in from the rest of his house as he grabbed at the blue painter's tape. He tore vicious strands of tape from the roll, each movement of his hands hard and pressured, but every step of labor consoled his own rage. He rounded the corners of his closet with the tape, continuing to the baseboards, and finishing with his bedroom door. Eventually, after all the work he could possibly do in one night had been done and his anger slid back under the surface, he turned the radio off and fell into bed.

Hours passed into the quiet of night as Sloan slept heavily in his sheets. Barely moving, his face gave away his only signs of pain. His eyebrows turned down-ward and his lips pursed while he bit at the inside of his cheek. His fists rolled into balls and, as suddenly as he had slipped into a rage filled slumber, his eyelids tore open while he struggled against the bed beneath him.

After calming his rattled nerves, he found his phone tangled in the sheets and looked at it. An annoying four in the morning smiled at him from the screen. Rubbing his eyes as if that would erase his dreams, he refused to go back to sleep. Instead, he cracked the door open to see if his father and brother had finally made their way to bed. The living room was quiet and dark. It appeared foreign in comparison to the scene it had previously held, like a warzone now empty except for the still remains of shrapnel. Sloan quietly edged to the kitchen and filled a glass of water in the sink. Bottles and papers littered the floor, their presence fueling the resentment flowing in his veins. His teeth clenched as he thought of how he would be forced to clean his father's mess the next day.

Sloan crossed to the fireplace and rearranged some half-charred logs to make a small fire. He stood from the hearth and, as he turned to sit, he leered over at his father's chair. A few photos were jammed into the creases near the arms and its over-stuffed back cushion sat squashed and misshapen, smelling of sick liquor. Sloan aptly decided to sit in a different chair, the one that his father had crammed into the corner of the room. His exhaustion masked the jabs and bumps of the antique high back his mother had purchased long ago.

He struggled to stay awake. Every second that passed his eyes grew heavier. Sloan could feel his limbs sinking into the chair, and the temperature of the room mocked his futile attempts to stay awake. He hated to be warm in any way. Only the cold could console him. It was a reminder that he was alive, and it kept him moving. The movement of a cold breeze was quick and bit at the world around it, whereas the stifling heat of a summer wind forced people to move slower, think slower. One of the many reasons Sloan hated the South. It was like moving through molasses. But the heat proved to be so inviting this time. The air in the cabin enveloped him in a blanket of warm repose. It was as if the world wanted him to fall asleep, beckoned him to relax.

The fire licked at the surrounding air and sent shadows across his eyelids. He attempted to remain alert, awake. Every time his eyes closed, he would immediately jump, startling himself. Five minutes seemed like an eternity and the rhythmic swinging of the pendulum in the clock on the far wall began to hypnotize him. Click, click, click, click. He couldn't resist. Click, click, click. The room began to warp around him. Click, click. His vision tunneled. Click, click. The noises faded. Click …and as he slipped into the corners of his mind his head dropped to the side and came to rest on his shoulder…

I feel the warmth of the sun still lingering on the metal bars of the playground even after the daylight had dissipated minutes ago. Sand forms little mounds and hills in my shoes, bothering my feet, but I refuse to stop long enough for her to untie them, empty them out, and lace them back up. I move around the slides and walls of the playground as I chase imaginary soldiers and dragons. I hang from the monkey bars, afraid of the spewing lava licking at my toes. I climb up the ladders like they were the very rocks of Everest. She watches the whole time, smiling and waving from her bench. I can see the love in her eyes even through the darkness of night encroaching in the distance. He went back to the car for our camera, and every once in a while she looks over her shoulder to see if he is on his way back yet. But when I reach the top of the tower and look down at her there is something else. It comes down off the hill from the tree line. It seems to bring the night with it like a thick wool overcoat. It moves so quickly that in those few seconds everything about life changes…

Sloan woke with a scream, his lungs tearing at the air. He gasped. It was as if all the air in his nightmare had been water, and he was finally able to rip through to the surface. His throat scraped dry with each clawing breath. He gripped at his chest and tried to force his beating heart to slow. Skin crawling, he doubled over in nausea. He cradled his head in his hands. There was no escape, no bargaining with the thoughts that swam through his mind every day only to emerge through the surface at night. They were so intense. They were so real. They imprinted onto his eyes, and their shadows stained his memory.

9

Laughter drifted under Marlowe's doorway as she turned in her gray flannel sheets. She rolled out of bed and crossed to her window, pulling back layers of heavy curtains to reveal the night sky. Yellow lights looked out of nearby windows to streetlamps on the road below. As she peered into the windows at her neighbors going about their bedtime routines, the laughter grew stronger as someone finally reached the crescendo of their story. Marlowe quickly dressed and twisted her hair into a loose bun before making her way downstairs.

The house was beginning to look as it had before they left for their trip East. The rich oak furniture had been polished. Tall lamps and low chandeliers sent a soft glow around the room, and splashes of books and antiques dotted shelves and tabletops. Instead of sheets and boxes, there now was a collection of sentimental, historical memorabilia delicately dotting each surface. Homes like this only belonged to the very old or the very wealthy, and in Marlowe's family's case, both.

Dorian stood, smiling, next to a dark leather couch. He poured their most expensive brandy into the snifters of an attractive brunette and her male companion. Upon entering, Marlowe was immediately flung into polite introductions and cordial chatter before she was able to take her usual seat in her corner chair. Oliver walked in carrying a small tin delicately between his thumb and forefinger. His leather Oxfords excitedly padded across the wood floors.

"I don't know if you remember this Emily," he said to their guest.

Marlowe had seen the small tin on his bedside table many times but thought nothing of it. Emily turned her head and looked curiously at the box.

Taking it from his hand, she opened it and asked, "Tea?"

Oliver looked expectantly at her, and there was a thick pause before they both burst into laughter. Marlowe looked across the room at Lydia. They both glanced an awkward stare at each other and shrugged. Evidently, this wasn't one of those inside jokes people liked to explain to the rest of the group. Evangeline dramatically laughed in her chair, trying to appear as if she knew the punch line. She didn't. She held up her empty drink with a smile toward Oliver.

"Where have you been staying?" Dorian asked Emily.

"We are actually renting a house across town. We knew that you had found this city suitable for a residence, so we decided to visit," Emily replied as she took a sip of brandy.

"And how are you finding your hunting? We left to head east about a decade ago because it was becoming too dangerous here." Dorian's eyes momentarily flashed around the room.

"Some of us were becoming impulsive..." Evangeline added.

Dorian interjected, "Minor cabin fever, if you will. We slowly travelled back west, and it's nice to be home."

Emily nodded politely. "I see. Well, hunting is average. We started rationing ourselves when we heard of your arrival into town, so as not to cause a stir. We really should find some other feeding grounds, but the few we frequent are prime. There's the Rusty Hook, the Clancy, and..." She turned toward her companion, "Benjamin, what's that last one, with all the older women?"

"I don't remember the name, but the locals call it 'The Den'," Benjamin replied.

"We'll be sure and stay away from those areas then. With fewer and fewer of us, it will be nice to share the territory." Dorian poured himself another glass of brandy and sat on the arm of the couch next to Emily.

Sensing her exclusion, Emily turned politely to Marlowe. "So, Dorian tells me you're originally from Cape Cod? That must've been nice."

"Yes. I suppose it was." Marlowe tried to remain light. Lately, all the talk of hometowns was beginning to make her feel nostalgic, but in the terrible way that makes you want to bury your head in the sand. She changed the subject, "How do you all know each other?"

"Well, I met Oliver back in the 1700s at a tavern called Cromwell's Head. I was serving porter and he just walked in for some lodging and food, although the food wasn't that good. We were amicable, talked for some time, and became...friends." Emily's reciprocated smile to Oliver made Evangeline bristle and erratically clear her throat, and Marlowe smiled at her discomfort. "And then I evolved in 1798, but that is an entirely different story. Some time passed until I came across Oliver again, but this time he was with his brother. And that's how I met Dorian."

Dorian cut in, "And we ended up meeting again after the turn of the century, under much better circumstances, and Oliver and I introduced Benjamin to Emily, and one thing led to another..."

"We fell in love," Emily cut Dorian off with a smile.

Benjamin blushed and added a small, "...and I didn't find out what she was until after we were married." The whole room escalated into another roll of laughter.

"How did you keep it a secret for so long?" Marlowe asked.

"He only courted me for one month before I agreed to marry him, and then we were only engaged to be married for one month after that. I wasn't going to tell him until afterwards. What would he have done otherwise?"

"I would've put you away in an institution or tried to kill you, I suppose." Benjamin winked up at her.

"Either way, it would have been terrible, and I was in love and not thinking clearly," Emily trailed off, silkily grinning and looking into Benjamin's eyes.

Benjamin sighed and looked toward Marlowe, "The conversation the evening after our wedding was difficult. The risks...unimaginable. Nonetheless, I was in perfect health and Emily allowed me to decide. After the proverbial coin was flipped, Emily stayed by my side, listening intently to my heart. I actually don't remember much of those minutes that passed. But I do remember opening my eyes and seeing the relief in hers." His hand rested on her knee and they tenderly breathed a synchronous sigh.

Dorian quietly wandered from the room. "I'm going to put

the brandy away."

The conversation continued at an even ebb and flow as Marlowe followed him into the kitchen. The white cabinets and gray marble counters were in heavy contrast with the rest of the house, but the appliances were antique and barely functional. Dorian stood hunched over the sink, one hand gripping the brandy until his knuckles strained white.

Marlowe pulled herself up onto the counter to sit, her feet dangling and lightly hitting the cabinet beneath. "Are you all right?"

Her question unlocked his stiff shoulders and brought him back to himself. "Yes, I'll be fine." He cleared his throat.

"Did you love her?" she asked, her voice not louder than a whisper.

Dorian turned to face her. His eyes narrowed in confusion as he studied Marlowe's expression.

"Who? Emily?" he asked. An aching laugh left his lungs, and he became quiet again. "No...not Emily. Her and Benjamin's story just took me somewhere I didn't think would bother me. I didn't believe that the memory would be so fresh in my mind after so long."

Marlowe motioned to slide down off the counter, but Dorian caught her before her feet reached the floor. He lightly kissed her forehead and, as he moved away, he hesitated inches from her lips. He wanted to, and she knew it. They both felt the pull toward each other, to replace the ache of pain and memory with a fleeting kiss. He inched closer to her, his hands resting on the countertop on each side of her. She placed her hands on his upper arms, the cotton button-up softly wrinkling under her fingertips. He was almost to her, but just before their lips touched, she thought better of it and wrapped her arms around him as she hugged him.

A few moments passed as they lingered in their embrace. Their short-lived moment of desire turned to pity and, when they parted, Dorian sighed. They looked regrettably into each other's eyes before the arthritic silence was broken.

"Where do you go when you leave to be alone?" Dorian

asked.

Marlowe looked over Dorian's shoulder to avoid his eyes. "To the park. There's this bench. I just like to sit and watch people. Watch the grass. The sky. It's ridiculous, and I sound like an old eighty-year-old woman feeding the pigeons."

"You're older than an eighty-year-old woman," Dorian corrected with a smile. After a time, his face grew serious again. He brushed Marlowe's hair off her shoulder with the back of his hand. "I just want you to be careful."

Marlowe reassured him, "I always am."

"I know," he grinned as he parted from her to retrieve the brandy carafe. Marlowe hopped to the floor and turned to leave the kitchen. Dorian's voice stopped her, "I do love you, Marlowe."

She swallowed hard to force her voice steady, "I know."

Marlowe left the kitchen confused and ashamed. The last thing she wanted to do was eat but as she reemerged into the living room everyone was gathering jackets and sweaters from the coat closet. Forcing a weak smile upon her face, Marlowe rummaged through the closet for her boots and grabbed the new black jacket Lydia had given her. She quickly dressed among their lighthearted chatter and as she watched Emily and Benjamin playfully nudge each other she was overcome with a calm resolve. With their affection came companionship, and even though Marlowe was left without the first she was thankful to have the second. Dorian met them in the hall, and before they left the house to hunt, he offered his arm to her.

Marlowe gladly took it.

*   *   *

The others walked toward the elevator near the other end of the parking garage, but Marlowe stayed behind for a few beats looking over the garage railing into the teeming city. She watched as cars drove down the streets of Seattle, their rear-lights flashing as drivers pressed upon the breaks. Her eyes moved to the sky. Clouds rolled past in a deep haze as the lights from the city gave them a warm glow. No stars out tonight. A breeze rolled under her nose with the faintest trace of a child. Marlowe's jaw clenched. She opened her eyes, swallowed deeply, and placed the hunger in the back of her mind.

"Marlowe!" Lydia called. Everyone had already piled into the cab of the elevator, and they were waiting impatiently as they held the doors open for her. As she trotted over to them, Marlowe's eyes became warm and she let out a small sigh releasing the tension in her neck and shoulders. Dorian looked down at her and cradled her hand in his.

"Smell something nice out there?" he asked.

She mischievously glared up at him as she slid her tongue over the contours of her protruded canines.

Lydia clapped her hands together and let out a small squeal of excitement as she exclaimed, "What are we eating? I'm starving!"

"That's a surprise," Evangeline teased.

Oliver playfully lifted Evangeline in his arms and kissed her forehead. "This is why I chose you, the constant sarcasm. What would we do without your keen observations and witty retorts?" She pushed him away and gave him a quick roll of the eyes before fixing the slightly tousled waves of her hair.

"Are you sure it's no inconvenience?" Emily asked from the corner.

"Oh, of course not. There should be plenty to go around. Just go with whoever gets the twelfth floor," Oliver replied.

Lydia exchanged a puzzled look with Evangeline before asking, "Whoever 'gets'?"

"You'll see," he smiled around the elevator. Apparently, only Dorian and Oliver were in on the plan.

The elevator signaled their arrival with the quaint ding of a bell and the doors parted. Across the street stood a tall office building. It appeared to be entirely made of glass and reflected the night around it. The street was empty and the lights flashed red for the night traffic. As they crossed the street, Dorian urged the group to an adjacent, narrow alleyway. Marlowe watched as Oliver parted ways with them and moved toward the shiny revolving doors. He changed his stature as his expression became panicked and frightened. Benjamin and Emily exchanged excited glances.

"Have I mentioned how much I missed hunting with you lot?" Benjamin grinned from ear to ear and Dorian smiled as he looked over his shoulder at them skipping joyfully behind him. They disappeared into the alley as Oliver entered the building. The security officer glanced up from his late-night reading and stared questioningly at Oliver as he tried to hide his magazine into a drawer. Oliver took a quick glance at its front page before the fumbling man had a chance to stuff it away. He laughed to himself as he eyed the cover.

"You can't be here. It's after hours," the man said as he stood up and waved Oliver out of the building, but Oliver didn't budge. Instead, he breathed in and out with such velocity that the words came in animated waves.

"I know, sir. I just heard screaming from that alley next to your building. I was walking to my car after a late night and called the cops. But I saw you and figured I should inform you as well...it sounded pretty gruesome. I think a lady is in danger," he rambled. He had to keep from smiling because he was so thrilled with his performance.

The rotund security officer's eyes grew wide as he absorbed the story. He pulled up on his belt, grasped his taser, and moved from behind the counter.

"Stay here," he instructed.

"Trust me...you don't want to go out there," Oliver sincerely replied with a small hint of menace. The security officer hesitated before deciding to go forth and, as he exited the building, Oliver let loose his pent-up smile.

Marlowe had been waiting patiently against the brick wall. She chose to read the graffiti to pass the time, when suddenly a man with a small metal badge attached to his vest turned the corner. Before he could even make a sound, Dorian was upon him covering his mouth and pressing his fingers against his windpipe. Lydia ripped into his chest, her teeth tearing against his warm flesh. Blood soaked his light blue vest and ran down to his waist.

"Guests first, Lydia!" Dorian scolded in a hushed whisper as the man struggled against his grasp. Lydia pulled away and looked sheepishly at Emily.

"I'm sorry," she apologized as she dabbed at the blood dripping from her chin.

"You are always so messy!" Marlowe laughed.

"It's okay," Emily smiled. With an excited flick of the hair, she bent down toward the guard's chest.

They each took their respective turns and as Evangeline finished the rotation he slid from Dorian's arms into a puddle of his own blood. As they cleaned their hands and faces, Benjamin motioned them out of the alley and onto the sidewalk leading to the revolving doors.

They entered the building to see Oliver sitting mischievously behind the security counter. The television screens behind him revealed black, empty boxes. He had no doubt removed the security tapes and turned off the system while they were outside. He hopped over the counter and placed his hands behind his back as a devious smirk spread across his face. Walking up to Marlowe he asked, "Right or left?"

"Right."

Oliver held up two slips of paper. "One or two?"

"Two."

He handed her the second slip and moved to the others, playing the same hand game as he went. After each slip had been distributed, he cleared his throat, "In each of your hands is a small slip of paper. On each of the papers is a location…a floor in the building. You will go to the floor and find a surprise waiting in one of its rooms. I just want you to know that I have done my research. Every night for the last week the same people have been burning the midnight oil and every night they have not disappointed me. You have no idea how hard it was not to just act like a glutton. Try not to have too much fun." He winked at Lydia and Evangeline who had been given the twelfth floor. "Now, Dorian is going to stay down here and play look-out." Oliver looked down at the paper he had been left with and moved quickly to the elevators. "Happy hunting," he called over his shoulder. Lydia and Evangeline showed their slip to Emily and Benjamin before racing each other to the stairwell.

Marlowe sauntered to the desk and leaned over the counter. "You're not eating more?"

Dorian rummaged through the desk drawers and took out the crinkled and worn magazine. "No…I have to catch up on my reading," he replied sarcastically as he turned unabashedly to a page of a woman lying provocatively on some stereotypical black satin sheet.

"Have fun." Marlowe winked at Dorian and turned her attention to the ripped piece of paper in her hand. Transcribed upon it was a graceful number "16." She placed the paper in her pocket and pressed the up button on the elevator.

Once inside she leaned against the cold, metal wall. She closed her eyes and inhaled deeply. The smell of the day's inhabitants still lay lightly on the elevator's surfaces. One scent stood out from the rest. A child had been there. She separated each scent.

Sugar cookies. Grass. Sweat. Paint. Lavender.

As she exited the elevator, she knew without a doubt that a small child had enjoyed a wonderful day of finger-paints and outdoor activities before visiting someone for lunch. The slight touch of lavender perfume told Marlowe that the child was holding its mother's hand while waiting for the relieving ding of the elevator as it reached its destination and opened its doors.

The sixteenth floor was empty. She walked by rows and rows of desks spinning each office chair as she went, leaving a twirling line of chairs in her wake. After passing a few offices, she noticed that one of the far rooms was lit, the light barely slipping through the cracks in the horizontal blinds.

She scanned the remaining offices before deciding that this lonely office in the corner was Oliver's intended mark for her. Marlowe thought about the kill as she walked down the hall. She considered it as if she were deciding whether to broil, bake, or fry a freshly cut filet. The more anxious the prey was before the catch the more bitter it tasted; the chemicals of stress made the blood thick and heavy. The happier the prey was the sweeter it tasted; the endorphins added a light, almost citrus flavor. And the sudden surprise of an unsuspecting victim made it a delicacy; the adrenaline acting as a soft, creamy butter in the veins.

Marlowe toyed with the methods in her mind and decided that the element of surprise was her preferred fare for the evening. She positioned herself right outside the office door, and just before Marlowe was about to fling the door open she heard a noise. Instead of one voice coming from the other side of the door, there were two. One male and one distinctly female. The female's voice let out a teasing giggle that faded into low, carnal moans. Marlowe released the door handle and stepped back a few feet.

. *Oliver…you son of a bitch*, she thought with a smile. She pulled a rolling office chair to the door, sat down, and crossed her legs. Marlowe listened intently as she allowed her prey to finish their transgressions. It was the least she could do, and the endorphins and serotonin pumping through their writhing bodies was the *je ne sais quoi* to a perfect meal.

Clearly, the couple believed they were alone; their late-night escapade adding excitement and yearning to the sound of their loud, rhythmic poundings against the desk. A chair bumped across the floor and a metal container holding pens and pencils clearly fell to the ground as its contents scattered and rolled across the carpet. Marlowe could hear a clumsy shift in position as the two whispered awkward instructions and adjustments to each other. When the couple found their new placement, they started in quick and rapid, obviously moving toward a finish. The woman squealed and moaned her last into the night, and Marlowe snickered to herself, *Faker*.

When she was quite sure that they were basking in the aftermath, she rolled her chair to its desk and regained her position at the door. Her mouth began to water as she imagined the sweet, buttery tastes infusing her palate. Her teeth ached as she allowed her canines to extend into her mouth. They slowly tore at her gums; a process that was necessary and fulfilling, but painful to endure. With one final inhalation she thrust the door open and descended upon the room's occupants.

The female had just begun to button her skirt and, before she could even turn to stare at the intruder, she was overcome. Marlowe lunged behind her and grabbed the woman's hair with one hand while wrapping her arm around her bare waist. Her teeth tore into the her shoulder and moved up the neck. Blood poured from the wound and the woman quickly went limp as she lost consciousness. The male stood, shocked, in a corner of the office. He bumped up against the wall causing his many degrees and awards to teeter upon their hooks. Some fell and crashed to the floor. His striped tie was loose and askew, and his pants hung limply halfway down his thighs. As Marlowe finished one meal and dropped it to the floor, she turned her attention to the other. As she lowered her head, blood dripped from her jaw. She took a few steps closer to the quivering man. He mumbled and held up his hands in speechless defense. Marlowe paused and smiled, raised her right hand and brushed the remnants of blood from her face.

Her heart was racing and the veins and arteries under her skin were pumping feverishly as she geared up for her second attack. The male made a split-second decision and moved to the left, but before he could take two steps forward she slammed him against the wall and forced him still with one of her forearms. She grabbed his left hand and eyed the ring finger where she located a small, gold band. Marlowe spun it upon his finger. As quickly as she had grabbed him, she opened her mouth and bit into his chest, just above his heart. She could feel the pumping muscle slow just inches from her canines. His scream muffled into a tight gasp as his face fell into a taught grimace. As he faded, Marlowe let him slip to the floor. She crouched down beside him to observe the blood pump through the gaping hole in his chest and dump to his side. Her elbows perched on her kneecaps as she sat on her haunches and her eyes moved over his body, taking in every shiver and convulsion. She listened intently as his heart began to hammer from within his rib cage. His eyes grew glossy and rolled back into his head and a warm sweat broke out over his face. She watched as his shoulders quaked and his veins engorged under his skin. With awe, she couldn't help but observe his torment with the grotesque fascination that a child would have with an insect under a magnifying glass in the heat of summer.

Marlowe cocked her head to the side as his eyes quivered under the strain. The rhythm of his heart sped to untraceable lengths, the Morse code skipping through short bursts and pummeling into long, slow taps. His mouth hung open in one last gasp. His back rose in one last futile attempt. And his heart stopped, its muscle and resolve not fit for the metamorphosis.

Finished and exhilarated, she took a seat in a high-backed leather chair and surveyed the remnants of her meal as she allowed her muscles to cool. She closed her eyes and went into the calm blackness of her mind, away from the hunt.

As she sat still in her solitude, Marlowe felt the blood beginning to dry around her mouth and on her neck. She fumbled for a loose article of clothing upon the desk and found the woman's blouse. As she cleaned the blood from her skin, Marlowe kept her eyes closed. She wanted to wait until her canines had retracted, so she could relax in the joy and accomplishment of a satisfying meal. As her heart slowed to its normal pace, she gradually opened her eyes and peeked around the office. There was a tremendous amount of blood pooling upon the brown and white speckled carpet and the walls and desk had a fine red mist upon them.

Making sure her flats didn't hit any puddles or make any footprints, she moved quietly toward the door, but something caught her attention. Amidst the smells of blood and sex, Marlowe could sense the subtlest hint of lavender and sugar cookies. She turned and looked around the room, her eyes stopping on a set of small, framed photos sitting happily on a bookshelf. She walked to the photos and stared into the faces, and her attention quickly shifted to the smallest photo. The man she had just fed upon was at a beach with what appeared to be his daughter. They both had large smiles upon their faces, and the little girl lovingly looked up at her father.

Marlowe tore her eyes from the photo as distant memories screamed back into her mind. Her heart began to race and her hands rolled into fists. Marlowe grasped the edge of the bookshelf as she forced herself to keep from spinning out of control.

Very slowly, she moved to the office door, flicked off the light, and left the room. Fighting not to look back or acknowledge her momentary weakness, she walked to the elevators, and, after pressing the plastic down button, planted herself in front of the metal doors. She once was so strong - impulsive, but steady. Now she found herself slipping at every comment or photo. With every nod of a family member or sideways glance, she believed the worst. She was a rag doll slowly splitting at the seams, bits of fluff peeking out at the world and falling to the ground, lost forever to her mind.

The doors parted. Emily's thoughtful gaze enveloped her, and Marlowe walked into the elevator with an exhalation as she zipped her black coat.

"You need a break," Emily said from the corner.

Marlowe leaned against the walls of the elevator and picked at the crevice where two pieces of sheet metal met in the corner of the elevator. "I don't know what I need anymore. It just keeps getting worse."

"Have you tried being alone?" Emily pensively watched as Marlowe's fingers fumbled against the wall.

"Yes, but I ran into someone, so it didn't really work out." Marlowe smiled at the thought of Sloan.

Emily removed a small handkerchief from her pocket and gently rubbed a spatter of blood off of Marlowe's chin. "If they make you smile like that, then maybe you should run into them more often."

"Maybe," Marlowe muttered with a grin and a bite of her lower lip. She thought about the effortless conversation with Sloan and the warmth she felt around him. She took a sideways glance toward Emily and sighed, "Did Dorian put you up to this? Send you back up here for me?"

Emily laughed. "Yes, but don't tell him I told you."

"All right. As long as you don't tell him I'm losing it."

Marlowe held out her hand.

"Deal," Emily agreed.

The doors opened into the lobby, and Marlowe relaxed as her newfound friend gracefully walked to Benjamin. He slipped a delicate silver bracelet onto her wrist – a trinket he undoubtedly took from his latest kill. Emily cooed over the finely braided strands, and they batted at each other like kittens before filing out of the building onto the street. Pushing the fluff back into her tattered seams, Marlowe gathered herself together. She walked with heavy, unsure steps, but by the time she reached Dorian's waiting arm she had regained her composure and every inch of her screamed to believe that she was fine.

Bright, abrasive lights flashed yellow and red against the backdrop of night. With heavy stenches flaring from every direction and reaching toward his nostrils, he shoved his way down the path. Every now and then, a peel of screams would slice through the crowd, followed by the whooshing noises of spinning and heaving contraptions. Sloan walked through the state fair, accidently bumping into gawking patrons as he struggled to keep up. He followed behind his aunt and sister, and they would rush up to a game counter or food stand only to linger for a moment before ricocheting to another booth. Annoyed, Sloan was forced to change direction with each new decision. His arms were full of their winnings: bright pink teddy bears, inflatable baseball bats, and bags of popcorn and cotton candy. Occasionally, he would crane his neck to see if his father and brother were in sight, but they never were.

They had split from the group to find the restrooms at the edge of the fairgrounds and had probably become distracted by a game, or something worse - suspicious behavior that in the end would be harmless. Becoming paranoid, they would stalk someone whom they felt was a potential target only to find them eating a snow cone or chomping on a foot long hot dog, their misconceptions fading away until they found yet another person to watch with suspicious eyes. The fair was supposed to be a distraction from the ordinary, or at least that's what Aunt Mag said, so Sloan enjoyed these outings and considered them a type of mini vacation, but whenever the event would draw to a close, he would be faced with the same disappointment as they ventured back into that same terrible cycle.

"Do you mind if Mag and I go on the Condor?" Jess asked as she grabbed the popcorn and cotton candy from Sloan's arms. "It'll only be a couple of minutes and we can do whatever you want after. Okay?" She inhaled the food before Aunt Mag could even catch up to her.

Sloan laughed and sat himself at a picnic table at the edge of

the food pavilion. Jess had told him that they would do whatever
he wanted only about a million times that night, but as they
skipped off to the nearby ride Sloan sat alone. He watched people
pass chattering wildly or holding hands. He moved crumbs around
the table with his index finger and looked aimlessly at the
scurrying ants beneath his feet wielding large loads of food.
Laughing to himself, he compared the ants to the people around
him, their faces stuffed with grease and their arms bulging with
gluttony.

A woman walked out from between two booths onto the main
stretch of fairway, and when he looked up from the ants below and
saw her, he smiled.

Marlowe skipped over cables that had been run between the
game booths. With the state fair more than an hour away from her
family's home, she thought it safe to borrow the car and go out on
her own for a solitary hunt, but she was no longer alone. Marlowe
felt the burn of eyes upon her and scanned the fairway. Her gaze
landed on the picnic area where she found a dark-haired man
sitting behind a plush, pink teddy bear. She waved and slowly
walked over to him between the movement of crowds and strollers
as she briskly wiped her cheeks and neck with the back of her
sleeve for any sloppy remnants. Never before had she wanted so
much to look into a mirror before starting a conversation.

"You look like you're having fun." She patted the teddy bear
on the head.

Sloan's cheeks flushed. He rolled his eyes, "It's my sister's. I
swear."

She brushed the picnic table top off with her hand before
gracefully hopping up onto the table to sit. Relaxing onto her
elbows, Sloan and Marlowe watched as people wandered by,
looking at the rides or comparing their prizes with one another.
They quietly surveyed the gamut together, ranging from a first
date to a seven-hundredth date. Teenagers fidgeted with their
clothes or shoved their hands in pockets, wondering when their
date would finally hold their hand. Young couples shared pinches
of food between the batting of eyelashes and the occasional

longing stare. Families dragged kids along by the hand, the smart ones propping the youngsters up on their shoulders. Old couples strolled along the fairway, happy and oblivious to the other fairgoers who would hustle by them. As Marlowe watched the waves of crowds, she began to wonder what they thought as they looked at Sloan and her. If they appeared a couple at all, or maybe they were just two strangers sharing the same picnic table. Marlowe snuck a sideways glance at Sloan. His t-shirt was second hand, but the way he wore it gave it more of a vintage feel. His khaki shorts were worn at the cuff and frayed a little along the pockets. Spending a little too much time on his attire, Marlowe snapped her eyes back to the crowds.

Sloan caught a flick of Marlowe's shoe from the corner of his eye. "I'm sorry about a few weeks back."

"What are you sorry about?" Marlowe asked.

"That night we met and went to that bar didn't seem to end too well, and you kind of left in a hurry. So, I'm sorry if it wasn't what you hoped for," he apologized as he crossed his arms across his chest.

"It was great. Don't be sorry. If it was as bad as you think it was, I wouldn't have walked over to you." She pushed him playfully on the shoulder.

Sloan grinned. "I never thought I'd see you again, but here you are."

"Here I am," Marlowe sighed. Their eyes fixed on one another, the invisible strings once again being cast out and one by one attaching to one another. With a nod and a smile, Sloan stood from the table.

"Do you want to go on a ride or something? My sister won't miss me if she can't find me for a few minutes," he asked.

"Sure! I'd love to," Marlowe replied.

"You can hold this if you want?" Sloan made the puffy, pink teddy bear dance upon the table, trying to make it as appealing as possible.

Marlowe laughed and grabbed the bear by the paw. "What? It's not your style?"

"It's definitely my style, but you just don't have any prizes yet. I don't want you to feel left out...share the wealth, you know." He winked at her, making her face grow warm and cherry. Sloan shied away at her blushing as he helped her off of the picnic table.

They ambled back onto the crowded and hot fairway. Marlowe held her breath for a majority of the walk. The air held a pungent, repulsive quality that sent her stomach flipping. *Sweat. Vomit. Fried food. Farm animals.* She held the bear to her chest and leaned her head down to breathe through its fur.

Sloan breathed in deep and exhaled, "I love the smell of this place."

"Mmm-hmm." Marlowe caught a glimpse of the Ferris wheel at the edge of the grounds. Something slow and airy. "Ferris wheel?"

"Yeah. We'll get a good view." Sloan clasped her hand and led the way, making a couple of shortcuts between games and vendors before making it into the Ferris wheel's line. Her heart jumped at his touch. Unsure of herself, she pulled away. Sloan only had a moment to look down at her before they were quickly ushered onto the tilting bench of the ride.

As they made their way into the sky, Marlowe let out a sigh of relief. "I don't like the smell...but I do like the way the fair looks from up here." The noises of the fair hushed beneath them, and the lights quietly blinked and flashed across the grounds. A wind crept by their bench and brought a clean burst of air to Marlowe's senses. Sloan shivered in his seat.

Marlowe removed the bear from between them and passed it into Sloan's goose-bumped arms. "Here. This pink bear can now serve a purpose."

He sat it comfortably upon his lap and crossed his arms behind it. "Thanks. If he hadn't been given a purpose, he probably would have developed a complex."

"And then he would have resented you for the rest of his life, or until you handed him off to your sister," Marlowe laughed. Sloan's face felt relieved as he smiled in return, his cheeks and chin using muscles once forgotten.

The Ferris wheel swung through another rotation and headed back up to the top. They sat quietly in their gondola, enjoying the silence of each other's company as they slowly moved upwards into the air. With a silent push from their subconscious, they inched closer to each other. A billion Ferris wheels spun between them, and as they reached the apex of the revolution a cold chill caressed Marlowe's cheek, but betrayed her when it blew across Sloan's neck.

Sugar. Laundry detergent. Sweat. Barbeque charcoal. Sirloin. Mouth watering, her stare remained upon his neck, skin smooth in the darkness with hairs standing on end.

"Is there a bug on me?" Sloan gripped at his skin, brushing every which way.

Marlowe blinked back to reality. "Yeah. A small one, it's gone now." Staring ahead of her, she sat like a statue and watched as the horizon vanished behind game stands and roller coasters, only to reappear as they made their way up one final spin. She wanted the last rotation of this ride to be over. She clenched every inch of muscle to keep from turning to Sloan until he slowly dropped his arm over her shoulders. A shockwave of deep hunger and sensation brushed down her spine at his touch. His wrist was so close to her mouth as it dangled around her shoulder. Marlowe parted her lips slightly and breathed in. She leaned toward his wrist, his radial artery calling out to her from his arm.

"Did I say something?" His voice snapped Marlowe forward, and Sloan studied her face with worry. She didn't dare look back at him for fear that she might slip and do something careless. She grew hungrier with each teasing touch of wind across his body and the incessant thrumming of his wrist near her ear.

The ride stopped and a burly man holding a cigarette clicked the safety bar open. Marlowe jumped from the bench and hustled into the reeking crowds.

Sweat. Vomit. Fried food. Farm animals. The repulsive odor flipped her senses upside down and when Sloan caught up to her and laid his hand upon her shoulder, she neither flinched nor hungered for him anymore.

"I must have gotten motion sickness," she coughed into her hand while rubbing her stomach.

"Yeah, looks like it. You were really pale there for a moment." He gently rubbed circles between her shoulder blades as they walked back to the picnic tables.

"I should get going," Marlowe murmured.

"Before you leave this time, can I get your phone number? I'd like to call you." Sloan was surprised at his own courage and couldn't help but stand a little straighter and walk a little brisker. Marlowe didn't answer, fearing that if she spoke it, she would immediately regret it. Instead, she chose to scribble it down on an old receipt and hand it over to him before walking away.

He watched as the back of her long brown hair disappeared behind a ring toss. A new emptiness filled his chest and he wished that he had Marlowe's hand in his own, not the puffy, pink paw of an unwanted teddy bear. He slumped down onto the picnic table when Jess bounded up to him with a freshly powdered elephant ear.

"Look what we got you! But don't eat it all, cause I want some when you're done." She slid the plate across the table to him. He didn't touch it. "You okay?"

"Yeah. I'm fine." Looking slightly crazed, Sloan grinned from ear to ear. His sister and aunt looked at his uncommon smile before shaking their heads and turning to their sodas, but Sloan was ambivalent to their quiet shock. He was wrapped up in his own contentment, thinking of when he should dial the numbers in his pocket and what he might say when her voice spoke on the other end of the line. Even while Marlowe walked away from him in the distance as he sat at the picnic table staring dopily at an elephant ear, the strings had been cast out, attached, and would stretch however far apart they became.

11

He felt the give of carpet beneath his feet but heard no footsteps. Sloan moved silently through each room, rounding corner after corner, his heart racing with anticipation only to settle and relax after discovering that what he was searching for was not hidden behind the next corner. But he knew that after so many turns, he was bound to come upon his target eventually. Art hung on the walls. Glass tables and sculptures dotted the rooms. Everything in its place with not a speck of dust.

No children, Sloan thought, a wave of relief flowing over him.

The gun's metal felt heavy in his hands and he kept grasping and releasing it to prevent his sweaty palms from slipping when the moment would finally come. His stomach leapt up against his panicked heart as he saw Patrick silently pass outside by the tall windows of the living room that looked out onto a patio. Glimmering flashes of moonlight on pool water shined in upon the walls of the living room. He had to keep still so he didn't accidently bump into a table or lamp in his temporary fright, but he was relieved that his family had finally arrived at the house. Stretching his neck to either side, he forced his stomach back into place as he moved forwards toward the second floor. Every step up the wide stairs felt like an eternity, the staircase growing higher and higher. When he managed to cross the threshold onto the second floor, he heard whispering from down the hall. Their crisp voices drifted under the far door and wafted to his ears.

Barely audible, he heard the faint scuff of a patio chair catch against the cement beneath it. So did they. Their whispering stopped, and just before they opened the door down the hall to reveal Sloan, he sidestepped into a nearby room with the newfound agility that accompanies adrenaline. Two silent figures passed his room and moved down the long stairs, quieter than he could ever be.

He leaned forward to gain a better view from his hiding place out of the bedroom window, but the crinkle of plastic tore through the silence of the room as he took his first step. Sloan held his breath and movement, listening intently for any sound. No noise came for him, so he glanced down at his feet, and continued to look at the room he had so eagerly darted into. Plastic sheeting had been placed everywhere. The floor, the walls, and all of the furniture had been covered with tarps. As Sloan turned, he found the reason. Upon a plastic covered bed, lay a woman. The same woman he had observed at *The Den*. The woman who had looked happier than she had all night when a young man had decided to talk to her, to befriend her, and, at the end of the night, to ask her home with him. Her bracelets dangled from her wrists and her necklace hung lopsided off her neck. All of her jewelry dripped with blood, coagulating within the loops of the chains and forming tiny lakes and streams in the crevices of the plastic.

Sloan was too late. He saw the man approach her lonely table. She looked up at him with such eager eyes and a relieved smile. Sloan watched as the man worked his way into her trusting mind and, after an hour, she willingly got into his car. Sloan could see him toy with her hair and her neck as he followed them here to this house. She would laugh and swoon into his outstretched hand, but when she arrived at the neatly manicured home and they opened the door, she hesitated. Sloan could see another person inside the home, a woman, who had opened the door eager for their arrival; in that moment, Sloan felt so sure of his instinct. He called his family from his truck and then waited. He sat, picking at the worn-down seat of his truck and gnawing at his cuticles before finally mustering the courage to make himself go inside...but it was too late.

He stood in the middle of the room and quietly added the guilt of the moment to all of the rest - another brick of weight to his already laden chest.

Sloan left the room, one crinkling, pained step after another. Raising his gun once more, he went into the hall and squinted down the stairs toward the same whispering voices now pouring in from an open sliding glass door. Wind chimes rang from the patio, followed by splashing. The pool.

He quickly descended the stairs and found himself just feet from the open door. He stared out the window, gaze intent on the monsters who were so flippant about their crimes. It was a man and a woman. They made circles around each other, lightly splashing and talking. Their clothes lay next to the pool in unkempt piles. A small, red light caught Sloan's eye from the far bushes. His family was there, and they were watching and waiting. He relaxed as he gripped his gun. The time had come.

Exiting the house with a few smooth strides, Sloan began to shoot silent rounds into the pool, sending water reaching into the air in tiny columns. Following his lead, Jess stepped from the bushes as she shot into the water. One by one his family came out into the moonlight. Bullets hit the sides of the pool and sent chunks of cement flying into the bushes. The water slowly turned a shade of pink, and then gradually became a darker shade of crimson.

When all had settled, Jess and Patrick went into the house, but instead of following, Sloan walked to the edge of the pool. The water sloshed up onto the sides before it slowly calmed and two naked bodies floated on the surface, drifting toward one another only to separate on their wake. Sloan could smell gasoline as the others emptied cans upon cans into the house and onto the yard. Jess called for him to get in his truck and leave, but he watched the burgeoning fire reflecting upon the ripples of the pool. The flames lapped the inside of the house and crawled up to the ceiling. Windows began to break from the pressure of the heat as it gasped at fresh air by punching into all of the corners of the house. But he kept staring. Sloan couldn't stop himself from looking at those two bodies passing each other like driftwood. One came toward the edge of the pool, a silver bracelet clinging to its lifeless wrist. The burgundy water cleared from around its face. Her eyes stared up at Sloan. Dark brown eyes that had only just lost that spark of life.

12

Oliver counted the numbers on the mailboxes. 591. 593. 595.
The lawns were in immaculate order under the dim moonlight
and Dorian had to keep the high beams on to keep a steady
direction down the winding street. 597 passed, but around 599 the
street began to take on a life of its own. A few more cars lined the
way. The windows of houses glowed with the light from within,
and the curtains would rustle when an onlooker peered down their
once quiet drive. Lone joggers became gawking spectators, and the
smell of fire and ash hung on the air. Dorian, Marlowe, and Oliver
craned their necks every which way until they were overcome with
the scene that the neighbors had gathered to watch. Flame
engorged a house and black smoke darkened the already coal
night sky. The heat of the fire licked from the roof, tearing into the
darkness as if the night ran from the obtrusive light. A broken
mailbox read a bleak 605.

Fire engines blocked the street as they attempted to contain
the roaring fire, and police kept worried neighbors at bay, but
Dorian couldn't be contained. He swerved their SUV to the side
and, without thinking to mask the abilities of his age, he was out of
the car and at the police line in the time it took someone to blink.
Marlowe glanced around at the crowd to see if anyone had
noticed, but they hadn't. Their eyes were glued to the house, the
light of fire dancing off their faces.

Dorian looked chaotically from the ambulances to the house.
He pushed his way down the line to get closer to the medics, but
as he passed the crowded street, he shoved a few people to the
ground. Marlowe struggled to keep up with him. When she was
finally able to grab him by the arm she whispered into his ear.

"You have to calm down. You're drawing attention to
yourself," she warned.

He looked from one curious face to another and remade his
collar up around his neck before slicking back his hair. Dorian's
shoulders lifted in tension as he considered the police officers
milling about the area. They couldn't do anything for him. The

bodies would just be classified as another couple of John and Jane
Does, just another file in some cabinet in the dusty closet of a
police station. Dorian felt helpless as he watched Oliver amble up
behind him; his eyes cemented to the house like stones and his
mouth partially open as if he were drowning, lungs fighting for air.
And in the midst of their pain, the world kept moving and talking.
A couple of neighbors clucked like hens a few feet from them.

"They think it was drugs," said one woman with the remains
of wrinkle cream in the corners of her eyes.

The other woman gasped as she tucked her blue robe around
herself. "In this neighborhood?"

She let out an excited sneer. "They were renting. Whose to tell
what their business was? And that beat up truck the McGrady's
thought they saw. I've never seen that car around here. Probably
some 'visitors'."

"That's true." Stories and lies began to weave around in her
mind. "And how else do you explain a house fire like this. It just
doesn't make sense. It was probably drugs…or worse."

Dorian didn't even need to hear the rest. He grabbed Oliver
by the elbow and calmly walked back to their car, looking around
to be sure no one was watching them too closely. Ashamed of
what they had just heard, Marlowe trailed behind him. Once
inside the SUV they spun back onto the street, barely clipping
some parked cars in the process.

"They had to have escaped. I mean that was probably their
feed at the house," Marlowe tried to reassure Dorian, but it was no
use.

Dorian's mind paced back and forth like a caged animal. "No.
Emily and Benjamin are dead. If they were alive, they would have
come to our house or called to warn us about the attack. We can't
handle another relocation, and we need the stability. I want
everyone to act like everything is fine; we are going to be careful
and thoughtful with our movements, hunting on the outskirts of
town, on derelicts. Eventually, this will pass, and we'll be able to
relax into our lives again, but for the time being, at least for a
couple of days…no mistakes. No impulses. No episodes. We have

to be extra careful with our movements now. All of us do." The way he addressed her made the hair on the back of Marlowe's neck bristle, but she decided not to argue.

Dorian's breath became heavy and low making it difficult for Marlowe to hear, but she didn't want to look him in the eye. By his voice, she could tell he was fighting an avalanche. He was trying hard to hold it together for Oliver, who hadn't said a word since they first turned the corner and saw the house.

There was nothing stranger than losing an acquaintance. Marlowe felt awkward and out of place. She was unable to cry for someone she had only known for a few days, but she felt the twinge of pain that comes with loss. Marlowe empathized with Dorian and Oliver's sorrow, but couldn't console them because, after all, she never really knew Emily. And she could think of a few nice things to say about her but thought better of it when comparing those miniscule compliments to the years of stories and moments locked away in Oliver's memories. So, Marlowe sat quietly in the backseat, casting her eyes to the outside world rushing by, pained by the grief shared between the two people sitting in front of her.

One wheel of the cart wiggled in all directions. It was the black sheep of the four and it fidgeted uneasily against the path on which the others were being guided. They moved up and down aisles, around corners, passed other carts, and would stop whenever needed to wait patiently for their load to become heavier.

Sloan pushed the cart forward after Patrick pulled something off of a shelf and ticked another item off of the list. Then the cart would sway momentarily with the weight of it all before being pressed forward. Sloan hummed to the music playing over the store speakers while lightly tapping the handle of the cart with his thumbs. He stood a little taller, walked a little straighter. His eyes didn't dart around the store like they would have a month earlier, and the muscles in his hands didn't clench or spasm with each passing wave of anxiety. The moments that had tortured him before were now replaced with different, self-assured ones, and he had an idea as to why. It had only been five days since he did it, since he took the initiative. That's what his father had called it, and that so-called initiative made Sloan's hands steady. It made that final moment before he pulled the trigger easier. It was becoming smoother. It was becoming more natural, the killing. The floods of guilt or uncertainty were dammed to the sides of his mind with every pull of the trigger. But that same initiative also scared him, and it was only when he looked into their faces that he didn't recognize himself, that the dams would begin to leak and the uncertainty would slowly trickle back into his thoughts.

Patrick looked over his list. "Looks like we're just about done with dad's list. Shelving. PVC pipe. Hardware. New ratchet set. And a hand-held miter saw. What was it you wanted?"

"Paint," Sloan answered.

They made their way to the paint section and stared at the walls upon walls of swatches. Whenever Patrick pointed to a color he thought would work, Sloan pulled up a corner of his mouth in disapproval or shood him down the line.

"Blue?" Patrick suggested.

Sloan laughed at his attempt. "What kind of blue?"

"I don't know? Blue! Like normal...just blue." He grabbed a deep primary blue from the wall.

Sloan splattered the blue color upon his walls with his mind. He didn't like what he saw. "No. No blue."

"Red?" Patrick grabbed the deepest fire engine red he could find from the wall.

"So my retinas can burn every time I walk into my bedroom?" Sloan moaned.

Patrick paused before surveying the wall one last time. He skimmed the rows of paint swatches. "Then how about..."

"No yellow," Sloan mumbled.

"Well, I don't know what to tell you then. I'm all out of colors." Patrick switched places with Sloan to let him mosey through the swatches.

Sloan crisscrossed the wall dozens of times while his brother tore at the corners of his list out of boredom and leaned against the cart.

"Just pick a color," Patrick huffed when his supply of paper had run out.

"Brown. I'll go with brown," Sloan grabbed a rich chocolate off of the wall and headed toward the paint technician.

"Why brown?" Patrick asked.

"I don't know. A friend of mine likes the color. I guess it suits me right now." He blushed a little at the thought of Marlowe and grinned while he watched the paint cans shake in the mixer. After a few minutes of waiting, he grabbed his two gallons of chocolate paint off the counter and placed them into their cart. He and Patrick finished weaving up and down the aisles of the hardware store, purchasing miscellaneous things for the house and restaurant.

With each pound of weight, the fidgeting wheel grew more accustomed to the burden, and the struggling that it was once so eager to cause ceased. Instead of fighting to go every which way, it clamped down upon the path that the other wheels had chosen for it. The wheel suffocated its own frenetic impulses and glided unthinkingly in the direction it was being pushed.

14

Dorian moved to the jukebox in the far corner of the bar and flipped through the rows and rows of music selections. He lightly tapped the buttons to the rhythm of the song playing over the speakers. He passed the country, the rock, and the rap, and made his way slowly and diligently through the alternative before deciding on a new favorite. He pressed the "D" button and clicked the nearby "2". He turned toward the moderately crowded bar and leaned against the machine. His eyes grazed down to his own attire; the dark blue button-down, nice jeans, and Italian leather shoes were not conducive to the local dress of this particular establishment. Around him were worn-in, tattered jeans, t-shirts, and the stains and fray of manual labor, and even though this atmosphere was unusual for Dorian's particular tastes he was happy for the change. Blue-blood fare was becoming monotonous, and it was pleasant to be around genuine conversation without the yuppie predilections that often come with status.

As Dorian selected the song for their one-song hunting rule, Oliver played an uninterested game of pool under dim billiard lights with a gaggle of attentive females. His sour mood and depressed expression couldn't hinder his audience's affection and his meal wasn't going to be difficult to subdue tonight; it seldom was. Evangeline and Lydia lingered by the bar closest to the door talking quietly to each other. Evangeline's blonde locks were pulled into a French twist and every now and then a piece would fall out of place leaving Lydia to put her back together again.

Marlowe leaned over the bar farthest away from any of her family and pensively toyed with a small glass of whiskey. She yearned to lean her elbows on the wooden bar in front of her, but the boozy stickiness of it all repelled her. She wanted nothing more than to spend her evening at home while the rest of them brought her dinner to her, but with Dorian finally lifting the house arrest implemented for their safety Marlowe decided to tag along. Dorian's concern for their imminent safety had waned and after a few weeks of Lydia and Evangeline's nagging he agreed to a hunt out at a new bar on the outskirts of the city. Nestled in the woods and sitting just past a bridge over a flowing creek, this local watering hole proved a perfect choice.

Marlowe fidgeted in her seat trying to readjust the black skirt that Lydia had convinced her to wear. Even worse was the light pink, plunging top that Evangeline thought would be perfect to finish the ensemble. Marlowe felt cheap, but it only made the evening more successful. Her fidgeting and readjusting had caught the attention of a nearby patron.

A middle-aged man grasped the wooden bar with both hands to prevent himself from swerving and weaving to the floor. His dungarees were much too big for his gaunt frame and his facial hair was in desperate need of landscaping. Marlowe glanced over at him and looked him over long enough to catch a pronounced wink in her direction. He slid closer to her.

"Hey there. I've never seen you in here before," said the bedraggled man, the stench of skunked beer emanating from every pock mark.

Marlowe looked over to Dorian to see that he was leaning against the jukebox waiting for the current song to end and the next to begin.

"Wait until the end of this song and then we can talk." Marlowe finished her glass and placed it delicately in front of her.

The man continued as if he hadn't heard a word she had said. "I haven't seen you in here before, so you must be from somewhere else...heaven." He leaned onto the bar and a crooked smile spread across his face. Marlowe laughed and looked into his weary, drunk eyes. He wasn't the pick of the litter; he was the runt. And she always had a soft spot for runts.

Marlowe caught Lydia and Evangeline glaring at her from down the bar and turned back to her empty glass. Their eyes spelled a clear, *Cheater*. They had only one song to find their meal and begin engaging with it; if the fish didn't bite the hook, then they would go home empty handed or move on to a different lake. This was Dorian's new "safe way of hunting". The less time spent in a location the less memorable you are. If you talk to more potential meals, weighing all of your options, the more witnesses will have things to say about you. Fewer breadcrumbs, fewer trails. It was becoming a fun game.

"Tell you what…at the beginning of the next song I would love to talk about whatever you want." She motioned to the bartender. "Can I get another two fingers of whiskey and my friend here will have another of whatever he's been having tonight…on me."

The bartender paused before moving to fulfill her request. Completely perplexed at the match, she looked at Marlowe's new companion and back to her. As she walked away, the song switched over and Dorian moved around the bar. The night had officially begun. The energy in the room suddenly shifted as Oliver quickly chose one of his admirers and began to show her how to play pool, and Dorian moved to a male playing darts asking about his top scores and the like. Lydia found her way to a group of chattering females while Evangeline played the coy, lonely woman at the bar.

Marlowe turned to her admirer. It wasn't much of an act of skill or prowess, considering he had come to her, but she didn't mind the easy kill. She spun on her bar stool and handed him the bottle of beer the bartender had placed next to her whiskey. She cleared her throat. "What's your name?"

"Tom." He took the beer lightly in his hands and clinked it to her glass before taking a large gulp.

She nodded in approval. "Good, strong name."

"It's a family name." He smiled. "What's yours?"

"Marlowe."

"I like that name, unique. First time I've heard it." He grinned heavily and began to blush either from the onslaught of alcohol hitting his circulatory system or his flattery. As he drank another swig of his beer, Marlowe smiled and looked into his eyes. They were light tonight, but she could tell that they usually held a heavy quality as if the labor of his life had affected the soul behind them. He had crow's feet that dug into his leather skin and they revealed a soft yet despairing quality. For a split second, Marlowe wanted to back out of the kill and simply talk to the man until she left the bar and his company empty-handed, but someone walked through the door.

Out of the peripheral of her eye Marlowe could see a tall, dark-haired man make his way into the bar. Sloan couldn't have looked more at home in this local, working class dive, but his face was stern and careful. He stepped to the side in order to let the other people behind him enter the bar and disperse. Marlowe was unaware that he and his family had just walked into this bar to do a little hunting of their own.

Sloan's palms felt clammy as he forced them into his pockets. He looked at the inhabitants of the bar one by one and couldn't believe that a few of these humble locals were killers, but all of his surveying and tracking told him that this bar was the next best guess at their new target's hunting-ground. He was positive that they were here somewhere. He lightly shuffled the hair lying on his forehead and watched as his sister walked up to the bar and began talking to the patrons. Summing up those around her, Jess kept her eyes moving. Every movement could be potentially dangerous. A couple going to the restroom could easily change from a seductive tryst to a potential kill.

Sloan tried his best to look casual and carefree and as he moved to walk, he stopped himself. He felt a jump of happiness and a sudden lurch of concern.

"Marlowe?" His voice caught him off guard.

Marlowe awkwardly skipped toward him attempting to keep her skirt and top in place. "Hey you!" She smiled.

Sloan struggled to keep his eyes on hers and away from her fidgeting hands resting on her hips saying, "You look...ummm...nice?" He laughed a little at his stumbling compliment.

Marlowe felt more uncomfortable than she already had and crossed her arms across her chest. "Don't lie; I look ridiculous. A friend made me wear it."

Her ears could hear the song beginning its last chorus and she watched as Evangeline, empty-handed, began to eye Sloan from the bar. Marlowe had to act fast before anyone decided Sloan looked appetizing. She touched the collar of his shirt, rubbing the material between her fingers. Sloan bristled for a split second at her unexpected touch and then relaxed into it, his heart quickening.

Marlowe trudged on. "Listen. This may sound a bit...well...hasty, but do you want to go outside and get some air. I've been in here all night."

Sloan paused a second and looked around for his family. He couldn't spot them around the bar and figured they wouldn't miss him, and he knew that they could handle themselves if anything developed.

Nervous at his hesitation, Marlowe shifted her weight and eyed Evangeline at the bar. She daintily touched her blonde hair to make sure it was orderly upon her head, grabbed her purse, and moved toward Sloan. Marlowe had to act fast. She couldn't let Sloan become tonight's kill; at least not by anyone but her. She moved to the door.

"Come on. It's just some air." Marlowe paused by the door holding it ajar. *Come on. You have to get out of here.* "Or are you waiting for someone?" Her spirits fell at the thought of Sloan leaving the bar with anyone else, leaving her slightly surprised at her jealousy.

"No. I'm not waiting for anyone." Sloan walked through the door; as he passed, Marlowe wrapped her arm in his while the song playing on the jukebox came to a close.

Marlowe and Sloan took a few steps outside into the parking lot. He looked down at her dark brown hair and wanted nothing more than to spend the rest of the evening with her, but the responsibilities of what lay inside the bar clawed into his mind. Marlowe looked more nervous than she had inside, and Sloan was beginning to think something was wrong. Her mind was racing with different methods of deceiving her family as they exited the bar with their quarry, but only one unoriginal thing came to mind.

Marlowe pressed Sloan against the nearest car, her hands

curving around his sculpted shoulders. She pushed her lips to his and caressed the back of his hair with one hand while clasping a shoulder with the other. Sloan slowly reciprocated. His lips gradually changed from hesitant to hungry, full kisses. His eyes closed as he inhaled each moment, and her hips grazed his as she attempted to make this kiss the most believable thing her family had ever seen. She opened her right eye just in time to see Oliver and Lydia passing by with a meal under each of their arms. Oliver must have snagged double and generously given Lydia one before they left. They both eyed Marlowe's scene. Evidently, Marlowe had found an entertaining catch.

Dorian passed behind them, empty-handed, but he didn't look displeased at his lack of food. His mood suddenly shifted as he stopped just feet from Marlowe and Sloan, shooting a worried glance at her open eye. Marlowe slowly parted from Sloan's lips, lingering more upon his scent than she had anticipated. She dropped her hands to his chest and turned toward Dorian.

"Can I help you?" Sloan glowered at Dorian, a puzzled look forming over his face. He wasn't used to public displays of affection, but Dorian's stare made him feel more uncomfortable than he should have.

"No...I thought I recognized you." Dorian coldly replied before moving off toward the direction of Oliver and Lydia. He quickly looked at Marlowe before passing, a warning in his eyes. Leaving Sloan and Marlowe to themselves, they disappeared into the woods to a small picnic clearing near the creek.

"What was that about?" Sloan asked as he positioned a loose strand of hair behind her ear, amused by the attention that their scene had caused.

"I don't know." She played with his shirt before dropping her hands to her sides. "But I have to go...I guess I'll see you some other time." She walked backwards a few steps, her boots tapping on the pavement, and slowly turned to leave. Marlowe wanted to get back to the car before anyone could spot her leaving without taking the kill. Sloan grabbed her forearm as she turned.

"Wait." He couldn't believe she was just going to walk away

after that. Marlowe scrutinized his hand on her arm and looked up at him.

He quickly released her and placed his hands in his jean pockets. "I'm sorry…I just…" He couldn't stop stammering and looked at the ground. Sloan could feel his face flush with embarrassment. *Shut up and just walk away*, he told himself.

Marlowe tapped his chin with her finger and knowingly asked, "What?" She quickly looked around the parking lot to make sure they weren't being watched.

Sloan took a second and looked into her dark, chestnut eyes. He breathed in once and spoke clearly, with control and a hint of pugnacity. "Nothing. Have a good night." Sloan couldn't believe he was just going to let her go, yet again.

As he sulked away, Marlowe gazed after him with a mixture of confusion, admiration, and intrigue. She trotted up behind him and grabbed his forearm. Sloan spun toward her. He was closer to her than he meant to be and as he turned her chest lightly grazed his own. They were both immediately aware of their close proximity.

"I…just," she stuttered.

"What?" Sloan looked pleased like he knew what she was thinking.

"Shut up. Which car is yours?" Marlowe grabbed his hand as he pointed to a nearby truck. As they reached the green, beat-up passenger door of the cab Sloan pressed his body up against Marlowe and fervently kissed her. His palm held her jaw and he could feel her muscles moving underneath his body as she reciprocated his zeal. He toyed with the key as he attempted to unlock the passenger door behind her.

"Let me get that," she whispered as she demurely grabbed his keys, inserted them into the lock, and the door clicked open. Marlowe never even once looked away from his brown eyes, and she made no attempt to hide her dexterity; tonight, she was going to enjoy herself.

The green truck lumbered toward Sloan's house. He attempted to remain focused on the speedometer, but occasionally it would slow far below the normal range or race above the speed limit. Marlowe toyed with the palm of his right hand, tracing her fingers up and down his forearm. She lingered near the crook of his arm and then continued to follow to the nape of his neck, her fingers lightly touching his skin leaving a tingling sensation in their wake. She shifted in the bench seat and inched closer and closer to Sloan, eventually kissing just below his ear. She inhaled his scent.

Trees. After-shave. Rain. Firewood.

The smell was familiar and subtle, like a waft of a friend's perfume. Yet underneath it all, there was something there, something strong and definitive. A scent that she knew and at the same time never truly *knew*. It was the first time his scent had carried itself into her memory. It struck a chord in Marlowe, and as she pulled away, she tripped over a line of recollections, but before she could reach the one moment for whom the scent called into her mind, Sloan shifted in his seat bringing her back to the present.

He inhaled with her as his heart raced with each of her touches. Marlowe continued to skim his neck and jaw line with her lips, pausing every now and then to remain in control of her canines. They throbbed with the ache of hunger, bearing hard against her upper jaw.

Slowing the truck to stop, Sloan pulled next to the cabin. He removed the keys from the ignition and turned to Marlowe. He placed her face between his two hands and kissed her. Marlowe rested her hands upon his shoulders and steadily moved to the back of his neck, gripping and releasing the ends of his hair. He pulled away and looked across the yard to the front door of his home, Marlowe following his gaze. He placed his finger to his lips to show that they had to be quiet as they went inside, and Marlowe nodded in understanding. They made their way into the house, down the hallway, and through his bedroom door, which he quietly locked behind him. Marlowe lunged at him, her thoughts only centering upon the next kiss and touch. Amidst the tangle of arms and legs, they managed to undress without disconnecting from one another's craving lips before they fell upon his mattress.

*   *   *

Marlowe lay contently beside Sloan, her chest rising and falling to the steady thrumming of rain on the window. His head rested against hers as she ran her finger over his clavicle. Empty of cares and thought, he felt completely at ease listening to her breathing and only concentrating on the tender patterns her fingers played upon his body.

"Your heart is still thrumming pretty fast," he observed.

"Still excited, I guess." Marlowe was only half-lying. Curling up next to him, she looked over the walls of his room. "Redecorating?"

"It's been this color forever. I figured it was time to change something, and paint is the easiest thing to change, right? I bought everything, but I've been pretty busy lately so haven't actually started. It's a step though."

"Your roommates won't mind?" Marlowe slid out of bed and, retrieving her underwear and bra, peered at the paint cans in the corner.

"If by roommates you mean my siblings and my dad, no, they won't care, and if they do there isn't much they could say that would make me change my mind." He watched her from the bed as she surveyed his color choices.

"Brown?" She looked up at him with an amused expression. "I thought you hated brown."

"What can I say, it grew on me. Besides, it's a mature color." Sloan winked at her before she continued to wander about his room peeking into drawers and flipping through papers. He usually would have minded this invasion of privacy, but this time he didn't care in the least. Her eyes were curious and interested as she skimmed through things, and he could tell that if she did find something of concern or amusement she wouldn't mind or judge. She flounced around the room, a graceful flutter of energy in his usually solitary space. He was pulled into her movements, mesmerized by each touch of paper and he wanted to jump from the bed and have her again, but he held firm to the sheets around him not wanting to ruin the casual image of her peering into his childhood.

"Who are these people?" She handed him a picture she had picked out of a stack.

Sloan looked it over, remembering the vacation that Aunt Mag had forced them to go on, requiring that they all wear the same cartoon character sweater. "That's me when I was eleven. My brothers Patrick and David. My sister Jess. My dad. And my aunt. She forced us to wear those stupid sweaters. I actually think Jess still has hers." He handed the photo back to Marlowe.

"You don't look like you minded wearing it that much."

"It was the first vacation I had ever gone on. It was fun, but my dad was pretty absent the whole time."

"Yeah, I can tell. He isn't even looking at the camera. Eleven? I haven't been a kid in a while, but isn't that kind of late for your first vacation?"

Sloan sat up in bed and pulled the sheets around him. "I didn't notice at the time, but I guess it is late. Our family hasn't ever done anything like 'regular' families though."

"What do you mean?" Marlowe found some other family photos lying haphazardly in a desk drawer.

"My father treats us more like employees than his children, at least I've never seen him act emotional about us…unless he's drunk of course."

"What about your mother? What's she like?"

"I don't know. She died when I was five, but from what I remember she was wonderful. But after she died…I think it probably all changed."

"Death does that, it changes things…changes people," Marlowe said as she picked through a crate of old eight-tracks, cassettes, and CDs.

"It's still changing though. It's like the world still exists out there, but my family was swallowed up by this other place and we can never get out of it. The harder I try, the more I get deeper into it. The more I find myself becoming more and more like someone I don't want to be."

"Like who?"

Sloan could barely look at her, "My father."

Marlowe handed the photo of their first family vacation back to Sloan. "You are nothing like your father."

Sloan examined the photo and after comparing the smiling, energetic boy with the ghostly, shell of a man beside him he placed the photo back into the desk drawer and smiled up at Marlowe. "What was your first family vacation?"

Marlowe finished picking through his desk and flopped down on the bed. She pensively looked at the ceiling. "My first family trip? There are two."

"Two first family trips?"

"Two families. One trip each."

"Were you adopted?" Sloan asked as he leaned against the wall.

That's a good way of putting it, Marlowe thought. She answered matter-of-factly, "Yes. My first trip with my first family was to New York City. I think I was nine. It was amazing. It felt like the city was breathing."

Sloan found her hand and began to trace the lines on her palm and around her knuckles. "And the second?"

"My first trip with my second family was to Atlantic City. It was chaotic, stressful…and wonderful."

"How old were you for that one?"

"Twe…" Marlowe was so lost in her honesty with Sloan that she almost slipped and said twenty-three, but she barely caught herself, hoping that he wouldn't notice her slight pause. "Twelve. I was twelve. I really don't remember it."

She's lying to me, Sloan thought, but he didn't mind. "Do you have any siblings?"

"It's confusing." *I have Oliver…but he's more of an uncle as well as a brother. Dorian, I don't even know. Lydia, daughter and sister? And Evangeline…*, Marlowe drew family tree lines in her head and decided that the jumbled mess of relationships was too confusing for regular familial terms. "We're all sort of foster kids. Oliver and Dorian you could consider brothers, and Lydia, Evangeline, and myself you could consider half-sisters…maybe. I don't know."

"You don't know? How do you not know if you have siblings?" Sloan stopped scribbling on her hand and looked down at her face. Marlowe's brow had furrowed up and lines creased the area between her two eyebrows. He took his thumb and rubbed small circles into the worried lines, just like Dorian. "If it's confusing, I understand. You don't need to talk about it."

"Oliver and Dorian are brothers. Oliver and Evangeline are a couple. Lydia is like my sister, but I'm also like a mother to her. And Dorian and I…" She wanted terribly to describe their relationship, but she couldn't understand it herself, let alone put it into words.

"You're not married are you?" Sloan laughed a little and then faltered, considering for a moment that what he said might be true.

"God no. No. Dorian and I are…best friends. It gets complicated sometimes. He kind of got stuck with me."

"No offense, but why doesn't he just leave if he got stuck with you?" Sloan was relieved.

"He can't. He has an obligation to me. He's like a guardian of sorts, but he's not stuck with me anymore. We stay around each other out of choice now."

"This Dorian…he won't hate me, will he?" Sloan yawned as he scooted back down into his bed and wrapped his arms around Marlowe. She curled into him and shut her eyes.

"No. He won't have that choice."

Marlowe took her hand and grazed up one of his arms to his neck and then started tenderly tracing the right side of his spine. She could feel his ebbing blood flow through his veins and arteries like tributaries and rivers. As she came to each vertebra, the hairs on his skin stood and quivered to her touch. Sloan was magnetic to her, and she thought of Emily and Benjamin. She wondered about the point at which Emily weighed the risks of attempting to change Benjamin and thrust him into this next evolutionary phase.

After all, you couldn't control it; you couldn't control who the venom successfully changed and who it led speedily to a painful heart attack. Marlowe eyed Sloan's chest next to her as they laid on their sides; he was strong and healthy. She had listened to his heart enough times and seen enough of these deaths to believe that Sloan could survive.

He sighed and focused every nerve onto her gentle touch as it lingered down the right side of his spine and hovered near his ribs behind his heart.

"Just below here", she started as she lightly pressed, "is a small vein that empties into your heart. It can act like a detour if the major veins are blocked - pretty ingenious of the circulatory system." She moved her fingertips in small concentric circles down and back up his spine. "It flows up, steadily and surely, and in some people can even form differently. A rarity." She smiled to herself as she felt this exact rarity in Sloan, but unable to say anything more she lightly sighed and snuggled into him.

"What's it called?" Sloan asked.

"Hmm?" She whispered sleepily.

"This." He grazed her spine and outlined her ribs above her pulsating heart.

"Azygos. It's the azygos vein. It doesn't have a match on the other side."

Sloan moved his hand to the other side of her spine. "You mean there isn't one over here?"

"No. It's not symmetrical; no pair. Just a single vein."

They talked for hours more, drifting in and out of conversation while following the peaks and valleys of each other's skin. Sometimes they would pause for a few minutes to simply listen to the sounds of each other's breathing, savoring every second. The night was unending and seemed to be a lovely circle of caresses and divulgences. In the middle of their soft whispers, Marlowe and Sloan drifted into sleep, their minds feeling light and empty, as if they had cleaned old closets and finally sorted through some long-forgotten boxes. Their eyes grew heavy, and, curled up beside one another, they relaxed into a dreamless night, but just as

Marlowe felt the final pull of slumber, she thought she saw a blonde flash of hair pass quickly by Sloan's window.

15

Marlowe's eyes slowly opened. Her dreams had been empty and calm, something she hadn't experienced in more years than she could remember. Sloan's arm lay lightly over her stomach, and their legs tangled comfortably around each other. The morning was proving to be beautiful. The morning. She darted out of bed and quickly closed the curtains to his bedroom window. A small rash tinged the side of her face and arms where the first beams of sunrise had lingered into the room and found her skin. Her mouth felt parched, and she noticed a pressure on her temples as an onslaught of pain began to meander up her shoulders and surround her head.

"Good morning," Sloan greeted as he rolled over in bed with a stretch.

Marlowe cleared her throat, "Hi." She stumbled over her feet as she gathered her clothing and painfully dressed.

"You okay?" He moved from the bed to her side and gently skimmed his hands over her arms. His touch seared into her body and she shivered to the unwanted sting. Sloan shifted at her repulsion and saddened at the sudden change from their gentle touches in the night.

"I need to get home." She looked under the bed for her missing shoe. As she bent forward, she was overcome with dizziness and slumped onto the carpet.

"I'll drive you. Just let me get dressed." Sloan hurried around the room grabbing his car keys and wallet.

Her head throbbed and her stomach heaved. She pulled a blanket off of his bed and tugged it toward herself as she huddled on the floor. Gathering the blanket around her shoulders and the sides of her face, she attempted to shield herself from the soft sunlight.

"Do you know what's wrong? Do you need to go to a hospital?" Sloan looked extremely worried, and Marlowe slowly stood up off the floor, forcing the discomfort at bay.

"I think it's just a hang-over, and I'm just cold." She shut her eyes.

"Take this." He handed her a sweatshirt from his closet and helped her into it. Marlowe closed the hood in over her face.

"You have a rash all over you." He brushed a hair out of her face and she winced in pain.

"Just get me home," she murmured.

Sloan held her up as they meandered down the hallway to the front door. When he opened the door, Marlowe was immediately pummeled with the intense heat of the sun. She pushed Sloan away and bent over double into the nearby bushes, heaving and retching.

He looked past her shoulder into the bush that was now stained red. "Are you sure you don't want me to take you to the hospital? That looks like blood."

"No. Let's just hurry. It's wine. I drank a lot of wine last night." Sloan helped her into the truck and as they drove away from his house, she found some sunglasses and put them on.

"You have a migraine?" He asked as he made his way onto the highway.

"What? Oh...maybe." Marlowe focused all of her energy onto settling her churning stomach.

"Whenever Jess gets one, she shuts all the curtains in the house. She says the sunlight makes it worse."

Marlowe murmured, "Then let's call it a migraine."

The trip to her house was only a thirty-minute drive, but to Marlowe it felt as if it would never end. Every once and awhile she would open her eyes to look around and give directions or repeat the address, only to close them as she attempted to ignore the torment. She could feel the rash on her face beginning to solidify and she couldn't open her mouth very much to speak without the pain of a potential crack in its surface. Her head hammered as if it would explode for lack of room. She could feel her heart palpitating in her chest as it struggled to fend off what she considered a deadly allergic reaction. Forcing her entire body to fit into the sweatshirt, she curled herself up into a ball. Marlowe's vision began to spin and right before she thought she was going to faint Sloan pulled up to her house.

"We're here." He quickly jumped out of the truck and helped Marlowe stumble up the steps to the front door. She rasped a quiet "Thank you" and slipped into the house, locking the door behind her.

"I'll get the sweatshirt later. Feel better," Sloan stammered from the doorstep into the wood of the slammed door. He hesitated before leaving and rubbed his hands in concern. After a few tense moments by himself, he walked back to his truck, revved it to life, and headed back home.

Marlowe curled into a ball on the cool tile of her front foyer. The darkness of her home was beyond welcoming, and as she drifted into the cold sweat of unconsciousness she heard Dorian's anxious voice and rushed footsteps.

*   *   *

I sneak back into my house around midnight. My heels dangle in my hands, since I decided to take them off before I came inside. The wood grain of the floor feels cool beneath my bare feet and as I saunter to the sink for a glass of water I trip on my own accord. I suppress a giggle at my clumsiness, the nerves in my face tingling and warm to the touch. But as I fill the glass of water under the tap a loud shotgun blast rings through my house. I peer up at the ceiling, frozen and scared, all qualities of the liquor in my veins disappearing. Heavy and stumbling footsteps move upon the floorboards above me.

"Mother?" I whisper to myself.

I find the courage to go up the stairs, and every time my foot lands upon a step I pray that the wood be kind enough to remain silent, to fight against its impulse to creak and bend from my weight. I slowly round the corner to my parent's room, hiding and trembling from those heavy, stumbling footsteps moving about the house, and upon entering I suffocate a petrified scream. I can't see her face. It's her body in her nightdress. I can't see her face. It is her hands curled up in slumber. I can't see her face. It's her foot, dangling out from under the sheet. But I can't see her face.

Those dragging footsteps come down the hall. They are so heavy and pounding, like an enormous drum sounding its way across a field, a cannon fire with every step. They get closer and closer. They're by the stairs now.

Step. They're by the guest room now.

Step. They're hidden in the darkness.

Step. They're getting closer. Step. They're getting closer. Step. Closer.

I stumble backwards on an empty bottle. It rolls across the floor of my parent's bedroom. It betrays me and sounds my presence throughout the house. I frantically search for a place to hide. For any place. Any place that keeps me from those heavy steps. I slide under the bed. Under the bed where my faceless mother sleeps without breathing. I grip my shoes so tight in my hands that the heels start to dig into my flesh and make me bleed.

Step. In front of the door.

Step. Inside the room.

Step. He stops the bottle from spinning.

Step. He moves closer to the bed.

Step. I can feel the floorboards bend under his weight.

Step. I stop my breathing.

Step. He's at the side of the bed.

Step. I can see the toes of his shoes from under the bed skirt.

Step. I pray. Step. I look up at the mattress. Step. The mattress stained blackened red above me. Step. I pray. Step. The mattress drips with my mother's blood and lands upon my silent lips. Step. The blood covers my face…

Marlowe screamed and shook. She was paralyzed to her bed. Moving would have required energy; energy that she didn't have. She couldn't stop herself from crying and when she was almost to the point of hysterics she sat upright against her headboard. Marlowe kept her eyes wide and unblinking. Sunlight clawed the edges of her curtains. It was the afternoon.

After slowing her breathing, she began counting the slats in her closet doors. When she was finished with that, she started to count the stitches in her sheets, anything to keep herself from slipping. When she couldn't hold back anymore or keep her mind focused on menial tasks, she finally drifted back into unwanted sleep. The sleep where dreams were fires and memories the kindling for their flames.

16

Marlowe teetered uncomfortably down the stairs with one hand cradling her head and the other gripping the banister for support. The walls of her skull still reverberated with the echoes of earlier pain and her stomach flipped and turned with the demand for sustenance, but the mere thought of food caused her to pause on the bottom step. It was well after midnight and there wasn't much time until the sun came up. She would then have to crawl back up into her room to sleep for another day.

"Feeling better?" Dorian walked over to her from his study, his hands nervously jammed into his pockets.

"Yes. I just need some food." Marlowe brushed past him as she headed toward the kitchen. She listened to Dorian sigh. "I'm fine. I swear." She didn't need any more concern than she was already being given, and the incessant coddling didn't mix well with the pain. It was beginning to rub her nerves raw.

"Did you see Evangeline?" Dorian's eyes scanned the back of Marlowe's head as he followed her around the house.

"No. Why would I? Have you seen Lydia? I need some food, but I don't think I'm up for going out myself." She trailed around the house, searching for Lydia and finding no one. Dorian opened his mouth to speak as she passed him, but she pretended not to see, instead ignoring his presence as she focused on her throbbing head and aching stomach. After brushing by him a few more times, Dorian lost his composure.

His voice boomed through the house as it bounced off the walls, "Would you stop! There are more important things than your food right now!"

Unable to argue, Marlowe leaned against the arm of the couch with a deflated sigh. "What?"

"She didn't come home after we left the bar last night. I thought that she might have gone with you somewhere, since you went missing as well."

Marlowe eyed him like he was speaking another language. "Why would I go somewhere with Evangeline?"

Dorian's patience with Marlowe's childish retorts was thinning. "But did you see her or not?"

"No," she answered, short and defiant.

"Then where were you?"

"I don't have to answer that. I didn't see her, okay?"

A stiff silence passed between them. Dorian wanted nothing more than to dig just below Marlowe's surface. She was hiding something and he knew it, but he didn't have the strength to argue so his penetrating stare melted away. He crossed to the couch and slowly sunk into the cushions. His usual composure was failing not only his voice, but his body as well. "Oliver and Lydia are looking for her."

Marlowe placed her hand on Dorian's shoulder. "She's probably on her way home right now. Got caught at dawn and crawled into a hole somewhere."

"Let's hope so. Oliver wouldn't be able to handle another one, especially if it was Evangeline."

Marlowe had overlooked his concern until now. She watched as Dorian's face fell. He had stumbled through the last few weeks, but suddenly the grief and worry were becoming entirely too personal. Not simply some force that lurked outside of their home, it was beginning to affect his family and to intrude upon their lives from the inside. It had finally invaded the privacy of their family.

Marlowe wasn't accustomed to seeing others fall apart around her. She was used to receiving the sideways glances and the worried lectures, not doling them out. She reached to his hand and held it in her own. She wanted desperately to console him, but she didn't know how to form the words.

He glanced up at her, the heart in his chest beating a little slower and labored beneath his ribs. A quiet moment of affection was shared and with their unspoken tension he leaned in toward her ever so slightly. His fingers curled up around hers and he brushed the loose wisps of hair from around her neck to lay upon her back. He licked his bottom lip and inched in toward her neck, and Marlowe could feel that same electric current pulling her toward him, beckoning her to reciprocate. She knew better than that and pulled away from his tender advances.

Acting like she was nervously looking for Evangeline, she moved from the couch and stood in front of the window. But Dorian knew what she was feeling; her rejection was made out of habit and that he deserved it. He exhaled uncomfortably upon the couch and tousled his hair with his hands before rubbing his face in defeat. After a few labored seconds, he anxiously cleared his throat a little as he moved from the sofa into his study.

Once inside his sanctuary, he poured himself over his shelves and grazed his fingers over the smooth surface of an ivory doorknob, the face of a broken clock, and his fingers finally came to rest on the crevices of a jeweled brooch. He brought the brooch into his hands and held it like it was fire, carefully turning it over and over until its memory poured out from the crevices of the blue jewels into his hands and washed over him. He had to put it back upon the dark shelf to keep from feeling a familiar pain of regret.

"I want to hear about that one," Marlowe whispered from the doorway of his study.

"Out of all of the ones on my shelf, this is the one you ask me to explain?" Dorian tried to push the brooch into the corner behind the other artifacts like it wasn't worth talking about.

"Every time we…you…Every time *you* slip and turn to me for some kind of comfort, whatever that may be…and I decline, you retreat into this study. Go to that shelf. And pick up that brooch. You don't think I watch you, but I do. I watch as you carefully brush over it and stare into each blue stone. And as you look it over, you become ashamed. I want to hear its story." Marlowe went to his leather chair and locked herself into it. She crossed her arms like a small child, pouting and stubborn, as she stared him down, refusing to budge. He owed her.

Dorian reluctantly retrieved the brooch and caressed its outline. "This particular memory is your memory too. You just didn't know it." He paused, allowing himself to become lost in the brooch before he continued. "I watched you for days and days. You were so fascinating to me. Your stubbornness amazed me. Denying all those men; I can't deny that I was pleased whenever you would dismiss them because they weren't good enough for you. But that night...the night that I...changed you. Afterwards, I went back to your family's house."

Marlowe bristled in her seat. She didn't want to hear about this, about this terrible memory. Her nightmares reached their boney fingertips from her subconscious and into her streaming thoughts. Images flashed before her. The blood. Those footsteps. Her mother. They flooded into her senses and made her want to scream, but she sat still, yearning to hear his side of things, to know what Dorian had kept hidden for so long in that small brooch.

"I thought that after I had fed on you that you had died, and I felt like I had killed something beautiful, something irreplaceable in the world. I don't know why, but afterwards I went back to your house. I crept in through the beachside doors near the kitchen. They were unlocked but the police hadn't yet arrived. The house was still silent. Still cold and hushed. I could smell the death on the air, all the blood...but my hunger had already been satiated." He became quiet as he met the end of his words, the guilt and shame still tinting this particular phrase after ninety-two years.

Marlowe moved to get up and made it to the door before Dorian's quick hand on her shoulder stopped her. He uncomfortably continued.

"I went toward the smell of the blood, and I found her. Your mother. Laying in her bed, unrecognizable to a stranger. The smell of the shotgun blast was still heavy on the air. And everything made sense when I saw her. The fear in your eyes...I'm so sorry, Marlowe. I have been so sorry ever since that night." Dorian choked back his words and gently handed her the brooch. She looked from the brooch to him and down again.

"So, you kept this thing to remember *that* night? That horrible night when you realized you didn't want me, that night when I *lost* everything!"

She could hear those footsteps coming out of her nightmares and intruding upon her sanity. Those heavy lingering steps. The blood. She wanted to scream at him, to dash his precious brooch to the floor, but she fought against her rage and urged him to keep talking to her before he bottled back inside himself. Before he was resolved to only stare longingly at bookshelves, losing contact with her once again.

"I turned to leave after I saw your mother, and I saw something on the nightstand. A small box tied with a light blue ribbon. Your name was on it. I opened it and there it sat - the brooch. I know I shouldn't have gone there, shouldn't have taken it, but I needed to remember that feeling. I needed to remember that guilt and how I had robbed the world of you."

"Did that feeling change when you realized I was alive?" Marlowe asked, her voice quivering.

"No." Pain and regret caused his eyes to become heavy and lost. He caressed her shoulder with his hand, but she flinched away from him. She placed the brooch back in his hand and closed his fingers around the cold metal and jewels.

"You can keep it. I don't need that reminder as much as you do. And every time our lives get complicated, you can run back to your things and self-flagellate to make yourself feel better, but I hope you know that I don't need this…or you." Marlowe turned her back on him and went into the living room.

*   *   *

A few hours passed in silence before Oliver and Lydia walked in with Evangeline. She hobbled next to them as they laughed between themselves even though she looked weary and sedated like she had just woken up from anesthesia. After finding her they had stopped to eat, but the revival in color hadn't yet peeked on Evangeline's face.

"What happened? Where were you?" Dorian feverishly asked. He paced around them as they slowly moved to the living room, while Marlowe stood apart from the entire affair like a spectator. Waving Dorian's worried expression away, Oliver helped Evangeline onto the sofa. She cuddled into the crook of his arm when he sat beside her.

"Well, where'd you find her?" Dorian asked.

"She called Oliver from a payphone. Probably the only one still in existence in all of Oregon," Lydia sighed. The night was less interesting than she thought it was going to be, and with a casual slump into the nearby settee she sat across from them, flipping through her newest photography collection.

"I broke into the trunk of some car and stayed there for the day. When I woke up after the sun had finally gone down, I walked into town and used the first payphone I could find," she quietly said from Oliver's cradled arms. Evangeline's voice was smaller than usual, but with every passing minute her body slowly recovered, and she transitioned from unwell to simply exhausted.

"What if someone had opened that trunk?" Lydia asked, her tone repetitive and annoyed like a scolding mother's.

"It was a broken-down car in someone's yard. Covered with weeds. I was thinking the chances of someone opening it the day I decided to crawl inside were in my favor," she replied as she glared at Lydia from the couch.

"The heat from the day made her a little loopy," Oliver explained while rubbing her hair. Even with Evangeline's obvious misstep in judgment, he always chose to make excuses for her. "It must've been like an oven in there, but we stopped to eat after picking her up."

"Did you bring me anything?" Marlowe prodded when the tone of the emergency had shifted. They all stared at her like she was an insensitive monster. They ignored her and moved on with the questions.

"What were you doing out all night?" Oliver gently asked Evangeline. She sat up and leaned heavily against the couch. Her eyes moved from face to face and landed pensively on Marlowe. They shared a knowing stare that made Marlowe incredibly nervous. Marlowe glanced at the others, but they weren't catching the message flowing out of Evangeline's eyes and into her own. She knew. Somehow Evangeline knew what Marlowe had really done last night. With one solemn confession, Evangeline could completely destroy the relationship Marlowe was building with

Sloan. She could tear open a new argument between Marlowe and Dorian. She could even cause another relocation. Marlowe began to feel nauseas and unsteady like the floor was moving out from under her and her legs couldn't balance. Evangeline's gaze moved from Marlowe's nervous eyes down to her own hands.

"I followed Marlowe," she murmured.

They all stared at Marlowe and back to Evangeline. Marlowe couldn't believe it. Leave it to Evangeline to destroy everything, to ruin Marlowe's only chances of a normal relationship. Hatred and loathing coursed out of Marlowe's body, and she clamped her mouth down to keep from exploding vicious thoughts into the room.

"And she didn't take the kill...of the guy she left with..." Evangeline continued. Dorian stared up at Marlowe like it was the last straw. Tears welled up in her eyes and she opened her mouth to defend herself when Evangeline cut her off with a lie.

"But she took another...after I saw her feed, I went off on my own. I had left the bar with nothing, and I was starving so I decided to go hunting on my own." Oliver huffed at her carelessness, but she kept weaving her story. "After I fed, I wandered around. I didn't get hurt or anything, and just before sunset I found this car. So, I climbed in. I'm sorry. I should've come home sooner, but I just wanted some alone time." Evangeline looked up at Marlowe. She had the appearance of a "you-owe-me" stare, but the rest of the family was so consumed with looks of disappointment and relief that they didn't even notice. A wave of calm overcame Marlowe as she sat onto the ottoman in front of Lydia.

"Is that what happened? You didn't take your first kill." Dorian asked. His suspicious eyes tracing between the two of them.

"Yes, that's exactly what happened." Marlowe mumbled. She couldn't look into Dorian's eyes for fear that her own would reveal their tangled lies to him.

"All right. Well, now that that's settled...I'm going to get something to eat. I'll bring you some left-overs, Marlowe." He gruffly went to the kitchen and retrieved a gallon freezer bag before leaving. The living room felt simultaneously lighter and heavier. Oliver and Lydia moved about the house like any normal Sunday night, Lydia skipping up the stairs to shower and Oliver moving into the den to watch some TV. But the thick tension was heavy between Evangeline and Marlowe. They didn't know what to say to each other, but for some reason Evangeline had decided to cover for Marlowe's actions. She had thought about revealing Marlowe's deceit to the family, and after seriously considering it, Evangeline changed her mind. The soft sounds of a laugh-reel from Oliver's favorite sitcom rolled out of the television when Marlowe had finally chosen what was best to say to Evangeline.

"Thank you," she whispered.

17

A pair of light knocks tapped upon the front door. Marlowe and Lydia looked across the living room at each other, confused eyes glancing up from books. Hoping that the noise would just go away, they didn't move from their spots.

"Its vision is based on movement," Lydia whispered from perched atop her ottoman with a wink and a low laugh.

The knocks thudded a little harder the second time around. Marlowe placed the cloth ribbon bookmark into the small leather-bound copy of *Doctor Faustus* before carefully stepping to the front door. Her footsteps were light and soundless upon the hardwood, and she lightly leaned in upon the door to peak through the eyehole. Her eyes widened as she recognized the face on the other side and she subconsciously adjusted her clothing. She took a breath and opened the door. Sloan smiled from across the threshold.

"Hey! I'm sorry to just come over like this, but your phone must be dead or something. I tried calling it all day," he explained.

Lydia heard his deep voice from the door. She craned her neck from her seat to try and see around Marlowe and leaned so far from the ottoman that she almost fell off its leather cushion onto the floor. Marlowe shifted uneasily at Lydia's attentive stares, so she placed her hand on the doorframe, creating a clear blockade into her house.

"It's okay. I was...um...at work," she mumbled.

Sloan nodded his head in understanding. "Yeah, the phlebotomist thing."

A roar of laughter peeled from the living room causing Lydia to slide down the ottoman to the floor.

Sloan teetered nervously on his feet at the sound. "I just came by to see how you were feeling."

"I'm all better now. It was just an allergic reaction." Her face grew hot and butterflies lifted off the walls of her stomach. She was flattered at his concern and wanted to giggle in excitement, but instead she bit at her bottom lip as she tried to keep up with the lies. Lydia appeared behind her, grinning from ear to ear.

"Hi! I'm Lydia. Marlowe's roommate," Lydia waved.

Sloan shook Lydia's hand under Marlowe's arm. "Hi. I'm Sloan. I've heard so much about you."

"Oh, you have?" Lydia smirked. She was enjoying this tremendously. "Why don't you come on in?" She kept hold of Sloan's hand and led him under Marlowe's arm into the house. "Sorry. We're just not used to company. Do you want me to show you around?"

Marlowe grabbed his wrist to keep him from following Lydia into the rest of the house. "No, Lydia!" They both looked at her sudden shriek with concerned eyes. "No...um, Sloan and I need to get going."

"You have plans? But I thought Sloan's visit was a surprise," she toyed, placing her index finger upon her cheek.

"It was." Marlowe's response caused Sloan to deflate a bit before she corrected herself. "I mean, it was a *pleasant* surprise. So nice of him to check up on me and all, but I'm hungry so we might as well get a bite to eat!"

Lydia covered her mouth to stifle a laugh, but as Sloan and Marlowe quickly left the house her rollicking energy sprang forth and rang down the walkway into the night.

"She was nice," he said as he jumped into his truck next to Marlowe.

"Yeah. She's a riot," Marlowe quipped with a thick layering of sarcasm.

They drove to a restaurant on a quaint historic street just outside of the city. A few tables had quiet patrons leaning across their plates talking to each other under dim lights, but for the most part the restaurant had the emptiness that follows a dinnertime rush. Marlowe and Sloan found a table in an empty corner right beside the window that looked onto an empty sidewalk. He awkwardly pulled the chair out for her and she smiled back at him with warm eyes, but after she had taken her seat Marlowe fidgeted with her linen napkin and nervously adjusted the silverware around her plate. This was a nice restaurant. One of those restaurants where the waiters wore white button-ups and pressed black slacks. One of those restaurants where martinis and wine ruled the drink list. One of those restaurants where you had to eat.

The server handed Marlowe and Sloan their menus before regaling them about the night's specials and the recommended mixtures of wine and food. Sloan listened politely, but Marlowe was lost in the menu. The words jumbled and jumped all over the page. She tried to find something to eat, something normal and non-threatening. She skimmed through the pastas, the seafood, the appetizers, the soups and salads, and feverishly landed on the steaks. A wave of relief washed over her, and she shut the menu with a grin.

"I'm glad you're feeling better," Sloan said across the table.

"So am I. I just have to be careful it doesn't happen again." Marlowe made a mental note to remember that sleepovers weren't the best idea.

Sloan threw some conversation topics around before deciding that he should just ease in with some small talk. "How has your family been?"

Marlowe fidgeted at his subject of choice. He could've picked anything in the world to talk about: sports, weather, or even world peace. Instead, he chose the one thing Marlowe wanted to talk about the least. "We've been better. A family friend just passed, so it's been hard on all of us. Putting us on edge."

"On edge?" Sloan asked, puzzled at her choice of words.

"What death doesn't put one on edge?" Marlowe looked around for the server so they could change the subject. She nodded in the woman's direction and after a few uncomfortable minutes she was at the table. "I'll have the filet mignon, rare. No gorgonzola crust." Marlowe handed her the menu.

"Um. I'll have the same, but I'll take mine medium with the crust. Thanks." They sat in silence for a few beats while the server bustled back to the kitchen. "Rare?" he asked.

"I like it rare. I think it's better for me…but that's just my opinion." Marlowe laughed.

The food came to the table on contemporary square plates.

Marlowe gently shoved the steamed vegetables away from her steak as she made compartments for each of the types of food on her plate. Sloan chalked it up to a small amount of OCD, but in reality Marlowe didn't want any of the pungent flavors of potato or asparagus tainting her steak, it was going to be hard enough as it was. Cutting small pieces of the red meat, she choked them down between sips of water. She swallowed just enough to pass as normal in Sloan's eyes, and whenever he looked down at his plate Marlowe shoved a forkful of vegetables into the napkin waiting in her lap and dumped them onto the floor. After a few bites of her steak, her stomach began to flip just enough to force her to consider what she was eating. A bite hesitantly swallowed here, a stalk of asparagus flung to the floor there. The night's meal labored on and on, and when she finally looked down at her plate and it was clean she smiled from ear to ear with personal accomplishment. Sloan finished off his meal and looked across at Marlowe.

"I assume you liked it?" he asked.

She smiled and nodded her head as the toe of her boot grazed a mountain of mashed potatoes on the carpet under the table. A small part of her felt terrible that the server would be cleaning at the end of her shift only to find a cornucopia under one of her tables.

Marlowe brought her clutch up onto the table to pay for her half, but Sloan insisted. They left the restaurant just before the kitchen closed and while they walked down the sidewalk to his truck, he grazed her hand and latched onto it. Marlowe became soft at his touch, so happy that she momentarily forgot about the churning of her stomach.

"Should I take you home?" he asked politely.

"I was thinking we could go back to your place," she grinned. He didn't say another word but quickly opened the door for her and jumped behind the wheel. He had to control himself so he didn't look too eager, even though a broad smile gave him away. Marlowe enjoyed his excitement.

The tension between the two was electrifying. The strings

didn't just branch out between them like they had in the past. Instead, they became wires that wrapped around them both, pulling them closer and closer together. Sometimes when one of them would shift in their seat it would send a shockwave through the taught wire and cause the other to tingle and shiver in its aftermath. The minutes it took them to reach his house felt like an eternity of shallow waiting breaths.

When the truck had finally reached the end of his driveway and the engine was turned off, they both exited without saying a word. Marlowe coyly walked to the back of his truck and leaned against the tailgate with her hands in her pockets. He met her with a smile.

"If we make a habit of this, I may have to meet your family," she said with a wink.

Sloan laughed and put the tailgate down before he lifted her up onto it so she could sit. He positioned himself between her legs and very slowly brought his lips to hers. It wasn't with the awkward pressures of a first kiss or the tentative pecks of a self-conscious couple. They moved their hands and lips in synchronization, as if those attractive strings were pulling them in the right direction. Taking a deep breath, Marlowe hesitated between kisses. Something was familiar.

Grass. After shave. Sweat. Gasoline...

It was the gasoline that made her stop. It was strange and thick in the back of his truck, and she hadn't noticed it before but the odor was laced with the faintest trace of charcoal or burnt wood. She parted from his lips and turned her gaze behind her.

"Do you always have gas cans in the back of your truck?" she asked.

"Um, uh...Yeah. Just in case I run out of gas on the interstate. I like to have a can available. The fuel gage doesn't work sometimes," he replied. He turned her head to keep kissing, but she pulled away from him with a smile. The wheels were spinning in her head like they were feverishly trying to tell her something. Marlowe's thoughts became preoccupied, and she could barely focus on Sloan's ramblings about the woods behind his house as they moved away from the truck and walked to the front door. And then it hit her.

As Sloan moved to open the creaking screen door, Marlowe let her hand slip from his. She repositioned the pieces of her thoughts like a puzzle and the wheels slowly came to a grinding halt. The gas cans. The familiar smell. Even the speed of his heart when she had asked about the contents of his truck. She tossed around the possibility and every time she had a doubt, she tried to make excuses for him. Suppressing a terrible grinding feeling, she tried to convince herself that she knew nothing, but her attempts weren't working. It was true that Sloan didn't know anything about Marlowe, but Marlowe felt she really knew Sloan, until tonight.

"You know. I think I'll just go home. I still don't feel all that well," Marlowe said from the walkway. Unable to look at him, she scrutinized her feet.

"Um, okay. Let's go." Sloan didn't want to make her feel uncomfortable for wanting to go home. He could understand that she might still be sick. He could even understand that after her last experience and the allergy attack that she might be reconsidering wanting to stay over again. But what he couldn't understand was that Marlowe might have just figured something out about him that he worked so hard to keep from her.

She climbed back into his truck and sat pensively in the passenger seat. As she waited for Sloan to walk around the back of the truck, she anxiously fiddled with the seatbelt. Her hand moved past something that didn't quite belong and she grasped at its delicate braid. Slowly pulling it from the crevice of the seat, she studied a fine silver bracelet. Sloan opened his door, and she quickly buried the jewelry in her fist. As they drove back onto the highway, Marlowe peered across the dash at his fuel gage. It was working just fine.

18

Marlowe went, even though she didn't want to. She followed them to their prey's house, her stomach in knots and head aching with pain from the day earlier. She sat, slumped against the cement retaining wall, in the dirt and mulch of a front garden listening to voices rise and fall in argument. The five members of her family crouched there looking furtively into the windows of the house. Marlowe's hand reached into her pocket and fumbled with the small trinket of silver that looped its way in and out between her fingers. She considered just giving it to Oliver or Dorian now in this moment of quiet and calm. And then quickly changed her mind. She had to wait for the right moment, but she also wasn't entirely sure she even wanted to tell them.

Marlowe's family patiently waited until the fight surging from within the house calmed and the living room light went out, but when it was time to move, she stayed sitting in the darkness as they made their way inside.

Lifting her head, she looked through the front window. Her family moved through the house like ghosts. Dorian stopped behind the couch and looked at her as she looked at him. He motioned for Marlowe to come inside, giving her that "or else" look. She could feel their annoyance, the irritation at her hesitance, but she couldn't just forget about Sloan. How could everything she thought she knew about him be wrong? Most of all, why didn't she hate him more? She didn't feel disgust or vengeance and, after all, he was still the only person she could breathe around, as if everyone else was either a judge or jury.

She reluctantly rose from the mulch and brushed herself off before pushing the door open, slowly shutting it behind her without a sound. Even though Marlowe didn't want to be there, she refused to hurt her family's chances of a successful meal.

No mistakes tonight, she thought to herself.

Marlowe's stomach groaned as she meandered around the living room furniture. The mantle was littered with portraits of an annoyingly happy couple positioned in annoyingly fake poses of tenderness. Painful smiles graced their faces as if tape had been pulling their cheeks apart and when the shutter closed and opened the tape was removed, snapping their faces back to their lonely, bitter expressions. Even though she could see the lie in their eyes, a part of her yearned to remember what it was like. To have a bond with someone out of choice, instead of the accidental impulse that bound her to Dorian or Lydia.

A stream of water could be heard from a faucet. One of their prey was washing their face before bed. Her family inched closer to the master bedroom. Dorian looked at Marlowe before they turned a corner and motioned for her to stay in the living room. She flipped him off and flopped onto the uncomfortable couch. They forced her to come with them, and now they forced her to hang back to avoid an "incident."

The cushions of the living room sofa were stiff and unwelcoming. It was obviously bought for aesthetic purposes instead of comfort. She crossed her arms and drew in a sharp breath. Stomach burning, she refused to satisfy her hunger. Everything was building up against her like a dam about to break. Boston. Emily. And now Sloan. Her family didn't trust her, and she didn't care. As she sat on the awkward cushions of the sofa, Marlowe realized that her defenses were falling all around her, and at the worst possible moment in her realization a wall of aroma struck her across the face.

The sweet, heavy smell of blood permeated her senses and ripped down her throat. Marlowe's insides heaved and lunged forwards willing her body up and into the bedroom. She swallowed hard against her throbbing throat. Every inch of her being was telling her that she needed it. Even the hairs on Marlowe's arms screamed and split, longing and reaching from their pores. She felt like she was jumping out of her skin and Marlowe tried to stay back. She tried to keep away. She tried to place that incessant hunger in the back of her mind, but she failed.

Rushing into the room, Marlowe fell to her knees and picked up where her family had left off. The woman on the floor was not yet dead, and she looked up at Marlowe with worried, searching eyes. Blood gurgled from the wound in her throat and as she tried to speak her utterances were helplessly silent. Marlowe looked into her troubled eyes, but that painful longing shrieked amongst Marlowe's thoughts, confusing her vision and suppressing her guilt. A fragile tear ran from the corner of the woman's eye and dripped down the side of her face into her hair, but the pain within Marlowe's body was too much to control, and she gave in.

She was ravenous. She chewed into the woman's flesh until her stomach stopped burning. Her throat relaxed. Her mouth satiated. The hairs on her arms calmed. The longing in her lurching body became a murmur. When Marlowe was finished, she looked up into their faces. They looked at her as if she were an animal, as if she had done something different from what they had just done. She slowly stood and adjusted her clothing. Her face dripped with trails of syrupy blood, and even though Marlowe had no reason to be ashamed in comparison to the others, she looked down in embarrassment. As she moved to the bathroom, she heard whispering behind her.

The porcelain of the sink was cool beneath her hands, and she looked up into the mirror. The woman's blood masked her face. Marlowe's breath became panicked and coarse as the mirror in front of her warped, becoming a tunnel of light. A shattered memory pieced itself back together and gripped its bony fingers around her lungs. Marlowe couldn't breathe. Lately, she couldn't look at her bloody face without thinking of that terrible night that so often haunted her dreams. Without thinking of her fear. Without thinking of her mother.

She splashed cool water onto her face with such velocity that it scattered throughout the bathroom and ran down the front of her shirt, turning the deep red of the blood into a diluted pink. With every wave of water, she temporarily washed that terrible memory away as well. But even when her face was dripping with water instead of blood, she felt like there was more hidden beneath the surface. She scrubbed at her skin with water until her cheeks were rubbed raw and a few traitor tears mixed in with the deluge. And just when she was about to reclaim her sanity, and plaster over those cracks that had chipped into the surface, Lydia, without thinking, opened her mouth.

"Just like Boston," she whispered to Dorian with nervous eyes.

In a few breakneck steps, Marlowe was out of the bathroom and upon her. She forced Lydia onto the far wall like a speeding train. A lamp shattered beside them, and the room went dark. Evangeline moved to help Lydia, but Oliver held his arm in front of her. The three of them watched as Marlowe lifted Lydia up off the floor and pressed her against the wall, yelling between sobs and screams.

"What about Boston? *Boston has nothing to do with it!* Do you want to know what I remember about Boston?! We went to that fancy neighborhood and stood outside a brownstone that you had been watching for weeks. When I looked into the window and saw those teenagers making out on the couch I couldn't wait to eat. And I remember laughing to myself. And then we finally made it inside…and I got to kill them! No, not just kill them - I got to tear them apart!" Marlowe laughed as she cried, her eyes wide and crazy. The fine points of her teeth glinted in the streetlight filtering in through the window.

"And I could hear the girl screaming as I murdered her boyfriend. I could smell the sweat and fear on his body as I ended him, and I couldn't wait to taste her blood too! I wasn't even hungry, but when does hunger tell us when to eat anymore! Is it hunger or a hobby? Can you answer me that? I did the same thing to that girl. She tried to run into the kitchen, but I stopped her by picking her up and throwing her down on the counter, her ribs cracked on the granite, and I tore into her throat. She stopped twitching after a few seconds and when I finally looked up there was blood everywhere, trailing from the living room to the kitchen, on the walls and soaked into the rugs. And this…*amused* me! I went from room to room, wiping the blood off of my hands as I ransacked their drawers and cabinets. I was robbing them. First, I killed them, and then I robbed them." She pushed Lydia so hard into the wall that the drywall cracked around her shoulders. Marlowe's nails dug into Lydia's flesh. Bearing down on the pain,

Lydia let Marlowe finish. She wanted her to explode, to release what she had been holding on to for so long.

"But then I saw my face! I passed a mirror in the hall, and it stopped me. My face was hidden! Unrecognizable! Covered in blood! *In her blood*! Just like before! Just like the last time! What am I supposed to do, huh? What?! I heard you guys downstairs laughing and turning the place upside down, and for the first time in decades I was ashamed. Why? For what purpose but our own impulses!? We weren't even that hungry, were we? ...And then I smelled it. Another person. Shaking, I went to a room at the end of the hall, and I opened the door. I heard a small shuffle, but I didn't just *hear* it. I could feel their heartbeat coming at me through the air, hitting me in the chest. A heartbeat...a heartbeat like a hummingbird. Small and quick...and scared. And I went to the closet and slid the door open, and there was...a boy, not older than nine. He was crying, but I couldn't do it. I couldn't finish it! Not another one. So, I grabbed him and rushed him to the window. He was fighting me...he even wet himself. But I had to get him out...if I didn't, *you* would have gotten him! And I flung the window open and pushed him onto the fire escape and he made it to the street below and he ran. I just leaned out that window until I saw him get away and I was so happy. I was so ecstatic that *you all couldn't get him*! I felt so alive. And I didn't even care what any of you had to say! I couldn't do it! I couldn't do to him what Dorian did to me!"

Lydia let Marlowe finish before she slowly unwrapped Marlowe's hands from her shoulders, leaving nail punctures in her skin. She slid Marlowe to the floor in a heap of shock.

"I'm sorry," Dorian whispered. He walked from the bedroom, and they could hear his footsteps recede out the front door and down the sidewalk toward their car. Leaving the dark bedroom in ruins, Oliver and Evangeline followed in silence. Lydia sat next to Marlowe and cradled her head in her arms. She had finally felt release, and even though Lydia was the one she had attacked, Lydia was also the one to stay and comfort her. She held her and brushed the top of her hair with a tender kiss, but as Marlowe leaned limply against her shoulder, she was numb to all thought, except for one. She wanted to be in someone else's arms, someone she didn't have to explain herself to. In that moment, she decided to let that braided loop of silver stay hidden forever.

19

Sloan poured himself over a large, wrinkled map on their coffee table. Newspapers littered the floor and the buzz of the nightly news chattered from the small television in the corner. They had been following the patterns of their newest targets for quite some time, but for some reason they were proving to be more unpredictable than the rest. Just when they thought they were upon them, Sloan's family would leave the bar, park, or hospital empty handed. It was as if they were one step ahead of them and it was infuriating knowing that they kept missing their mark. Sometimes, Sloan's gut could even feel that they had been there, and that's when he felt like he was so close they might even be staring him in the face. The map was littered with coffee stain rings, and sharpie marker lines that had been scribbled out after being given more thought. He tossed a pen across the table in bored frustration and apathy.

A strange feeling comes over someone when they become who everyone wants them to be; they feel like they betrayed some part of themself, but a sense of accomplishment clouds that betrayal until all they can recognize is this strange, new person in their place. Sloan was wrought with this feeling. He had finally transitioned into the hunter his father had always wanted him to be, but he had given up some valuable parts of himself in the process. He still enjoyed the planning, but it wasn't bringing him the same satisfaction or feeling of contribution to his family. He didn't want to be a tracker or strategist anymore. Instead, he longed to be out in the field with Patrick and Jess.

His father sat in the kitchen reading the day's local newspaper, flipping through page after page cutting certain things out with scissors and placing them into a binder. Clippings that read "Missing Person" or "Second Homicide Hits Familiar Neighborhood." They would flip through them later in the night, observing the patterns and similarities between the victims just like detectives. And the next day would be a schedule full of follow-ups and questions. More than likely, half of the articles in his father's binder would need to be crossed out, but there was always that one single page that set off the alarm bells.

The big hand on the grandfather clock clicked over to 11:10. The night was growing late. Sloan stretched on the floor as he folded up the map. He was almost to his room when the doorbell rang. His father grumbled from the kitchen that it was too late for company as Jess skipped to the front door. She opened it to find Marlowe on the other side, disheveled and weary. Her brown hair pulled back into an unkempt bun and a pained smile tugged up on her cheeks.

"Is Sloan home?" she asked as she picked at her clothes and her fingernails.

Jess nodded as Sloan walked down the hall and approached her with a hug. After he reached the door, Jess moved back into the living room and began to clean up all of the evidence of her family's hidden life.

Marlowe wrapped her arms around Sloan's neck as if she hadn't seen him in ages. The very sight of him relaxed her and brought comfort to her thoughts. The only consolation she found that evening was in Sloan. He stood separate from her family and her life. He was unbiased and unaware. He didn't judge her or think her cruel. And he didn't know about her past, about her memories, or the things that kept causing her to slip deeper and deeper.

When she released her arms from around him, Sloan could see that something was wrong, but he knew that she would never tell him, and he was fine with that fact. They shared a few wordless seconds before Marlowe realized that her hands were still gripping his shoulders tight. With an awkward fumble, she reached down around her waist and untied Sloan's sweatshirt.

"I had to bring this back to you," she said as she placed it into Sloan's arms. "Thanks for letting me borrow it."

She hadn't come that far just to return his belongings and Sloan knew it. The sweatshirt was just an excuse, just a reason for her to come to Sloan. She hesitated as she let go of the hood of the sweatshirt, avoiding his eyes.

"Thanks," he said as he moved away from the ↖

He gestured for her to come in and she tentatively ste↗ inside while the screen door creaked shut behind her. Sloan took her hand and walked down the hallway into his bedroom as Jess and Patrick looked out from the living room sofa with ogling eyes. Sloan shot a sheepish, annoyed grin in their direction before he clicked his bedroom door shut. Putting the sweatshirt on a hanger, he nervously filed through the clothes in his closet. Marlowe was more reserved than she usually was as she sat upon his bed, her arms crossed and eyes flicking around the room like she was following a fly.

"Quite a difference it makes," she observed as she pointed around the room. The walls had been painted brown and framed black and white photos hung above his desk. They were now standing in a room devoid of the innocent yellow that once bounced across their vision. The deep brown wrapped around them with new maturity and responsibility. It was Sloan's room, but a different Sloan. An organized and confident Sloan. A Sloan that in some ways frightened Marlowe. She fidgeted upon the bed like she didn't quite belong.

"You okay?" Sloan asked as he sat next to her.

"Yeah, it's just different. Takes some getting used to, I guess. I mean...I like it." She stumbled over her words, trying to find a way to say what she really wanted to say, but she didn't have to struggle for long.

He grabbed her trembling hands and held them in his own. "Is something wrong?"

She thought about it and considered telling him everything. She wanted to, needed to be anyone else, but she wasn't sure if he would understand, or even feel empathy for her. Marlowe knew things about him that he didn't know she knew, and that was dangerous enough as it was.

"No, nothing is wrong," she mumbled, deciding that the time would never be right.

"Do you want to go out for a walk, the park or something?" he asked with a smile.

She agreed with a nod, and they headed back down the hallway to leave, but just as they were reaching the front door Sloan's father came out of the kitchen. He juggled a glass of water in one hand with the remaining shreds of newspaper in the other and as he slowly looked up and caught eyes with Marlowe he froze in his tracks. His fist clenched tight around the glass and the newspaper clippings fell to the floor. Marlowe knelt down to pick them up with Sloan. They shuffled the shreds together into a haphazard pile, Sloan's father not tearing his eyes away from her for a second.

After they had placed the pile onto a small side table in the hallway, Sloan introduced his father to Marlowe. She held out her hand, but he couldn't take it, and upon his rejection she put her hand back into her jean pocket with an uncomfortable glance at the floor. Sloan's father refused to move, all the while the glass in his grip shaking dangerously. After a few wordless glares from his father, Sloan ushered Marlowe out of the house and into his truck. They drove away into the darkness of the night.

The glass smashed to the floor.

20

Marlowe and Sloan gradually walked toward her familiar bench as they talked softly to one another. The empty park quietly buzzed with the lampposts that dotted the paths across the hillside. The amphitheatre at the bottom of the hill that had once emitted classical music across the grass was now bare and lonely in the stillness of midnight. Clouds rolled above them on a crisp autumn breeze carrying something in addition to the wind, the gift of solitude. They reached the metal bench and sighed as they sat next to each other. Although this time they were noticeably closer than before. The strings that had once branched out to tug and pull them toward one another had now comfortably tied themselves in small bows around their joined hands.

"I'm sorry my family was so…" Sloan struggled to describe his father's actions and, even though he was quite used to this steady ebb and flow of angry episodes, Sloan couldn't quite finish his thought or find the usual words to describe his dad.

"Different? It's okay. You weren't expecting me, especially at this time of night. I was intruding." Marlowe took his arm and leaned against his shoulder.

Sloan took a deep breath of the wind and sighed, "I love the fall."

"I don't know. I prefer the summer, warm weather that wraps you up and surrounds you. It's easier to feel relaxed."

"I'd rather be awake than relaxed. Sleeping doesn't do much for me anymore." Sloan bristled, but not for the wind.

"Me neither. What I see when I dream gets in the way of things when I'm awake." Marlowe found herself skimming through her dreams like a playlist. "Why can't you sleep?"

"The same thing as you…dreams." Sloan could feel his shoulders bunch as tension rolled upon them.

"What do you see?"

He started off slowly, choosing his words and phrases carefully. "I dream…about the day my mom died, the day she was killed."

"Are you scared?" Marlowe asked.

Sloan paused. "Yes."

She searched his eyes. "I dream about death, too. But instead of my mother, it's me who dies."

He leaned back into the bench and scanned the sky. The clouds hovered over the earth on the windless air as if they had decided to sleep for the night. His eyes searched back and forth as if he were looking for something distant in the heavens, but all he was looking for were the words. "You know, we're a lot a like...you and me."

Marlowe painfully smiled at his observation. She wished it were true as she watched him watching the sky. "Sloan, can I tell you something?"

"Sure." He folded his hands over his chest and closed his eyes.

"You aren't going to believe me, and I don't expect you to say anything or even want to see me again after this."

Sloan chuckled to himself. "It's not one of those 'If I tell you, I have to kill you' things is it?"

Marlowe shifted uncomfortably in her seat. "Actually. It's just like that."

He opened his eyes and turned toward her, and with a shake of the head and gentle touch he replied, "Then don't tell me...and I promise I won't tell you mine."

Marlowe smiled and wrapped her fingers in his. She knew that he had killed Emily and Benjamin. She knew that he had probably killed a lot of her kind, but she didn't want to ruin what she had found in Sloan. Reaching out to the stubble that grazed his cheek, she leaned in to kiss him.

But with a loud bang from across the park she felt a sharp sting just above her chest in the crook of her left shoulder. Her skin grew warm and wet, and as she dabbed the spot on her shirt she pulled away gasping, blood lingering on her fingers. Sloan's eyes grew wide with panic and he pressed his hand upon her shoulder. She recoiled in pain while Sloan's eyes jerked about as he scanned the park. It wasn't long before his frightened eyes came to rest in the direction of a man stumbling as he ran toward their bench. His outstretched arm shook with a gun. He staggered to a stop and wiped his face with his other hand.

"Dad?" Sloan yelled, anger tinting his voice.

"Get out of the way!" his father roared.

Sloan jumped from the bench and screamed, "What are you doing?! Put it down."

Even from a distance he could smell the liquor wafting through the air. As he slowly walked toward his father, Marlowe stood and made her way behind the bench. Her eyes never left the gun in his hands as she contemplated running at the first chance.

His father kept his gun on Marlowe's quivering form. Sloan stepped into its path, no sign of anxiety except for the pounding of his heart. "Calm down. Just give me the gun."

"Don't think that I won't shoot you to get to her! *Do you know how long I've waited for this?* Get out of the way!"

"I'm not moving. Give me the gun."

But his father didn't move an inch. His hand stayed firm on the slick metal of the trigger and his eyes were empty and filled with rage. It was then that Sloan fearfully realized that his father was actually going to kill him in order to get to Marlowe. Sloan swallowed the lump in his throat and as he shut his eyes, for what he thought was going to be the last time in his life, his father moved to pull the trigger when a flash of movement was suddenly upon him. Limbs struggled against each other upon the grass in a huddled mass. Sloan backed up from the brawl, unsure of what to do or say, but relieved that he had lived to open his eyes. And as suddenly as Sloan's father had been stopped, the trigger was finally pulled. The grappling movement became still. The silence rushed over the park like a flood, and Marlowe and Sloan held their breath.

Sloan's father pushed the interfering body away as he shuffled out from beneath the stranger. He looked down at the man and his face grew pale as he glanced at his hands and the foreign blood staining his shirt. He didn't know this man. He only knew that police sirens rang in the distance, so he grabbed Sloan by the hand and pulled him to the edge of the park. Sloan fought against his grasp, but his legs were limp with shock and his father gasped a breathless, "Let's go."

Sloan took one last fleeting glance at Marlowe as she stood defeated next to the bench before he disappeared out of the park. She stared at the man on the ground who lay like a statue. The clouds became still.

"Dorian?" she quietly inhaled into the cold night air.

Slowly moving from behind the bench, her arms hung by her sides in shock. It was as if her mind was only telling her muscles what had to be known, leaving all things unnecessary to fend for themselves. She fell to Dorian's side and brushed the grass off his face. His eyes stared blankly up into hers. His chest lay flat and unmoving. His lips parted open and hung fruitless.

Marlowe let Dorian fall from her fingers. The scene around her began to change. The noises became softer as if their sources were miles away, and even her own breathing became muffled in her ears. Everything seemed to move slower, except her heart. Marlowe's heart began to beat faster than it ever had as her chest buckled in upon itself and her lungs tore at the air. Relief didn't come. Her vision grew distorted as tears welled up in her eyes, and just before the ensuing tears surged from her eyelashes a hand grabbed her by the arm.

"Come on, Marlowe! We have to leave. Now!" Evangeline had appeared by her side unbeknownst to her. She dragged Marlowe from Dorian's body as police sirens barreled closer and closer to the park.

They hurried to the car and sped onto the street toward their home. Marlowe sat limply in the passenger seat and stared blankly at the dashboard. She couldn't even feel the wound bleeding near her shoulder. She couldn't feel anything. If Evangeline was speaking, Marlowe couldn't hear it or understand it. Instead, it was as if all of the energy and thought in her body had coiled itself into a small ball inside of her chest, expanding and contracting with every breath. With every passing second the ball grew larger and larger. Eventually she wouldn't be able to hold onto it anymore. She tried all she could to keep the ball inside her heart, but the more she compressed it the more it pushed against her. As Evangeline leapt from the car and rushed into the house, Marlowe erupted from every seam of her body. The ball violently uncoiled itself with screams and tears. She pounded her fists against the dashboard and closed her eyes so tight that they hurt.

21

"Did you kill her?!" Mag demanded from the door. Patrick and Jess hovered over her shoulder as they all peered out onto the driveway where Sloan trembled from behind the steering wheel of his truck.

"No!" his father yelled as he exploded from his sedan and pushed his way into the house. He teetered into the doorframe as he passed.

Sloan pensively stepped from his truck. His face was pale and dripping with worry. It was as if his body was being quartered in different directions by galloping horses, but instead of snapping and breaking apart he stretched and stretched with every inch of pain.

"What did you do?" he choked, the words catching behind his teeth and landing on unhearing ears.

The screen door slammed shut in front of him. He could hear the others arguing from the kitchen. Cabinet doors battered open, and fresh bottles shattered upon the linoleum. Sloan stumbled to the door and tripped over the threshold. His thoughts raced from the dead man lying in the park to Marlowe's wounded shoulder. Skin tightening, he stared angrily across the kitchen table at his father.

"What did you do?" he called out.

His father's fingers jutted into the inside of his jacket as he pulled the gun out and tossed it into the sink in a fit of rage. Their yells of questions and curses pummeled through the air, and Jess began to cry into her hands. Aunt Mag paced quietly back and forth like a crazed animal before she barreled out of the house to retrieve gallons of gasoline. Amidst the piercing chaos, the room began to spin like a top, uncontrollable and wavering.

"WHAT DID YOU DO?" Sloan roared.

A thick silence slapped every surface. The chaos slowly spun to a stop. His father collapsed in front of the sink upon the jagged silence. His limbs in a jumbled mess. His eyes weak and heavy. A bottle of beer fell to his side and poured out over the floor like a wound.

"I had her. She was right there, just sitting there, and I missed. *I fucking missed!*" They all looked down upon their father, angry and defeated.

"Her?" As Sloan found the word, the room began its revolution once more.

His father scrambled to his feet as he stopped just inches from Sloan's face. Each pointed syllable of his words pierced Sloan's ears. "She did it! She is the one we've been hunting! *She killed your mother!*" His shouting landed upon Sloan's mind with mortar and bricks. He felt as if he could fall into a million pieces under the weight, but his father refused to let up. "I followed you. I followed you to that park. And there she was, curled up beside you like a bitch, and you wanted it. Anyone could see from a mile away that you and her...how could you? A fucking blind spot...You are worthless to me! You are no son of mine."

His father left the kitchen and ambled outside, the stench of liquor barely concealing his animosity. Sloan remained pressed against the counter as Jess and Mag went in and out of the house loading the truck with gas cans. Patrick slammed a few gray bags onto the kitchen table and began checking each one for ammunition.

"Where does she live?" Patrick murmured from the table, his back to Sloan.

Sloan fought against his question as endless possibilities hurtled across his mind. He didn't know why, but he decided to lie. "I don't know."

"Yes, you do." Patrick continued his cold and calculated inventory of each bag, his voice lined with distant misery.

Sloan's confusion swept through his body. His thoughts stretched thin across the seconds, debating over the consequences of either telling them where she lived or protecting her. He tried to convince himself that his father, in a fit of liquor, had mistaken Marlowe as the killer. That he had placed all of his rage and agony onto her as an easy out. But what if he hadn't? What if he really had recognized her and she was the one that had ruined his life? He didn't know what to think or do for that matter. As he stared numbly down at the beaten linoleum beneath his shoes, Sloan chose silence over self-incrimination. Patrick turned to face him, weary and overcome, and in the second that Sloan met his eyes he saw his brother David.

"Someone has already died tonight," Sloan begged his brother.

Patrick took a few steps toward him. "But it wasn't *her*. I know you know where she lives, and I don't want to talk about why you know, but you do. Sloan, where does she live?"

Sloan turned his eyes back to the floor. He couldn't be forced to make that decision. He couldn't decide where his loyalties lay when he wasn't even sure if he had any loyalties to begin with. He couldn't face his family.

Patrick grabbed him by the collar and shoved him into the cabinets as he screamed, "WE HAVE TO FINISH THIS!"

The vision of David that Sloan had seen in Patrick's eyes suddenly shifted into the monster of his father, and within that revelation Sloan made his decision.

22

Marlowe idly walked into the house. Her feet dragged behind her, and every step only landed to keep her from falling to the floor. Face swollen from sorrow and head throbbing in pain, she looked about her home with empty eyes. Evangeline rushed up and down the stairs as she carried suitcases filled with the belongings of drawers and closets to the car. Lydia tore through the living room, gathering priceless heirlooms into her arms. The house seemed to be on edge with fear and as it swayed forwards and backwards on its keel Marlowe stood to the side, motionless and alone.

Sounds came to her ears like moving trains, approaching her only to leave in a retreating pitch. There were the sounds of panic as feet went from room to room, and then there were the sounds of rage. All too familiar sounds to Marlowe, shattering screams as all of the energy came breeching to the surface before it left its now hollow shell. The sounds of pain came bursting out into the hall where Marlowe met them with understanding. She slowly turned her head to look into Dorian's study. Oliver had just finished slamming a chair into the ground only to grab a nearby table lamp to launch into the wall. When the furniture had been destroyed, he turned his attention to the shelves.

They looked back at him with such reserve, those smiling faces of china and clocks. Oliver's body began to quake as he lunged to the top shelf. He gripped onto the wall hanging off of the shelves and in a matter of seconds he tore the wood from its braces with ease, throwing it to the side. Hacking the shelves and objects to splinters, his arms became a blur of rage and he inhaled with great difficulty as he fought against his pain. And then, as suddenly as it had come, it dissipated and in its place was left the shivering remains of paralysis.

"He was my brother." Oliver let out a heavy sigh as he looked down at the splintered ruins upon the floor. He knew that she was standing there, absorbing his every movement, but he couldn't yet acknowledge her presence. After a pained moment, he slowly rummaged through the broken remnants of flotsam and jetsam upon the floor. With the turning of a board, he paused on a small wooden box that had survived his rage. Oliver picked it up with his finger and thumb, the container able to fit squarely in his palm, and he clicked open the worn and well-polished lid. In one brief but palpable glance, he surveyed the single, lonely inhabitant – a piece of wound rope, as insignificant as an inchworm. He clicked the box shut and tenderly slid it into his pocket before he breathed a sigh of longing and ache.

Marlowe stood motionless and numb in the doorway. They shared the stillness together before he walked past her and laid a quiet hand upon her shoulder.

"You should pack quickly. We need to leave." His voice was an empty whisper falling upon her empty ears. She nodded, and when he disappeared into the house she went up to her room.

Marlowe's hands went through the motions as she diligently packed a bag. A few shirts taken without much thought from her second drawer and a few pairs of jeans gathered in a heap, but as she looked around her carefully decorated room, she couldn't find anything worth holding on to, so she stuffed the bag and shut the door, light on and drawers hanging open. Amidst Marlowe's empty motions, Lydia and Evangeline called feverishly to each other from across the house.

"Did you empty the safe?" Evangeline yelled.

Lydia's eyes darted around the house, double-checking everything in her line of sight for importance before she called, "Yeah. I think we're done."

They all piled out of the house with their bags bulging and pockets overflowing. The front door hung open as if to wave them goodbye, but when they reached the SUV Marlowe hesitated.

"He shot me," she breathed as she replayed the night over and over.

Lydia and Evangeline exchanged glances. They were beginning to feel the tinge of fright that comes from watching someone slowly lose control, and Lydia looked blankly at Marlowe before she softly spoke, "Get in."

Marlowe's eyes shifted into the SUV with a blank gaze, but she couldn't look at any of their faces. "He shot me. He meant to kill *me*. Not Dorian...Dorian's dead because of me."

"Why would that man want to kill you?" Oliver asked.

"It was Sloan's father." At the sound of Sloan's name, Marlowe began to feel panicked. She was worried and lost, finding it difficult to put anything in perspective.

"Marlowe, get in." Lydia's voice came in a quick waver from behind the steering wheel. She looked out of the windshield, eyes flashing from side to side.

Thoughts jumping from Sloan to Dorian, Marlowe didn't move. All she could think of were Dorian's glazed eyes staring up at her from the grass, and all she wanted to do was run to the comfort of Sloan's arms. In the chaos of her thoughts, she began to confuse Sloan with Dorian and Dorian with Sloan. Their places switched back and forth until she was met with the dread of ever meeting Sloan's dead eyes and the longing to be consoled by Dorian. Everything was backwards, and she couldn't suppress it any longer.

"Do you love him?" Evangeline asked, as she looked deep into Marlowe's frantic eyes.

Marlowe threw the word around in her head before murmuring, "No."

Lydia's stern voice slowly cracked, "Then get in."

Marlowe looked from each of the faces staring out at her with fear and love. She wanted desperately to face Sloan, but she needed to leave with her family. Marlowe couldn't make this decision and as she turned her head back toward the house, Lydia grabbed her by the hand.

Sloan trudged up the stone steps to the charred cinders of the house. The smells of damp wood and gasoline filtered through the air as he snuck by the yellow caution tape. A light wind stirred around his face, brushing his hair across his forehead. His arms hung limply by his sides and with every step came a resounding thud as if this walk was a long time coming. His family had come the night before with their gas cans in hand and the satisfaction of vengeance upon their minds, but Sloan had decided to stay behind slumped in the corner of his bedroom. He had betrayed Marlowe, and a small voice within him told him that he couldn't be a part of her destruction. He felt weak as he sat in his bedroom waiting for the sound of cars on their dirt driveway and the creaking of the screen door as it shut. He prayed that it would finally be over, the work that they had built their lives around would be complete, but it wasn't. When he listened as is father went stumbling and sobbing to bed, Sloan knew that that night hadn't changed a thing, and as he walked to the house his rib cage felt as if it were attached to long hooks pulling him toward the front door with the urgency that she might be inside and the hope that she wasn't.

The blackened door teetered haphazardly from its hinges. As he pushed it forward it scratched upon the ground, the slats of the hardwood floor curling up and wilting under the weight of his feet as he walked. The house breathed a sigh of pain and creaked upon the wind, screaming Sloan's arrival. The staircase jutted upwards to the second floor but failed to reach its goal as if it were an arm broken clean through. The windows had become large gaping holes in the sides of the house, and the metal shutters sagged to the floor on each side. The cold night air lazily moved throughout the house like a ghost.

Sloan carefully took each step. A solid lump stuck in his throat and his hands cemented into his pockets. His heart was heavy, matching his footsteps, and the shattered remains of the house caused him to feel dizzy with emotion. As he passed the stairs he stopped and looked into the small bones of a room. Wooden shelves lay scattered and piled around the floor, their once gleaming oak now the image of charcoal. Glass trinkets lay shattered among pieces of cloth. Metal twisted in upon itself. Baubles and rhinestones lay delicately in the blackened dust. He walked to the shelves, across sticks of broken wood and furniture, seared lamps and severed books. He grazed his finger along the blistered edge of the wood until he stopped inches away from the handle of an ivory doorknob. The scarred face of the doorknob was still soft and inviting to the touch and as Sloan wiped the rounded surface, he was glad that he had come. The small voice of regret crept into his thoughts but only long enough to announce its arrival before Sloan suppressed its cries.

"I never did find out what that was from," a small voice whispered from the corner.

Sloan quickly spun and as he did the ivory doorknob slipped from his fingers and crashed to the floor, splitting down the center, the handle forever separating from the ivory sphere.

"Marlowe?" Sloan cracked. His voice sounded miles from his throat and his heart began to sprint as his vision warped around him. There she was, as if she knew that he was going to come to her home, all tattered and broken. Marlowe sat curled up in the corner grasping tightly to the burnt remains of a small leather-bound book.

"I came back to see if anything survived," she murmured, "I couldn't go with them when they left. Lydia begged and pushed me, but as I got into the car...I couldn't go with them." Unblinking tears began to run idly down her face.

"I thought you were dead." Sloan took a few hesitant steps forward. "They just said they burnt down the house, and they wouldn't tell me if you were inside or not, but when my father went to sleep last night...he went the same way he always does. And that's when I had a feeling that you might still be alive."

The air in the room hung heavy upon them and the suffocating stillness reverberated around the walls. Marlowe stood weakly from the floor. Her limbs were slack as if the same hooks that had pulled Sloan's bones into the house dragged her to the floor. She looked down at the mangled book in her hands.

"After your father came to the park. After Dorian...I thought about what I had done to make this happen." She paused as she struggled to remain standing. "I'm sorry, Sloan." She looked up into his face from across the room. His eyes were lost and begging as she confirmed what he knew deep within himself.

"You have no idea what you did to our family." Sloan's words softly cut through the damp air.

The book hung loosely by her side as she moved toward him. "I am sorry for what I did to *you*," she cried, the words barely falling from her lips.

Sloan backed up onto the wall's dangling brackets and splintered wood, and with an exhausted sigh leaned against them. "I have dreamt about that day my entire life, and the dreams kept getting worse and worse as I started to hunt with them. I was just a boy, barely able to sleep without her as it was, and then you had to take her from me. I couldn't move from the top of that tower on the playground as I saw her get ripped apart in the mulch. It was like my worst nightmare had come out of my head and decided that my mother was the best place to land. It was you. You watched us from the park. I saw you walk up to her. I saw you ask her what time it was. You saw *me* looking at *you*! And still, you did it! When she looked down, you went at her. And I saw you finish her off before you sauntered away. And my father...retreated into himself and filled our house with hate. You condemned us to a life of resentment. He actually blames me for not doing anything, but I was...just a boy."

Sloan's face grew into stone and his heart slammed against his chest over and over again. Her stomach twisted in knots as she fought against its deafening rhythm.

Marlowe spoke painfully as if each word was a needle jabbing into her throat. "I don't know why I did it, but I did. I was on a walk, and there you were. I could smell you on the wind. The smell of your hair, your clothes, your sweat. As I came up to the playground I saw a woman, and it just happened...but I never meant to kill her...I meant to kill you."

Sloan stepped away from the charred hollow cavity, his heart tearing from his ribcage as it clawed up his throat. He couldn't speak, so Marlowe did.

"But I never forgot that little boy. That little boy who looked down at me. That little boy who I knew would never forget me either and that little boy haunted me." She paused and considered him before speaking and turning her attention to her pocket. Removing the bracelet from within, she held it gingerly in front of her with one hand, the book in the other. "I didn't tell Dorian. I should have told him. And now he's dead because of me." She looked up into his eyes. "I found this in your truck. And the way you smelled, the gas cans, everything. You killed them – Emily and Benjamin. And you kept this. As a what…a memento? A reminder of what you did to them? Something to…" Her words began to stick in her throat. "Collect?... I know it started with me, what I did to you, but you're no different than us. Your family – my family. We're the same." Marlowe's words came to a close as if a door in her mind had been slammed shut. She dropped the small book to the floor onto the haphazard waste of the funeral pyre that had been their lives. It landed with a deep thud. She turned the bracelet over in her hands and then tossed it to Sloan's feet.

As she turned to leave the room, Sloan's heart began to slow. It released its claws from his throat, and it settled into his chest, it's rhythm steady and untroubled. For the first time, he felt relaxed as if the spinning of the world hesitated just long enough for him to catch up. Everything slipped into place - the memories, the waiting, the knowing, the conviction. And in that moment, he stepped away from the wreckage, reached into his jacket, and retrieved his pistol.

With one earnest pull of the trigger, Marlowe's long life came to its finish.

Epilogue

Marlowe lay, sprawled on the floor, staring up at the ceiling above her. Noises turned silent to her quiet ears. The coldness of the floor crept up her welcoming limbs and lingered before moving up her veins. The unrelenting stillness loosened the grip of loss upon her mind; her senses whispered their final thoughts until they had said all they had to say.

Death was lenient. In the second before Death finished wrapping its gentle tendrils around Marlowe, it briefly paused. The pain in her spine just to the right of her heart became a mute voice in the back of her mind where it stayed locked away. Like a slowly spinning fan, long buried recollections sprang forth for a moment only to be swept away and replaced by others. The dancing touch of a hardwood floor beneath bare feet. The smell of a mother in a passing brush. The taste of a kiss.

But just before Death pressed the final breath out of Marlowe's lungs, she felt the fear and sorrow of a single memory belonging to a lifetime long past. She heard the ocean rolling over itself. She could feel the sand beneath her feet as she ran toward refuge. And like Death, she paused...

All
Stressed
Up and
Nowhere
to Go!

All STRESSED Up AND Nowhere TO GO!

A Guide to Dealing With Stress & Creating a Purposeful Life

 Bill Crawford, Ph.D.

Humanics Trade Group
Atlanta, GA USA

HUMANICS

All Stressed Up and Nowhere to Go
A Humanics Trade Group Publication
©2001 by Bill Crawford, Ph.D.

Humanics Trade Group Publications are an imprint of and published by Humanics Publishing Group, a division of Brumby Holdings, Inc. Its trademark, consisting of the words ``Humanics Trade Group´´ and the portrayal of a pegasus, is registered in the U.S. Patent and Trademark Office and in other countries.

Illustrations: Victorian illustrations from Dover Pictorial Archive Series, with special permission from Dover Publications, Inc.

Brumby Holdings, Inc.
1197 Peachtree Street
Suite 533B Plaza
Atlanta, GA 30361

Printed in the United States of America and the United Kingdom

Library of Congress Control Number: 2001091316
ISBN: 0-89334-352-8

To Georgia,
Christopher, &
Nicholas
with all my love

Contents

Part I

Part II

Part III

Appoendix

Foreword

Melissa England

Babies cry to get their basic needs met. When the response is late, or worse the needs go unmet, babies grow anxious. All babies.

So, let's say we're the baby. We get fed, changed, and mom's burned out, she needs a break. Anyway, Grandma said it wasn't good to spoil us, so we cry for a few hours. Sigh. We are helpless, crying is all we've got but now we add a marker to life's map. The marker is anxiety or stress. For some of us, it's life's first sobering experience in the nursery.

We know nature is always streamlining, therefore, if stress is still part of the human condition, it must, in some way, be life-affirming. Let's go back to the nursery. Baby cries, mom assesses the sound. *Wa*, not too loud, not too urgent. Cool, Mom's still got time to fold the laundry. *Waaa*, nice tempo, Mom looks at the clock, five more minutes and she will have time to throw on a clean T-shirt for dinner. *WAAAAAA!* Baby's screaming, shaking, maybe hyperventilating. Mom is alert, she hears it, her baby is in trouble. What she hears is stress, and what that sound creates in Mom is stress. Both Mom and baby need to reconnect to ease their discomfort. It's life in the nursery.

Stress or anxiety keeps us close as children. Separation anxiety is what causes that toddler to come running, after you announce you're leaving. It kept us safe in the jungle and, as a

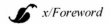

valuable signal, it keeps us safe today. As life-affirming as that process is, however, stress is also a lesson that needs to be redesigned for life outside the nursery. Stress and anxiety can also be paralyzing. This is where a little was good, and a lot is toxic.

One golden sentence Bill shared with me was that stress, and anxiety can be controlled and even partnered with, as part of the solution versus the problem. He also shared the notion that I was not alone in my struggle and that we all are dealing with the challenge of understanding how fear has shaped our lives. The sentences sounded so matter-of-fact, yet so powerful. As I've come to understand myself, I have realized that I feel stress when I feel I have lost control. I have also experienced stress from a helpless viewpoint. I was at the mercy of the emotion, out of control, and frightened.

But, I can do something, and something means everything to me at this point. I breathe, and then tell myself to relax. I usually emit a nervous giggle at this point, realizing that I have just commanded myself to relax, in the tone of some drill sergeant. Then I try it again, much kinder, much more caring. Then I imagine a more relaxed setting, Cocoa, my daughter still carries a small blanket with her when she leaves home. I imagine the blanket wrapped around me, it's comforting and warm. For me, stress signals a lower body temperature and thus warm is a good feeling. Then I talk to the part of me that has reacted with fear.

I ask myself if this is about my survival. If the answer is no, I ask if it's a new or old feeling. The answer has always been an old feeling, but I still need to ask the question to set it into perspective. Then I can ask if I can respond to it differently, if this tension is helping me resolve my problems, I ask if I have the power to change what is happening, or is this something I need to accept so that I can go on with my life. Each question and each answer quiets my mind, I am focused on what I want versus what is disturbing me, and I feel some control in the process. All these questions prepare me for the last step, connecting with a higher power. Knowing in my soul that I am not alone allows me to breathe in the fullness of this life.

In the past being alone has frightened me. With no other voice, I thought I always needed to know the right answer, and my fear was that I would make a mistake and the mistake could be fatal to me or to someone I loved. Knowing that a greater power hears my fears, knowing this loving power wants what's best for me offers me a peace of mind I never experienced in childhood. Peace is priceless. Now, I have me back, my intellect, my sanity, my faith and my peace. Now, I can begin again much better equipped to handle my day. With a purpose and in control, of all I can really control... me.

Bill, thanks for sharing your light. Your purposeful life helped to illuminate mine.

Preface

This is not the first time I have attempted to write a book. As a speaker, and trainer, as well as, a psychologist, I have always wanted to put on paper the ideas and concepts that I believe to be important in creating a meaningful, fulfilling experience of life. However, in the past, when I attempted to write these down, I was never able to get past the first paragraph. Now that the book is almost finished, and as I sit here composing the preface, I can reflect on what changed. Why now?

What has allowed me to be successful this time is that I have not tried to write a book. Instead, I have simply decided to give you my thoughts in much the same way that I would if we were engaged in a conversation (albeit one-sided). This, as it turns out, is both the good news and the bad news. The good news is that it was an enjoyable process for me and therefore contributed greatly to my actually finishing the book. I can't imagine putting in all the time and energy necessary to bring a project such as this to fruition if I wasn't enjoying the process. In addition, many of those who have previewed preliminary manuscripts have commented favorably on how the conversational style made the book easy to read.

The bad news is that I have broken some rules in the process. For example, I understand that when you write a book, you are not supposed to use the phrase *I believe* as a prelude to your thoughts. It is assumed that because you are the author of the book, you believe what you have written. This makes sense, and yet I

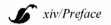

found myself using this phrase often. When I tried deleting it (because I kept hearing that it was against the rules), I was not pleased with the results. Finally, I discovered why. If I were having a conversation with you, I would want to make sure that whatever I said was represented as my beliefs. I would not want to imply that these should be your beliefs or anyone else's. I would want you to know and understand my perspective, and at the same time, I would want to be respectful of yours. Therefore, I would say *I believe* as a prelude to giving you my thoughts out of respect for your beliefs and your ability to make up your own mind. To me, just saying *This is the way things are* would be implying that there is only one perspective that's valuable, and that is mine. Now, I do believe in the value of my ideas, and I know that in order for you to benefit from any suggestion you read here, you must see how these concepts fit or resonate with you. Acknowledging your participation in this process is the purpose behind my conversational style.

One concept that you will read about during Part II is my belief in the value of being authentic or true to who we are. My style of writing is congruent with who I am. In some way, I would like to think that we are engaged in a conversation, you and I. Therefore, if after you read the book, you would like to write back, please feel free. I would love to hear your response. In any case, my hope is that you have as much fun reading this book as I had writing it, and that if you find some ideas that are meaningful, you will pass them on. That's what I have done here.

Enjoy, In Joy, Bill

Acknowledgments

As you might imagine, no project such as this becomes a reality through the efforts of just one person. I am grateful for the opportunity to acknowledge the contributions of all who have been instrumental in creating this book.

First, I want to thank my wife Georgia for her love and support, both in tending to the needs of Christopher and Nicholas (our two boys) while I was writing, and her tireless efforts in proofing and fine-tuning the final product. She also is responsible for the title of the book and choosing much of the art work. In addition, her consistent love, warmth, and wisdom as co-creator of our relationship continues to be a source of inspiration and a foundation on which my life is built.

I would like to thank my father and mother-in-law, Dr. and Mrs. Socrates Rombakis for their love and support as well. In addition to being wonderful grandparents to Christopher and Nicholas, Dr. and Mrs. Rombakis have also given me the gift of a loving extended family. This is especially meaningful to me given that my mother and father are both deceased.

As I think of all the people I want to acknowledge in the preparation of this book, one person, Robert Pennington, Ph.D. comes to mind who, as my mentor and partner during the early part of my career, has had a tremendous impact on my thinking. Many of the ideas in this book have grown from my work with Dr. Pennington. In addition, I attribute much of my success as a speaker and trainer to my work with Rob and the current and former members of Resource International: Stephen Haslam, Myrrh Haslam, Sue Lemaster, Tasneem Virani, Harriett Brittenham, Terry Cavanagh, Nancy Neptune, and Wayne Doris.

As I mentioned before, this book is based on a special that was taped at KUHT, the PBS affiliate in Houston. I would like to thank all the people at KUHT for their support, especially Adele Arneson, Caroline Woodruff, Ann Crider, Leon Collins, Jim Fisher, Jeff Wiess, and Jill Pickett. The acronym POWER for the final model in the seminar and this book was suggested by Jim Fisher, who is the senior producer at KUHT, Houston Public Television, and producer of the special on which this book is based. I had already developed the BRAIN model and had a second group of concepts that included purpose, past, serenity, spirituality, responsibility, etc. When Jim asked if this second group could spell "power", I immediately fell in love with the idea, because the concept is right in line with what I want you to get from the book.

Finally, I want to thank all my family, friends and colleagues that read early manuscripts of the book and offered their suggestions: Effie Rombakis, Georgia Crawford, Andy Rombakis, Peggy Broussard, Melissa England, Sue Lemaster, and Steve Butler. The quality, and consistency of the book has improved dramatically as a result of their efforts.

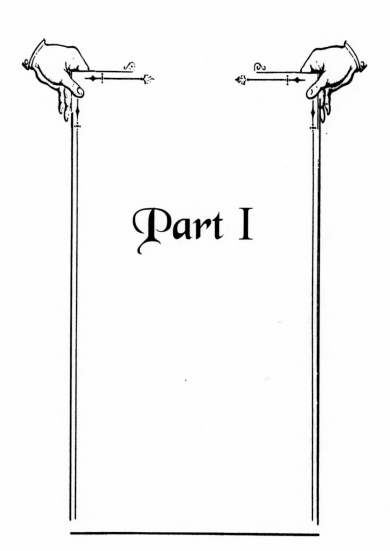

Part I

Chapter 1

How Stress Is Like Diarrhea

ave you ever noticed how much attention we give to the signal of diarrhea? I mean, really! When we become aware of this powerful signal, we immediately stop what we are doing and take care of it. Notice, we never say, *Well, I don't have time to attend to that now,* or *I'll just take care of it later.* No! We stop work, driving on the freeway, phone conversations, you name it, we stop it. At that moment, diarrhea becomes the most important thing in our lives. Moreover, because we give the signal of diarrhea this priority, we generally do whatever it takes to deal with it successfully.

Why am I going on and on about diarrhea? Because it demonstrates how effective we can be when we listen to our body's signals, and take action based upon these signals. Dealing with diarrhea is *a very purposeful experience.*

Unfortunately, the way we deal with other signals, such as stress or anxiety is less purposeful and more unconscious or habitual. I believe that this is one of the reasons we have so much difficulty with these aspects of our lives. For example, what are some of your "stressors" or situations that you find stressful? If you were to make a list, what would you come up with? Would you list your job, traffic, deadlines, difficult people, lack of money, time, taxes? We could probably spend the remainder of the book making this list, but for brevity's sake, let's just allow these to represent all events or experiences that you believe might be the cause of your stress. Now, when you find yourself dealing with these stressors, how do you generally react? In other words, how do you feel, or what do you do? Do you feel frustrated, angry, overwhelmed? Do you find yourself snapping at people? Do you overeat, drink, or smoke, strike out, or withdraw? We could spend a great deal of time making *this* list, as well, but for the sake of this discussion, let's just say that these responses represent our reaction to stress.

Okay, let's look at how all this works (or doesn't). First, we experience various situations as stressful. We then react by feeling frustrated, angry, and overwhelmed, which may lead to behaviors, such as, snapping at people, overeating, drinking, smoking, etc.

STRESSORS	REACTIONS
TRAFFIC	ANGER
DEADLINES	FRUSTRATION
DEADBEATS	OVERWHELMED
KIDS	SMOKE/DRINK
PARENTS	OVEREAT
TIME	STRIKE OUT
TAXES, ETC.	WITHDRAW

THE CYCLE OF STRESS

In other words, the stressors, over which we generally have little to no control, are triggering a reaction that consists mainly of unpleasant emotions and behaviors. That would be bad enough if it stopped there but have you noticed that it doesn't? In fact, when we react to the stressors by feeling angry, frustrated, or over-whelmed, doesn't the situation *seem to become worse*? Take traffic for example. Have you ever been stuck in traffic and found yourself feeling angry, frustrated, and/or stressed, only to find that these reactions seem to make the experience of traffic worse? Further, because this realization just triggers another reaction, which makes the stressor seem even worse, which triggers another reaction, which makes it seems worse, etc., this escalating interaction creates what I call the *Cycle of Stress*, which for many of us represents our experience of life. One thing is for sure however, if nothing changes . . . nothing works!

So, what can we do about this situation, and what does all of this have to do with diarrhea? Remember, I said that the reason we deal with diarrhea so successfully is that we give it priority. What this really means is that we deal with diarrhea very purpose-fully. That's not the case with stress. Unfortunately, our reaction to stress is rarely purposeful. For example, nobody ever says *I know, when I find myself in rush hour traffic, I'll feel really frus-trated and angry. Yeah, that's a good idea.* Again, our reaction to stress generally isn't purposeful, it's habitual or unconscious. Therefore, instead of dealing with this signal of stress successfully, we unwittingly create an ever-escalating cycle. This has us feeling worse and worse until we crash, burn, explode, implode, or what-ever. That's the bad news.

The good news is that this doesn't have to continue, and that's why I wrote this book. The purpose of this book is two-fold. First, I want to give you a way to deal effectively with the stressful situations in which you find yourself on a daily basis. Given that what we experience as "stress" is actually a chemical reaction to some real or imagined stimuli, what I really want to do is to teach you how to change the chemical make-up of your body when you find yourself in a stressful situation! Second, my purpose is also to describe a method of creating your life in such a way that you find yourself in fewer and fewer of these "stressful" situations in the first place!

There is a wonderful quote by Albert Einstein that might serve us in achieving these goals which says:

"Problems cannot be solved at the same level of awareness that created them."

—Albert Einstein

I believe that this is why we find dealing with stress so problematic. We are trying to solve the problem at the same level of awareness that created it, meaning that (as I mentioned earlier) we are seeing the stressors as the cause of our problems, and therefore defining the solution as changing the stressor so that we won't be stressed. How's that working for you? If you are like most of us, it isn't working at all because as we have discussed, most of the aspects of life that we define as stressors are not subject to our control. Therefore, trying to change them only makes us feel more frustrated, angry, powerless, overwhelmed, etc.

So what can we do? Well, we can take Dr. Einstein's advice and stop trying to solve the problem at the same level of awareness that created it. In other words, we need to raise our awareness of how to deal with stress effectively. You see, contrary to popular opinion, it's my belief that stress isn't the problem, stress is actually the solution!

For example, imagine you are moving your hand closer and closer to a hot stove (kids - don't try this at home!) You would begin to feel "stress" in the form of heat and pain. THAT'S THE GOOD NEWS!

If you didn't feel the stress, *you would destroy your hand.* I believe that seeing stress as the problem, and trying to change the world so that we never feel stressed, isn't working. In fact, I believe that our tendency to see stress as the problem, or as something that is being done to us, is a major factor in the creation of the *Cycle of Stress* and the problems that result.

Instead, I suggest we begin to see stress as a valuable signal that something needs to change, and respond more purposefully and effectively, as we do with diarrhea. In fact, there is a phrase that I like to use when I am teaching this in my seminars, and that is:

Stress is a signal that something needs to change. . . Suffering is when we don't make the change.

I like this way of describing the situation because it distinguishes between stress (as an important signal) from suffering (as what happens when we ignore that signal). The fact is that most of the time we receive very clear signals from our body and/or mind that something needs to change. Many of these signals come in the form of physical or emotional pain, or discomfort. A good example of how we might interpret these signals differently is in the way we view the little warning lights on the dashboards of our cars. When one lights up, we know that this is a valuable signal that something needs our attention. While we may not be thrilled with what the warning light is telling us, we are grateful for the "heads up." If we dealt with that warning light the way we try to deal with stress, we would just break the light out and keep on driving, thinking that everything was fine. You see, the light isn't the problem. It's part of the solution! Further, do you notice how much attention we pay to that signal? Often we take much better care of our cars than we do our bodies.

Unfortunately, most of us see the signals of stress as the problem and try to numb the signal. If we are successful, we shut off a valuable clue to what needs our attention. If we are unsuccessful, we become more frustrated and either redouble our efforts to numb the signal, or see ourselves as helpless failures.

ᑕhapter 2

ᗡhe ᗖive
Components of ᗡtress

So, what can we do? How can we respond more purposefully? Well, it's *not* about trying to change each stressor. That would be exhausting (and *stressful*). In addition, we will *always* be running into new situations that will be challenging. Therefore, rather than trying to deal with them one at a time, let's distill them down to five components of stress that are common to almost *all* stressful situations. We can then discuss how to deal successfully with each component and apply our new learning to *any* stressful situation, now, or in the future.

The first component of stress that most people agree is common to almost all stressful situations is feeling *out of control.*

This makes sense because, if we could control any of the stressors - hey, where's the problem? We can't, of course, but that doesn't keep us from trying. However, have you noticed that when we *attempt* to deal with stress by *trying* to change whatever situation we think is causing our stress, that often whatever we are trying to change doesn't seem to cooperate? For example, imagine you're dealing with a difficult person. You (graciously) try to let them know they are being difficult so they can stop. However, have you noticed they don't say "Thank you for sharing" ? In fact, they often respond by becoming MORE DIFFICULT. This, of course, has us feeling even more *out of control.*

Now, this doesn't mean that we should never try to deal with our stress by changing the situation. Sometimes this is exactly what's called for. In other words, sometimes *changing or leaving* a situation, is *exactly* what the stress is signaling us to do. The trick is to be more aware of those situations that are just not going to change no matter how hard we try, and respond to the signal (of feeling out of control) more effectively. We can then either leave the situation or change our response. I know, easier said than done, however we are going to discuss how to accomplish these admittedly challenging alternatives later in the book.

The second component of stress that is common to almost all stressful situations is feeling *tense.*

By "tense" I mean the experience of constriction or tightness we feel in our muscles, especially in the area of the neck and shoulders. Unfortunately, this is such a familiar experience for many of us, that we go through much of our lives "all tensed up." We *know* something's wrong, however, we have stopped paying attention to this "tension" long ago. Therefore, we are at a loss to know how to deal with it effectively.

In other words, our body is still giving us a signal that something needs to change. However, we have become so "skillful" at ignoring these signals, that we are unaware that change is needed. Instead, we find ourselves feeling constrained, or unable to move the way we used to, and we chalk this up to "getting old" or some other uncontrollable phenomenon. Sound familiar?

The third component of stress (more psychological than physiological), refers to the "little voices" in our head. These voices seem to complain about whatever's going on and ask questions like: *What is wrong with these people? How could they . . .? Why me?* and/or *What is wrong with me?* etc.

Often questions such as these create an internal dialogue which has us focusing on how "bad" the situation is. This, of course, *reinforces* our sense of feeling out of control and tense, and triggers an escalation of the *Cycle of Stress*.

The fourth component of stress, common to almost all stressful situations, is one in which we could *all* have earned Ph.D.s (given that we have done it so long and so well). . . *worry*!

Can you remember when you first started worrying? Most of us can't, because it seems we have worried about one thing or another for most of our lives. There's a reason for this perception that we will discuss later, but for now, just be aware of how much the experience of worry is tied to your experience of stress.

The fifth component of stress is what I call *the results.* These "results" represent all the ways we react when we feel out of control, tense, begin asking ourselves negative questions, and start worrying. This component has already been defined in the *Cycle of Stress* as frustration, anger, feeling overwhelmed, eating, drinking smoking, etc. (all the emotions and behaviors identified as "reactions")

Now, it is important to notice that, just as the stressors and reactions create an observable cycle, so do these five components. In other words, when we feel out of control, tense, start asking ourselves negative questions, and begin ruminating or worrying, we then feel *increasingly* out of control and our muscles grow even more tense. As a result, the negative self-talk becomes even *louder* and we *really* start to worry, which has us feeling even more out of control, and the cycle goes on and on.

The challenge here is to recognize what's not working and what we can do about it. What's not working is that we are reacting to the components (or signals) of stress in a way that only creates more stress. Let's look at what we can do about it by taking on each component of stress one at a time.

Chapter 3

How to Change the Chemical Make up of Your Body

et's begin our closer examination of the five components of stress by looking first at our tendency to feel *out of control*. By the way, are you a smoker, or do you know someone who smokes? What does stress have to do with smoking? Well, I've noticed that every time I have asked current or former smokers whether smoking helped them deal with stress, almost all have answered, *yes*. Now, don't worry, I am not going to recommend that you take up smoking as a way to deal with stress. I do, however, want to uncover what may be going on here. In other words, what is it that smokers do that might result in them feeling less stressed?

Well, first, they stop whatever they are doing and take a smoking break. Why is the ability to stop what you're doing important? Remember diarrhea? Just as we respond to the signal of diarrhea, smokers are also responding to a signal. At that moment, that signal (the desire to smoke) becomes more important than whatever they are doing, and they act on that priority. Can you imagine a time in your past when you were feeling stressed and out of control? Can you also imagine how stopping whatever you were doing and taking a short break might have helped you regain some degree of control in your life?

Now, my guess is that a small (or not so small) voice in your head is saying something like, *Sure, but I couldn't have stopped what I was doing at the time, so why consider this as an option?* Well, I'm sure you're convinced that stopping wasn't an option. However, I'll bet that if the signal were related to diarrhea you would have stopped whatever you were doing, whether or not it was convenient. You see, it's all about priorities, or what we give importance to in our lives. One thing we give a great deal of importance to is the signal of diarrhea!

Back to the smokers. Taking a break isn't all that smokers do. They also tend to go to the same place to smoke each time, (which in this day and age is likely to be the dumpster because that's the only place we will still let them smoke!) They also seem to have a certain routine that they go through. They may tap their pack several times and if it has been more than several hours since their last cigarette, many smokers will *really* try to get the most from that first drag by inhaling it *deeply* into their lungs. In other words, *they take a deep breath!*

I believe that this is one of the reasons smokers say that smoking helps them deal with stress. This may be the *only* time in their lives that they take a deep breath! Now, for the rest of us, being non-smokers means we probably *never* take a deep breath! We tend to go around breathing "normally," which means that our breaths are generally short and relatively shallow (especially compared to the smoker's first drag). The only time that our breathing changes is (a) if we exert ourselves physically, or (b) if we become very anxious or stressed. When we feel anxious or stressed, our breaths tend to become even shorter and shallower, or in a worse case scenario, our breathing stops altogether. Not good, because the latest report from the Surgeon General has confirmed that stopping breathing can be very detrimental to your health!

Remember, we are talking about how our reaction to feeling "out of control", can trigger the other reactions, and the *Cycle of Stress*. The good news is that when we are feeling out of control, there is one thing in our lives that we can always control . . . *our breathing!* That's why any "stress management" book you have ever read, probably included breathing as one of its components.

Actually, that's not the only reason breathing deeply three to five times can be helpful in times of stress. Another has to do with how our brain works. Brain research has discovered that we actually have three parts to our brain and that these parts evolved at different times in the life span of our species. For example, the oldest part of our brain (called the "brain stem") is where many of our instinctual, "fight-or-flight" responses are found. This is called the reptilian brain because we share this part of our brain with the reptiles. The second part of our brain to evolve is what is called the limbic system (or mammalian brain) and this is where many of our emotional responses are located. The last part of our brain to evolve (which is specific to our species) is called the neo-cortex and this where we do our thinking and planning.

OUT OF CONTROL? ☞ Start by controlling what you can!

Now, if you will, notice the nature of the emotions and/or behaviors on the right side of the Cycle of Stress, the "Reactions".

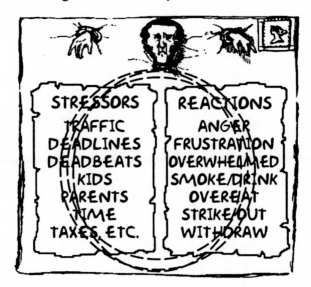

STRESSORS
TRAFFIC
DEADLINES
DEADBEATS
KIDS
PARENTS
TIME
TAXES, ETC.

REACTIONS
ANGER
FRUSTRATION
OVERWHELMED
SMOKE/DRINK
OVEREAT
STRIKE/OUT
WITHDRAW

THE CYCLE OF STRESS

Can you see how many of these reactions would fall into the category of fight or flight? What research has discovered is that when we experience some situation as "stressful," the signals tend to by-pass the neo-cortex and go directly to the older "less evolved" parts of our brain. This is why we sometimes looked back at something we said or did when "stressed" and asked ourselves: "What was I thinking?" Truth is, we weren't "thinking," at least not with the rational/planning part of our brain (the neo-cortex).

Since the brain interprets any "stressful" experience as fight-or-flight, it sends the signals to the fight/flight and/or emotional parts of our brain. That's the bad news. The good news, however, is that pausing to breathe deeply three to five times can allow our neo-cortex to "regain control" and allow us to be more influential in our next response. Further, this in turn gives our brain more of what it needs to function . . . oxygen!

Now, I must say that while this breathing technique can be very valuable in the process of using stress as a signal to regain control, it's not the entire solution. In fact, if all you do is breathe deeply each time you find yourself experiencing stress, the result is likely to be hyperventilation versus peace of mind! My purpose here is not just to tell you "Take a deep breath" and "Don't worry, be happy". My goal is to give you a complete and powerful model for using stress as a signal to deal with all the components of stress, so let's move on to number two.

Remember, we said that the second component of stress is feeling *tense*, or a tendency for our muscles to constrict or tighten.

Let me show you the effect this tension has in our lives. Just for a moment, become really tense, meaning purposefully tense every muscle in your body. I know, some of you are saying

"What do you mean 'get' tense? I've been tense for ten years!"

Now, as you are tensing all the muscles in your body, imagine trying to do something. Can you feel how difficult it is to even move, much less accomplish anything? It's as if we are fighting ourselves! This is why living with this tension is so exhausting, because in some ways we are fighting ourselves in the process of trying to deal with life while feeling tense.

Fortunately, there is a fairly simple antidote to these tense feelings, and that is to incorporate the word "relax" into our deep breathing. We can do this by taking a deep breath and saying *relax* to ourselves as we exhale. Try it. Take a deep breath through your nose, hold it for a moment, and then release it through your mouth while saying the word "relax" to yourself (as you exhale). Feels pretty good, doesn't it? Then why don't we do it? It's my belief that the reason we don't engage in this type of purposeful relaxation is that we, as a culture, don't value the idea of relaxation, except as something we might get to do *after* we have finished everything else. In fact, we tend to see anyone relaxing before they have gotten everything done as "goofing off" or "lazy."

For example, imagine you are working for a large corporation. You have decided to practice breathing and relaxing as a way to deal with stress. You are sitting in your office, breathing deeply, eyes closed, smiling at how good this feels, and your boss walks by your door. What do you imagine he or she will be thinking? Unless you work for a very enlightened company, your boss will probably be seeing you as goofing off, asleep, or at best, unproductive.

Now, imagine you are sitting in your office furiously typing into your computer. You have a worried look on your face, sweat is pouring from your brow, you are clearly stressed out of your mind, and your boss walks by. *Now* what do you imagine he or she will be thinking? That's right, they're probably saying to themselves, *Good...good, hard at work.* You see, the fact is, not only do we see relaxation as basically unproductive, it's almost as if our culture believes that if you're not stressed, you must not have enough to do! Some of us even go so far as to see stress and worry as a sign that someone is *doing a good job*, or that they really care, and relaxation as giving up, or giving in.

It's no wonder therefore, that even when we know that relaxing would be good for us (and we might even recommend it to our best friend) we will not allow ourselves to relax until we have checked everything else off our list. By the way, have you also noticed that we almost *never* check everything else off our list? We just add to our old list, or make a new list. Consequently, many of us never really relax.

This is evident to those of us who have received a professional massage. Often, after such a *thoroughly* relaxing experience, people say things like, *Oh, so this is what it feels like to be relaxed.* Now, we may not be able to stop and get a massage in the middle of a stressful situation. We can, however, stop and take a few deep breaths and say the word "relax" to ourselves as we exhale. This acts as a gentle command to our muscles, and guess what? They relax! In fact, you will probably feel yourself (and, therefore, your muscles) become more and more relaxed with each breath. (By the way, in the second half of this book we are going to deepen the impact of this aspect of the model by tying relaxation to the concept of serenity)

TENSE? ☞ **Relax as a precursor to regaining control!**

Now, the deep breathing combined with the word "relax" does a nice job of dealing with the physiological aspects of stress. However, what can we do about the *psychological* components? For example, those little voices in our head that love to complain about what isn't working and seem to ask questions like, *What is wrong with these people?* or *Why me?* or *What's wrong with me?*

The reason these questions are more of a problem than a solution is because they generally don't give us the information we need to deal effectively with the situation. You see, in many ways our mind works like a computer. For example, when you ask a computer a question, the computer will begin searching its data banks for the answer. It doesn't evaluate whether the question is good, bad, helpful, or not helpful. It just attempts to answer whatever question we ask. So does our mind.

Therefore, when we find ourselves asking questions like *What is wrong with these people?* our mind thinks we want the answer! It, therefore, goes searching its data banks and probably comes up with responses like, *Well, they're just stupid idiots who have never gotten it right and never will,* etc. . . . This doesn't help! In fact, the conclusion that we are dealing with "stupid idiots" will probably only add to our tension and stress!

The same goes for the question, *What's wrong with me?* or *Why me?* which are also questions we find ourselves asking during times of stress. Our mind will dutifully answer these questions as it did the first with something like, *Well, you're just a stupid idiot. You never were any good at this . . .yada yada yada.* You see, we are using our computer-like mind to ask ourselves questions that we really *don't* want the answer to, or at best, questions that don't help. In fact, they tend to make the situation seem even *more stressful!*

What if, instead, we begin to ask ourselves questions that we do want the answer to? For example, imagine you are in the middle of one of the "stressful situations" described earlier (traffic, dealing with difficult people, etc.). This time, however, instead of reacting in your usual way, you pause and take a few deep breaths saying the word "relax" to yourself as you exhale. You then ask yourseif a question that focuses your computer-like mind more on what you want than what you *don't want.* For example, what if you asked yourself, *How would I rather be feeling?*

For many of us, when we first ask this question, we may experience a momentary blank, because the idea of asking ourselves how we would *like* to feel is a new concept. In fact, "How would I rather be feeling?" may not only be a question that we have never asked ourselves, it may be a question that we have never even considered possible!   Contrast this with how quickly we are able to name *all* the things we find stressful, as well as, how these "stressors" are "making us feel."   Obviously, these stressors and reactions are very familiar to us which means that we are very practiced at focusing on "the problem", or "what's wrong". Again, that's the bad news.

The good news, however, is that as we continue to shift our focus from the problem to the solution, our brain *will* begin to answer the question: *How would I rather be feeling?*   As this happens, most of us will come up with words like calm, relaxed, serene, etc.   Now, while I see calm, relaxed, serene, etc. as very worthwhile goals, you might also want to include words like "confident, powerful, excited" and, "in control" as well.

I say this because often dealing with stress is characterized only as moving from chaos to calm, which, as I have said, is a very valid goal, however, there may be times when calm, relaxed, or serene isn't how you want to feel.   You might want to feel excited, powerful, confident, and/or in control, and if indeed this is what you want, then these feelings are just as valid as those traditionally associated with managing stress.

NEGATIVE SELF TALK & QUESTIONS? **Begin to focus on the solution vs. the problem**

Now, of course, we all know that when we are in the middle of a stressful situation, just asking ourselves *How would we rather be feeling?* and coming up with a few answers probably won't change how we feel. This, combined with the breathing and relaxing will help, to be sure. However, to make a significant difference in how we feel, we must do more than just breathe and ask more purposeful questions. This brings us to the fourth component of stress, which is *worry*.

WORRY!

Remember when I asked you if you could recall when you first started worrying? I believe the reason most of us *can't* remember that moment is tied to the reason we continue to do it (worry), even though it doesn't help. In other words, I believe in our youth most of us were taught to worry by people who loved us. For example, when you were very young and you were about to go out and play, what did your mother almost always tell you? Was *be careful* one of her frequent admonitions? What did that mean? It probably meant to watch out for bad things happening to you, and the implication was that if you did this well, you would be safe.

Now, this isn't about blaming Mom or implying that we shouldn't tell kids to be careful. My wife, Georgia, and I have two sons, and we tell both Christopher and Nicholas to be careful quite regularly. The problem is what "be careful" means to the child. You see, I would bet that when we heard our moms say "be careful" we didn't interpret this to mean "Be full of care (careful) for yourself and others". No! We heard "Watch out for bad things happening and this will keep you safe". The underlying belief here is that "Worry keeps you safe!"

To really understand how all this fits together, it is important to remember that our "job", or developmental task as a kid was (a) to have fun, and (b) figure out how the world worked. In other words, we were constantly creating a map, or manual of what to do, what not to do, and why. Part of the way we created this map was by listening to and observing those around us. Therefore, when someone who loved us and wanted us to be safe told us to "be careful" (or watch out for bad things happening to us), we listened. This was especially true when we were very young.

Of course, in order to watch out for bad things happening to us, we first had to know what those "bad things" were. For most of us, this wasn't a problem because, before we could talk, we heard scary stories (from our parents, or the media, or both) about what to watch out for. These stories were about mean people who abducted children and murdered or abused them in some way and/or what could happen to children that played in the street, etc. The implication, of course, was that if we weren't "careful," this could happen to us.

This was, understandably, a very frightening thought. It was meant to be! The idea was that if we held this vision in our mind (i.e., worried about all the horrible things that would happen if we talked to, or accepted a ride from a stranger, played in the street, etc.) we would be less likely to make those choices. Therefore, we would be safe, or at least safer.

Further, this was our experience for at least fifteen to twenty of the most formative years of our lives. It's easy to understand, therefore, why we, as adults, find ourselves worrying so much when we know (intellectually) that it doesn't help.

The good news is that most of us do understand that worry doesn't serve us. In fact, most of us would even go so far as to say that if we could learn to worry less, (especially about things that aren't happening at the moment), the amount of stress in our lives would decrease, and we would be a lot happier.

So why, when we know this, are we *still* worrying? We worry because at an early age, people whom we looked to for wisdom directly or indirectly encouraged us to worry to stay safe. Plus, to some degree, it works! Fear can be used to motivate behavior, however, there is a cost. For example, when you were in school and a test was coming up, what did you think? Do you remember saying to yourself, *Oh boy! A test, I'm sure looking forward to this?*. Not if you were like most of us!

Instead, we probably worried that if we didn't study, we wouldn't do well on the test. This fear (which was often reinforced by our parents and teachers) motivated us to study, and... guess what? We did well on the test! Or at least we convinced ourselves that we did better than we would have done if we hadn't worried (and, therefore, studied). This further reinforced the idea that the way to succeed was to fear failure and then use this fear to motivate ourselves to take whatever steps were needed to ensure success.

To some degree it worked, but the cost was to further solid-ify the core belief that worrying about bad things happening keeps us safe and fear of failure ensures success. Now, all of this would be just a minor irritant if it weren't for the effect that worry has on our experience of life. Let me demonstrate. For just a moment, imagine along with me (by the way, if you *really* want to experi-ence the full effect of this exercise, cup your hand, and hold it up to your mouth).

In your hand, imagine you are holding a lemon. You've gotten this lemon from the refrigerator, and it is ice cold. You can feel the coldness of the lemon against your hand. Now, slice your lemon in half and, as the lemon juice is running down the side on to your hand, you see the yellow pulp of the inside and even begin to smell the pungent odor of the lemon. Now open your mouth and *take a big bite of your lemon!*. . . What did you notice? Did your mouth pucker up? Did your production of saliva increase? Often people report similar reactions, and some even say they taste lemon juice! Now, what I'm about to say is very important. . . *there is no lemon!* However, you have just produced a dramatic change in the *chemical make-up of your body*, not by what you held in your hand . . .but what you held in your imagination!

The truth is that our imagination is one of the most power-ful tools we have for creating our experience of life. So powerful that it can change the chemical make-up of our body, regardless whether what we are imagining is actually happening!

Let me give you another example. Have you ever had a sex-ual fantasy? If so, you might remember that when you were hav-ing this imagined experience, you knew that it wasn't really hap-pening . . . but your body reacted as if it was!

So, why am I talking about imagination when we were dis-cussing the effects of worry in our lives? Because *that's what worry is* . . . the act of using our powerful imagination to create images about bad things happening at some point in the future. Further, just as you experienced a chemical change in your mouth when you bit into the imaginary lemon, when we engage our imagination by worrying, our body responds in a similar way.

You see, stress is a chemical reaction! When we worry, our brain reacts to the images we are producing by triggering a fight-or-flight mechanism. This, in turn, releases certain hormones in our body such as adrenaline, nor-adrenaline and cortisol. The most prominent of these fight-or-flight chemicals (the so-called "stress hormone") is *cortisol*. The function of cortisol is to rush throughout our body, inhibiting the production of protein and increasing the production of glucose. This would make sense if we were in a fight-or-flight situation, because we would need the energy provided by the extra glucose either to fight, or run away from the danger.

The problem, however, is that most of the time when we find ourselves worrying, whatever we are worrying about *just isn't happening*. Or even if it is happening (being stuck in traffic, for example) we can't deal with it from a "fight-or-flight" position, meaning, we can neither fight it nor run away from it. Now, of course, on some level we know that whatever we are worrying about isn't happening, just as you *knew* that you weren't really biting into a lemon. However, as you can see, our body's response is not based on just what we *know*, but what *we hold in our imagination!*

There is also another problem associated with the effects of worry, and that involves our immune system, which is the system in our body designed to fight off illness and disease. One of the building blocks of our immune system are white blood cells. One of the building blocks of white blood cells is protein. So, when we find ourselves worrying about this and that on a regular basis, our brain is constantly sending cortisol throughout our body to inhibit the production of protein. We then have less protein available to produce white blood cells. This results in fewer white blood cells available to strengthen our immune system, *and we get sick!*

That's one of the ways stress affects our health. Now, I don't want you to worry about that! I just want you to be aware of what is happening in your body, and what you can do about it. That's really what this book is about . . . awareness, because I believe that whatever we are aware of, we can influence. Whatever we are unaware of, however, will influence us in ways that may or may not help us create the experience of life we desire. Unfortunately, what we learned as children was not necessarily to be aware, but to "beware," which really means to "be afraid" (and we are), which is why we worry.

Okay, now we understand why we worry, and we have determined that it is a major cause of stress in our lives. So, what can we do? One thing's for sure, just telling ourselves to stop worrying, or trying to convince ourselves that "there's nothing to worry about" doesn't work. In fact, this tactic of trying to force ourselves to stop worrying often has the opposite effect. In other words, we often start *worrying about worrying*. Can you feel the *Cycle of Stress* beginning to form? So, what can be done?

The good news is that you already have created the answer. Really! Remember, you began this process by responding to stress as a valuable signal and breathing deeply (using the word "relax" on the exhale) to allow your neo-cortex to regain control and your body to relax. Then, instead of asking questions about the problem (like "What's wrong with these people?" and/or "What's wrong with me?"), you directed your computer-like mind to ask yourself a more purposeful question, *How would I rather be feeling?* Well, now the challenge is to engage your imagination (this aspect of your mind that has the power to change the chemistry of your body) to work for you, versus against you.

How do you do this? First, you look at the words or desired feelings that came up when you asked yourself, *How would I rather be feeling?* such as "relaxed, powerful, calm, in control" etc. Second, ask yourself if you have ever felt one or more of these feelings anytime in your past. I have yet to meet anyone who hasn't felt good (relaxed or powerful, or calm, or in control, etc.) at least once in their life, and most of us have had a multitude of these experiences. Third, begin to imagine this past experience in as much detail as possible. Imagine where you were. Were you alone or with others? If you were with others, who were they? What sounds did you hear? What aromas did you smell? What were you touching? Did it feel rough, smooth, etc.?

Several categories of "past experiences" can serve as effective resources. For example, because most pets almost always relate to us with unconditional love, one source of good feelings is any positive interaction you can recall between you and your pet(s). In addition, (as we have discussed) a positive sexual memory is also very effective in engaging your imagination in a powerful way. Finally, any memory of laughter, celebration, or relaxation would likely be effective in eliciting this response. Whatever you choose, the idea here is to immerse yourself in the experience using all your subtler senses, and imagine you are re-experiencing this memory in vivid detail.

In his book, *Timeless Healing, the Power and Biology of Belief,* Herbert Benson, M.D. (Associate Professor of medicine at Harvard Medical School and Founder of the Mind/Body Medical Institute), refers to a similar process of imagining a time in your past when you were feeling "well," or how you would like to be feeling now. He calls this "remembered wellness." Dr. Benson goes on to write how study after study suggests that this act of imagination, combined with relaxation can change the chemistry of the body in a way that actually helps our body heal. If this "remembered wellness" can reverse the course of disease in our body, just imagine how successful it can be in helping us deal with stress. (By the way, those of you who would like to include a spiritual, or religious component in this process, please feel free to do so. This can also add to the impact of the experience.)

WORRIED? ☞ **What you hold in your thoughts is reflected in your life**

Okay. So far you have practiced breathing deeply (three to five times), saying "relax" to yourself as you exhale. You then asked yourself, *How would I rather be feeling?* and allowed a few words to come to mind. Next, you have imagined a time when you were feeling one or more of these feelings in vivid detail. Great! Now, let's take this powerful concept a step further. Remember, this part of the book is designed to help you deal more successfully with stressful situations when you find yourself in the middle of them. It is not how to just escape from a stressful situation through mental imagery, or go to your "happy place". In other words, although there is value in our ability to change how we feel by what we hold in our imagination, let's not stop there. Let's also become clear about how we might affect our *present* experience of life as we bring those positive feelings from the past into the situation that we are dealing with now.

For example, imagine again that you are dealing with one of the stressors identified earlier (traffic, bills, difficult people, etc.).

Now, suppose that you are able to stop what you are doing, begin breathing purposefully, relaxing as you exhale, and ask yourself, *How would I rather be feeling?* Then you imagine a time in the past that you felt this way. You have already demonstrated how this powerful exercise in imagination might help you change the chemical make-up of your body (remember the lemon?), and therefore help you feel better. Now, suppose that you are able to bring these more purposeful feelings into whatever stressful situation you find yourself dealing with.

Can you see how this might help you respond to whatever is going on in a different, more effective way? Can you also see how you now might have more access to your interpersonal skills and problem-solving skills, and therefore, be more effective in the situation? If so, then I would encourage you to make this process as powerful as possible by continuing to imagine exactly *how* you would be different. For example, how would you be thinking differently, or interacting with those around you differently? Further, how do you think your more purposeful behavior might affect others? Again, the more you are able to create this vividly in your imagination, the more real it becomes, and the more likely it is that some form of your vision will become a reality.

Let's go a step further. Do you think that you will find yourself dealing with any of these "stressors" at sometime in the future? Pretty much guaranteed, right? Well, what if, as you were practicing using your imagination, you not only visualized bringing the good feelings from the past to the present, but continued to imagine how you would *like* to deal with this situation in the future? For example, you could create a mini-movie about finding yourself in a similar "stressful" situation, going through this process, and then responding more purposefully. Can you see how this would almost become a behavioral rehearsal for how you would like to respond to challenging situations in the future? If this makes sense to you, I would encourage you to practice using your imagination in this way, so that you can become skilled at using this powerful process to deal successfully with life now *and* in the future.

At this point, some of you may be protesting, *"Wait a minute, I can't do this, I don't visualize well"* which I interpret to mean that when you imagine something, you don't actually "see it" in your mind. Of course, this can be true, given that we all experience the act of imagining in a slightly different way. However, when I hear people say this, I often respond with, *Well, you must not worry very much then.* To which, almost everyone answers, *Oh no, I worry all the time.* I then ask, *Well, when you are worrying, aren't your images crystal clear?* You see, what they were really saying is not that they have trouble visualizing, but that they have difficulty visualizing what they want.

We often have no trouble at all creating crystal clear images (or worrying) about what we are *afraid* will happen. *Our* difficulty comes when we are trying to form a clear picture in our mind of what we *want*, or something that isn't tied to worry. For many of us, this is a new concept and just as with any new skill, it may take some practice before we become good at it.

The challenge is to view the act of dealing successfully with your stress as a skill that you would like to learn, much like playing the piano, or some other musical instrument. The reason this musical perspective works is that we *know* learning to play an instrument is a process that will take time and practice. Therefore, we don't judge ourselves (or the learning process) as a failure if we feel somewhat awkward at first, or even make some mistakes along the way.

Unfortunately, with psychological concepts, many of us have a belief that if we *know* it, we should be able to *do* it, and if we can't, we interpret this to mean that either *we* are failures, or the process doesn't work, or both. I would encourage you not to fall into this trap. Instead, recognize that learning how to deal purposefully with stress is much like learning to play the creative and powerful instrument in your brain. Allow yourself some time and practice to become accomplished.

Now, let's deal with the final component of stress, which is what I refer to as *the results*. As I said earlier, these "results" not only represent the reactions (feeling angry, frustrated, overwhelmed, etc.) that we identified as part of the *Cycle of Stress*, they also represent how we react to feeling out of control, tense, listening to the negative little voices in our mind, and worrying about things that aren't happening. We also know that these reactions often make the stressors seem worse, and therefore, trigger the escalation of the *Cycle of Stress.*

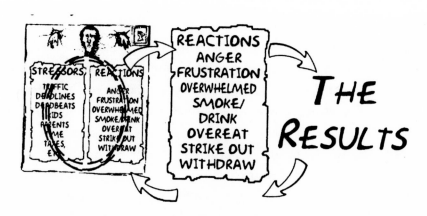

The good news is that up to this point, you have been practicing behaviors that not only break the *Cycle of Stress,* but actually produce a chemical change in your body (which changes how you feel). For example, what if you were feeling stressed, and instead of worrying, you chose to use this anxiety as a valuable signal? You could first begin breathing deeply and then say the word "relax" to yourself as you exhale. Then you could ask yourself the question: *How would I rather be feeling?* and allow several words to come to mind. Next, you could vividly imagine a time (in the past) when you were experiencing one or more of these feelings, and imagine how you would be reacting differently if you could bring these feelings into the present. Finally, you could imagine how you would like to bring these feelings into *potential* stressful situations, and how they would affect your experience of the future. If you were able to follow this process, can you see how this would change the way you experienced the "stressful" situation?

Can you also see how the feelings you identified in step three (ask yourself: *How would I rather be feeling?*) would be very similar, if not identical, to the feelings you have just produced, i.e., calm, relaxed, confident, etc.? If so, take a moment to acknowledge, or notice this positive change. The reason this is such an important step is that, for many of us, acknowledging what works, or what's *good* in our lives is an unfamiliar experience. We are, however, often very familiar with noticing what's wrong. In fact, we may have spent much of our lives practicing this selective vision. The problem with this learned perspective of focusing on what's *wrong*, however, is that *what we focus on expands*. In other words, as we focus on a particular aspect of life, that aspect becomes a larger and larger component of our perspective, and therefore colors our experience in a more profound manner.

For example, have you ever seen children spill their milk or make some similar mistake at the dinner table? Often, the parents will make a huge issue out of this and tell them over and over how bad this is, and how they should *never* spill the milk again. Of course, all the kids hear is how he or she is bad for making a mess and so they become very focused on "not spilling their milk." As they hold this focus, they are probably thinking thoughts like *Don't spill the milk. Don't spill the milk. Don't spill the milk.* These thoughts, of course, create certain pictures or images of . . . that's right . . . spilling their milk and how bad this will be, which of course guarantees that . . . guess what?

You got it. The child *will* spill the milk because this is the image that has been going through his or her mind.

Let's look at another example of how our focus affects our experience of life. Imagine that our mind is like a gardening hose and the water coming out represents our mind's energy (or where we direct our focus). Most of us find ourselves pointing the hose at (or worrying about) the weeds in our life or what's "wrong". The assumption here is that if we focus on what's not working, we will be motivated to take whatever steps are necessary to address the problem successfully. Often, however, this focus on the negative does nothing but color our experience of life in a way that actually paralyzes us, so that we take no action except to worry more about the fact that we aren't taking any action. *The weeds love this!*

While we are "watering the weeds," the flowers (the good things in our life) may be dying from lack of attention. This is evident in looking at the way many of us decide how much time and attention we give our relationships. We seem to spend a lot of time and focused energy on *creating* the relationship, and then we turn our focus to other areas that "need our attention."

As you look back over your experience of being in a relationship, can you see a change of feeling corresponding with your change of focus? In other words, can you see how, as you changed your focus from the relationship to other things in your life, your feelings around your relationship changed as well?

You have probably heard that, on average, married couples only spend approximately 20 minutes a week talking to each other. Can you imagine how long a business might last if the partners communicated that infrequently?

And yet, when we are asked what are the most important things in our lives, most of us would put family and our relationship with our spouse, at or near the top of the list. As a psychologist, I have found that couples often wait until their marriage/relationship is almost beyond help to begin giving their relationship the attention it needs, and even then, their motivation is often based more on their fear of failure than their desire to strengthen their love. In other words, we often don't focus (or re-focus) on an aspect in our lives until there is a problem. My point here is that this tendency to focus on the negative isn't working for us, or helping us create the lives we want, and therefore we should change our focus.

Now, I'm not suggesting that we should *ignore* problems, or that only "positive thinking" is valuable and productive. What I *am* suggesting is that when we become paralyzed by fear and worry, we often find ourselves making more mistakes and generally making the situation worse. I am further suggesting that as we regain control, we can bring our life skills to bear more effectively if we focus on the solution versus the problem. Finally, I am suggesting that it will serve us well to ensure that we are giving the positive aspects of our lives the attention they deserve and therefore allow them to expand.

For example, take this process of breathing, relaxing, asking, and imagining which leads to positive changes (i.e. feeling relaxed, calm, confident etc.) It's important to focus on, or notice, how this process works for us, meaning the changes, or the positive feelings it produces.

The reason it is important to focus on the positive changes is because doing so reinforces their effect on our experience of life... and isn't that what you want? In fact, what we really are talking about here is becoming more aware of what you *want* versus what you don't want, and then changing your focus so that your creative energy is concentrated in that direction. Wouldn't it have been great if we learned how to purposefully focus our awareness on what we want early in life? The good news is it's never too late to learn. Further, to support you in making these changes, I have created an acronym to help you remember this process.

Breathe Deeply 3 to 5 times

Relax On the Exhale

Ask How would I rather be feeling?

Imagine Feeling this way

Notice The changes you produce

That's right! It spells BRAIN. I did this for two reasons. First, I want you to be able to remember what to do when you find yourself in the middle of a stressful situation. In fact, this entire process is about purposefully engaging our brain to produce the kind of chemicals (hormones, etc.) that actually have us feeling good. Second, another advantage to the "good feeling of feeling good," is the fact this positive experience also helps us deal with *any* situation more successfully by giving us more access to our interpersonal and problem-solving skills.

Now, I'll bet that a small voice may be saying, *Yeah, Yeah, sounds great but I don't have time to stop whatever I'm doing and breathe, relax, etc. whenever I'm in a stressful situation. I'm a busy person!* Well, . . . remember diarrhea? Again, it's all about priorities. We have made diarrhea a priority, which means that it's so important that when we receive its signal, we'll stop what we're doing and take whatever action that is necessary to deal with it effectively. Our culture also supports the importance of diarrhea in our life. In fact, it's in the building codes. The truth is, you can't build a building unless it has a certain number of little rooms so that if anyone has diarrhea, they can go there! How many "stress reduction," or "peace of mind" rooms do you see?

So you might be saying, *Okay, I do think my ability to deal with stress, and my peace of mind, ought to be at least as important as diarrhea, but what can I do? I don't have a place where I can go in order to practice the BRAIN model and deal with my stress.* Well, I have a suggestion. You know those little rooms that they have built for diarrhea? Well, they are called "rest" rooms, aren't they?

Okay, so let's assume that you are in the middle of a stressful situation and you begin to feel somewhat "out of control," kind of like you are about to "lose it," so to speak. You say to the person or persons you are with, *Excuse me I need to go to the rest room.* Trust me, they will never say, *Oh no, you stay right here.* So, you go to the restroom and you sit in one of the little stalls.

Nobody knows what you are doing in there. So, you begin by taking a few deep breaths, which can be somewhat challenging in that kind of environment, but, hey, so much for aromatherapy! You then say the word "relax" to yourself as you exhale, ask yourself, *How would I rather be feeling?* and allow some words to come to mind. Then, imagine feeling these feelings in the past, present, and future. Notice the changes you have produced. First, you will have changed the chemical make-up of your body, and thus are likely to be feeling differently. Second, you might have a clearer vision of how want to respond to the previously "stressful" situation. Finally, just as a nice metaphor for what you've "let go of," I suggest that you go ahead and flush the commode and imagine all that tension and anxiety going down the drain. (Besides, if anybody else is in the restroom with you, they will feel better if you flush).

Now, when you return to the situation where you were previously feeling "stressed," I'll bet that several things will have changed. However, the most important thing that has changed will be you! You will be a different, more aware, more purposeful person, who is proactive versus reactive. Therefore, you are likely to be much more effective in handling the situation successfully. In addition, the other people may have changed as a result of your breaking the *Cycle of Stress*, and *they* may also be more open to moving in a different direction. Wouldn't it be great if this became so popular that the building codes were amended to include "peace of mind" rooms, as well as "rest" rooms? Until then, this is one way to break the cycle.

So far, I have described our tendency to find ourselves reacting to the stressors in our lives in ways that don't work for us (the *cycle of stress*), *and* I have given you rather specific ways of using the power of your brain to break this cycle. As promised, however, I want to give you more. If I could show you a deeper, more powerful model that would give you the opportunity to not only avoid stressful situations before they start, but *change the quality of the rest of your life*, would this be of interest to you? If so, read on, because part two of this book is designed to do just that... to show you how to create your life in such a way that you not only find yourself in fewer stressful situations, but also find yourself experiencing greater happiness, success, and meaning in your life, as well.

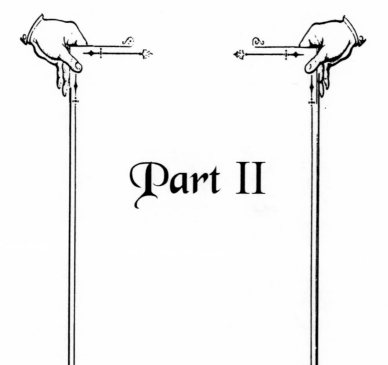

Part II

Chapter 4

Creating A
Purposeful Life Now

Y ou may have noticed that during the first half of this book, I have been using a word (other than diarrhea) quite a bit. This word alludes to what I believe to be a more successful way to live. The word that I'm referring to is "purposeful." You see, I believe that few of us are living our lives in a "purposeful" manner, or to put it another way, very few of us are living "on purpose." What do I mean by this? Well, for one thing, this means having a purpose, or reason for doing whatever we do, and using this purpose as a guide for our decisions and choices. However, it's more than just having a goal or a plan, or even a guiding set of values. Living purposefully also refers to the act of living life deliberately, not accidentally, but "on purpose."

For example, I don't believe that our tendency to react to the challenges (or stressors) in our lives (as we do in the *cycle of stress*) is purposeful. In other words, I don't think that we deliberately get frustrated, angry, or upset at the things in our lives over which we have little, or no control, nor do I think we view this reaction as effective. So why do we find ourselves continually reacting this way? Because we are reacting habitually or unconsciously, versus clearly, deliberately and "on purpose."

Choosing your purpose can mean becoming clear about what you want, who you are, and/or how you want to be in each aspect of your life. For example, what is your purpose, or who do you want to be in your relationships and friendships? How about your career, your relationship with your children, or your parents? It's really about focusing on what you want versus what you don't want, and allowing this focus to guide your choices and behavior.

Purpose

I believe that the more purposeful we are, the more successful we can become in all aspects of our lives. Further, it is my opinion that when we are doing something on purpose, we are more likely to do it well (or at least, we will be more aware of when something isn't working, and change). For example, assume that you wanted to deal more purposefully with one of the stressors identified earlier. Let's say, traffic

First, you would want to get a sense of your purpose and create a mini-movie in your mind or a vision of what your experience with traffic would look like if you were dealing with it "on purpose". What would you be doing differently, how would you like to be feeling, etc.? Chances are, the next morning as you find yourself in the same traffic patterns that you have found stressful in the past, you might choose to react differently.

For instance, you might pop in a cassette that you have been wanting to hear, listen to a book on tape, or tune the radio to a certain type of music. You could also focus on the fact that you are probably in one of the most comfortable seats that you will sit in for the rest of the day, and that you are in total control of the temperature of your environment. You could choose to take in more of the scenery than usual, be friendlier to those around you, etc.

Whatever you decided to do, your choice would be deliberate, or purposeful and, therefore, your experience of traffic (a situation that in the past may have been one of your "stressors") would likely change. This more purposeful experience will probably be either less annoying, or possibly downright enjoyable. Now, I wonder if there may be another small voice inside of you saying something like, *Yeah right! This will make traffic enjoyable!* Almost as if part of you is resisting the belief that you could actually feel good in traffic. You would *like* to feel good in traffic, wouldn't you? Isn't it interesting that, when we come across a new way of doing things, a part of us seems to argue for our inability to make a change? In effect, arguing against what we want, and for our helplessness.

In fact, it's not uncommon to hear people argue for their right to be anxious or stressed. For example, have you ever witnessed a situation where someone was feeling particularly upset or stressed, and another person walks up to them and tells them to calm down or relax? Often the "stressed" person will respond with something like *Don't tell me to calm down!@%#,* almost as if they are defending their right to feel bad.

Why do we do this? It's my belief that the reason we have trouble accepting the possibility that we could have more of what we want by changing how we think about or react to the outside world, is because we have spent so much time convincing ourselves that nothing can be done.   Now, part of this was our experience of childhood, where often, nothing could be done. In other words, as children, we could neither change nor leave our environments, and therefore, we learned that in some very significant ways, we were helpless.

In the mid 1970's, psychologist Martin Seligman did research on what he called "learned helplessness." In this research, he put dogs in a kind of sling from which they could not escape, and then administered a series of electric shocks. Of course, initially the dogs tried to escape. Eventually, however, they stopped resisting, seemingly resigned to the fact that nothing could be done. Twenty four hours later, the researchers put these same dogs in a two-compartment box divided by a barrier over which the dogs could easily jump. Then they administered shocks to one side of the box.

What happened was that two-thirds of the dogs that had experienced the previous shocks made no attempt to jump to the other side of the box. On the other hand, all the dogs in the control group (who had not received any previous shocks), quickly and easily jumped the barrier and escaped.

Dr. Seligman concluded that the reason two-thirds of the dogs from the first group made no attempt to escape is because they had previously learned that they were helpless. Therefore, when they found themselves in a similar situation, they reacted based upon this learned perspective of helplessness versus jumping to the other side of the box.

It is my contention that some of our tendency to resist

change is due to the fact that we have learned to experience ourselves as "helpless." We believe, therefore, that truly nothing can be done and based upon this belief, we do nothing, and even argue for our lack of ability to change.

Another reason that might explain why we may find ourselves arguing for our helplessness is that we need to see all the stress we have felt in the past as "unavoidable." In other words, if we are willing to believe that we can change our experience of traffic, it would mean that all the stress we have experienced in traffic up to this point didn't have to be. We might conclude that we have been "doing it all wrong" and we have "nobody to blame but ourselves"! In fact, I believe that many of us are so determined not to blame ourselves for our negative experiences of life in the past, that we will fight to preserve our inability to change them in the present. I have only one question... How's this working for you? If your answer is, "It's not!", then let's stop searching for who's to blame (ourselves or the world), and focus on what can be done.

What we can do is first become clearer and more purposeful about the way in which we live our lives. How? Well, we must initially become clear about our purpose for being on the planet. Now, this can be a big question, and while I support anyone who wishes to take the time to sit and write out their "purpose in life," I am speaking here of a more practical, applicable concept. In fact, rather than (or maybe in addition to) this purpose taking the form of a statement, I would encourage you to make a movie. *What? A movie?, you might be questioning, I can't make a movie! I can't even program my VCR!* Regardless, I believe that we are making movies all the time.

Almost every minute of every day, we are imagining scenes in our mind... scenes of us interacting with others, doing (or not doing) our job, scenes of what we have done, what we are planning to do, etc. We create little movies, and these movies have a profound effect on what we think and feel (or our experience of life). For example, think of the last time you saw a really good movie. Do you remember why you thought it was good? If you are like most of us, it was because of how it made you feel. In other words, whether it's proud, happy, excited, angry, or even sad... while watching a movie, *we want to be "moved!"* This means we want to be affected by what we are viewing.

Well, just as we are affected when we view a scene at our local theater, the images or movies that we constantly create in our mind (our imagination) affect us, as well (Remember the lemon?) In fact, they affect us even more because they are *about us!* Unfortunately, many of us are making "horror films," which is to say that we are worrying about the past, present, or future and, as we have seen, this only makes matters worse.

Instead, what if we began to make more purposeful movies? In other words, create a vision (or movie) in our mind of what each aspect of our life would look like if we were living "on purpose." A vision so clear that if a famous producer walked up to you tomorrow and said *I would like to make a movie about your purpose*, you could say *Great, I've just been waiting for you to ask!* You see, I believe that the clearer we are about what our purpose is, and especially what our life would look like if we were deliberately using that purpose as a guide for our decisions, choices and behaviors, the happier, more successful, and more meaningful our lives would be.

There is one problem, however. Often, when we begin to create a vision about what we want to accomplish, or the kind of changes we want to make, we tend to imagine this happening in the future. For instance, we might plan to start a new diet or begin exercising, but we almost always plan to begin this "next Monday," or "real soon."

The problem with this future orientation is that not only are we putting off our decision to begin living more purposefully, but we often use the fact that we are going to make changes as an excuse to do the opposite in the meantime. For example, we may think, *Well, since I'm going to start a diet on Monday, I'd better "pig out" now while I've got the chance,* or, *I'll start exercising regularly next week, so it's okay if I do nothing today.* Therefore, I encourage you to incorporate an additional component into your vision of your purpose that will make it even more powerful in helping you to create a life worth living, and that is the *present*.

Living "On Purpose" Now

The truth is, there's only one time that anyone can do anything about anything, and that is *now*, the *present*. Most of us, however, find ourselves obscuring this powerful time in our lives by worrying about the past or the future, sometimes to the point that we don't even remember what we've done. For example, have you ever been driving and found yourself so preoccupied with thoughts (or worries) about some situation in the past or future that you noticed you had driven a significant distance, and yet had *no memory of the experience?* Kind of scary, isn't it? However, this speaks to our powerful ability to ignore the present.

Actually, it makes sense that we would be very good at this. Many of us have been doing it (being oblivious to what's going on around us) for much of our lives. It may have even been a way we coped with being powerless to change our environment as children. However, I believe that in the present and as adults, this tendency isn't working for us.

Other ways in which we ignore the present is to create routines, or habitual ways of doing things so that we don't have to pay attention to what we are doing on a moment-by-moment basis. Now, I'm not saying that this is always bad. There may be times you would like to think about something other than what you're doing. However, I believe this stops working for us when whatever we choose to think about turns to worry, or when our mental preoccupation with the past or the future dulls our awareness of the power, beauty, and potential of the moment.

I'm just encouraging you to be purposeful about how you choose to spend your life, which means the present moments that make up your life. In other words, in order to find yourself in fewer stressful situations, and bring more fulfillment to your life, in general, I'm suggesting that you not only become clear about what your life would look like if you were living "on purpose," but that you also (on a regular basis) ask yourself, *What is my purpose in this moment?* Or even better: "What is my highest purpose NOW?" This question will go a long way toward keeping you focused on how you would like to create each moment and keep your purpose alive as a guiding principle and vision. This reminds me of a quote that I first remember reading on a greeting card, and have since heard said in several ways that reflects this idea:

The past is history and the future is a mystery. This moment is a gift, and that's why they call it "the present."

My hope is that the idea of "Living On Purpose" is becoming clear because this vision will be the foundation on which the rest of the model is built. However, because "finding one's purpose" seems to be a daunting task for many, let me add one more concept to the mix that might help you create this vision in a more powerful way. If you noticed, there is a word that I added to the concept of purpose in the last paragraph, and that word is "highest." "What is my highest purpose?"

I have found that in our search to define one's purpose, this adjective can be very helpful. For example, I'm sure that you have heard many people speak of their "purpose" in pretty mundane terms (i.e. "my purpose is just to get through this day".) When we add the word "highest" to the mix, however, we move from just surviving to thriving. Further, we clarify, as well as, elevate the concept of "living on purpose" (e.g. What is my highest purpose with my kids, etc.?)

If you like, we can define the concept of "highest purpose" even more specifically. This definition comes from the belief that everything that happens to us in life impacts us in some way. In other words, each experience, from the mundane to the profound, from the trivial to the deeply meaningful, has an impact on who we are, and who we are becoming. Now, most of us are fine with this "process of becoming" when the impact is positive. When someone tells us what a good job we are doing or how much they care, we feel good about how this praise accurately defines who we truly are.

The problem, however, is when the result is less than positive. When we find ourselves feeling frustrated, angry, resentful, etc., we feel bad about these feelings and look for someone, or something to blame for "making us feel this way." We are likely to verbalize this perspective as "Traffic makes me crazy!" or "That so and so made me so angry!" or "Rainy days and Mondays always get me down," etc. While this is understandable (no one wants to see themselves to blame for feeling bad) the problem is that when we identify the cause of our negative feelings and behaviors as something or someone other than ourselves, we give these people and situations the power to define who we are!

By definition, we become someone who reacts to traffic with stress, to difficult people with resentment, to deadlines with anxiety, etc. as if we have no choice, or no role in this process of self-definition! Further, not only do we create this definition of ourselves in the present, we project it into the future, ensuring that we will continue to be defined by the negative aspects of our lives for years to come! How is this working for you? Is it really the way you would choose to be if you were defining yourself "on purpose"?

You see, I believe that this is where the concept of "highest purpose" can serve us very well. What if we decided that our "highest purpose" is to take responsibility for this process of self-definition versus leaving it to chance or the behavior of others? We could then become clear about who we would be (the qualities and/or characteristics we would be demonstrating) if we were living, or defining ourselves, "on purpose," and look for opportunities to practice this self-definition.

Given that we are already good at being "who we are" when we are responding to positive events and people, we could see the "stressors" (or the negative events and/or people in our lives) as opportunities to practice redefining who we truly are. This process of purposeful self-definition then becomes our "highest purpose." If this concept appeals to you, I encourage you to keep it in mind as we continue discussing the rest of the model.

Okay. My hope is that you can see how important it is to be

aware (and purposeful) as we create our lives and, thus, our definition of who we are. So, if this is such a good idea, why do we have to be reminded of it, ...or, what gets in the way of our creating our present moments "on purpose"? Two words . . . *our past.*

Chapter 5

The Power of Our Past

W hen I refer to *our past*, what I really mean is our habits, tendencies, beliefs, and/or learned responses that may or may not be congruent with our highest purpose. Let's face it. Our past is where we formed our beliefs about who we are and our place in the world. It's where we learned what it meant to be a man, woman, child, how to react to conflict, interact with others, etc. It didn't matter that "the world" we saw was mostly what went on in our family. Most of us didn't think,... *this is just how my family is.* We thought, *This is how the world is.* For us, our family was our world, especially when we were young. From this experience, we formed our core beliefs about ourselves and the world, as well as, our habitual ways of reacting to the world, and we continue to repeat these habitual ways of being today. This shouldn't be surprising. The reason they call them habits is because *they're habitual*, which means we will do them without thinking, or we will seem to find ourselves behaving and reacting without our conscious thought.

Now, don't get me wrong, I'm not saying that everything, or even most of what we learned from our past is bad, or wrong. I'm sure that much of what you learned still serves you very well today. In fact, I'm going to suggest that you identify, and hold on to these valuable lessons. The good news is that you *will* (hold onto what you learned). The reason I can say this with such certainty is because this learning has taken the form of a habit, tendency, or core belief.

This doesn't mean that we can't change our core beliefs if we find they are incongruent with our purpose. It just means that we may want to hold on to some of this past learning and, if this is the case, we needn't do a thing, because it has become woven into the fabric of our being.

For example, when I think of my past, I remember growing up in the small town of Kilgore, Texas. My mother and father had been married twenty-five years before I was born, and I was their only child! My mom went to the doctor when she was around 45 and said "Doc, I'm sick" and he said "No, you're pregnant!" Quite a surprise, as you might imagine.

Now, in many ways, the fact that I came along so late in their lives was the good news because Dad had been drinking twenty-three of those twenty-five years. In other words, Dad had stopped drinking two years before I was born. This means instead of growing up in the home of an active alcoholic, I grew up in the home of a recovering alcoholic, and for those of you who know the difference, you can appreciate the benefit of this twist of fate.

When I was born, I was referred to as "their AA baby" because the way my dad stayed sober was through AA, or Alcoholics Anonymous. Kilgore was a small town in northeast Texas, and my dad was very involved in the program of AA. As a matter of fact, he was so involved that if you looked up Alcoholics

Anonymous in the phone book of that small town, you found *our home phone number!*

Our kitchen table was a place that people would come on a regular basis to pour their hearts out and often turn their lives around. Dad was always talking to someone on the phone, going out in the middle of the night to help people stay sober and attending AA meetings. Boy, did we attend meetings! Between my dad's involvement with AA and my mom's involvement with Al-Anon, we must have attended three to five meetings a week. *I thought it was what everybody did!* It was almost like going to McDonald's to me, because I remember playing around the meeting halls and watching my mom and dad stand up in front of all those people and tell their story, over and over again. Consequently, I have never had a fear of speaking in public.

Now, I understand that fear of public speaking is said to be the most common of all our fears, more so than snakes, heights, or even dying. However, because I saw my parents do this on a regular basis, it never even occurred to me to be frightened. In fact, I have a tape of myself at the age of five speaking at an AA meeting, and while I can't make out what I was saying, I was clearly saying it with confidence.

Given that this had been such a natural part of my growing up and learning about the world, to this day, I have never imagined that speaking in front of a group of two hundred or two thousand was anything to be frightened of. In other words, this part of my past, or the legacy that was given to me by my mother and father, is very congruent with my purpose.

As a public speaker, trainer, and counselor, this experience of growing up in this type of environment has given me a model for communicating and helping that has served me well, and continues to be a resource for my ability to be effective in those roles. In many ways, I am very grateful that I grew up in this type of AA household. That's the good news.

The bad news is that Dad seemed to use home as a place to recharge his batteries. When he was speaking at an AA meeting, he was "up" and "on" and "alive." Similarly, at home, when someone would call from AA, he would light up, and be full of all kinds of energy and enthusiasm. The rest of the time, however, he would sit and watch TV or sleep (at least, this is how I remember it). I have very few memories of him nurturing my mom and me with the same enthusiasm or intensity that he gave to those he was helping in A.A. I never remember being upset about this. . .

It just seemed to be "the way things were." Almost as if there was an unspoken rule that Dad's sobriety was essential for the stability of the family, and the way that Dad stayed sober was through A.A. Therefore, whatever supported this was essential.

Just to be clear, I want you to understand that I didn't, and still don't, see A.A., or Dad's involvement in A.A. as the problem. Quite the contrary, I see my exposure to the power of this twelve-step program as one of the most beneficial aspects of my childhood, one that continues to be a very positive influence in my work today (very congruent with my purpose).

What I *am* saying is that my memory of my father (and therefore my belief about what it means to be a father) was of someone who was very outgoing, nurturing, and supportive of those he came in contact with *outside the home* . . . and somebody who used his home as a place to recharge his batteries, and, therefore, didn't give the same energy to his family that he gave to others.

Now, I never remember saying to myself, "That's how I am going to be when I grow up." However (as you might have guessed), as I entered my late twenties and early thirties, I found myself drawn to speaking and counseling (surprise, surprise). I even earned a master's degree in counseling psychology and was working toward my Ph.D., and . . . guess what? I found myself speaking to large groups of people with relative ease, and with a great deal of enthusiasm (just like my dad). In addition, when I was working with someone in counseling, I found myself very focused and enthusiastic about helping them (just like my dad). Then, I would go home and (you guessed it), recharge my batteries (*just like my dad*).

Finally, as my style of counseling, or my way of working with others, became increasingly focused on helping them be more purposeful in their lives, I began to examine *my own* life in terms of this paradigm (what a novel idea). As I did, I discovered this discrepancy. Clearly, following this old learned perspective of using home as a place to just recharge my batteries was incongruent with my purpose, a big part of which was to be a loving and present force in my relationship with my wife and children.

As I became aware of this, I was able to change. Now, when I come home I purposefully give loving attention to my wife, Georgia, and my two sons, Christopher and Nicholas. Not because "I'm supposed to" but because it's congruent with my purpose. Then I say "Dad needs a nap!" and I go take a short nap. You see, I still use home as place to recharge my batteries, I just do this in a purposeful way, or a way that is congruent with how I want to define myself as a husband, father, speaker, and counselor.

That's the nice thing about becoming very clear about what our life would look like if we were living "on purpose." Once we have done this, we can use this vision as a criteria to determine which aspects of our past (which beliefs, habits, learned perspectives, etc.) we want to hold on to, and which ones we want to let go of, or better yet change, so that our new beliefs and behaviors are congruent with our highest purpose.

Remember the "purpose" of this book is not only to help you deal more successfully with stressful situations, but also to give you the opportunity to change the quality of the rest of your life! In order to become more influential in this endeavor, it would be helpful to discover how your "past" is affecting your experience of life in the present, and determine to what degree this is congruent with your highest purpose.

One of the most (if not *the* most) influential factors in how we create our experience of life is our beliefs, or what we believe to be true about ourselves, the world, and our place in the world. In fact, one way of illustrating just how influential these beliefs are is what I call the *"beliefs cascade"* or "how we create our experience of life."

As you can see from the illustration on page 63, the facts of our lives get filtered through our beliefs. These beliefs then create both our interpretations, or how we give meaning to what we see, and our expectations, or what we expect to happen next. These beliefs, interpretations, and expectations then create how we feel internally about the situation or our emotions. This creates our behaviors, or how we outwardly respond to the situation, and all of this combines to create our experience of life.

This is why so many people can have very different reactions to the same situation. It's not the situation that is causing (or creating) their reactions, it is their beliefs, interpretations, expectations, etc.

Further, it doesn't stop there. Since our experience of life is created by what we believe to be true, we often find ourselves experiencing situations the same way over and over. This only goes to reinforce the "righteousness" of our beliefs, which then goes on to influence our interpretations, expectations, emotions, and behaviors. All of this results in a cycle of sulf-fulfilling prophecy that is as powerful as the *cycle of stress* we spoke of earlier.

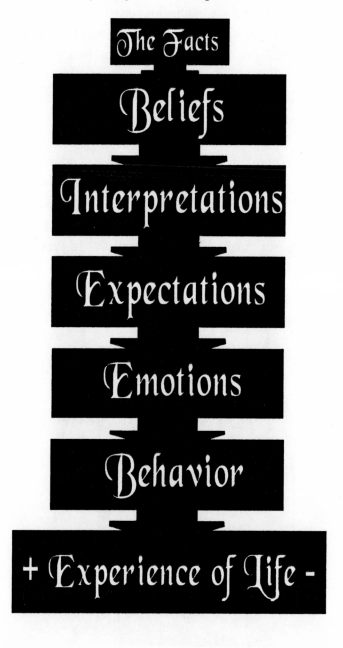

Now, the problem isn't that our beliefs create our experience of life. Actually, that's the good news, because our beliefs are an aspect of our life that we can influence or change. The problem is that very few of these influential beliefs were created "on purpose." They are the result of our growing up in a certain environment that was created by the (generally unexamined) beliefs of our caregivers which they learned by growing up in a similar environment, and on and on.

Again, I am not saying that all, or even most of the beliefs you learned as a child are problematic. I'm just encouraging you to be purposeful about choosing the ones you want to hold on to (those that are congruent with your purpose) and those you would like to change. How can we change the beliefs that are no longer congruent with our purpose? Great question! In fact, that's what the rest of the book is about!

Chapter 6

The Wisdom of Serenity

One of the most vivid memories I have of growing up in an AA home is going to the AA meetings. As I mentioned earlier, we spent quite a bit of time at these meetings, which was fine with me because they became my playground. As I became old enough to read, I began noticing all the signs on the walls. There were sayings like, "One day at a time," and "Let go and let God." My favorite, however, became the serenity prayer, which of course says, "God grant me the serenity to accept the things I cannot change, the courage to change the things I can, and the wisdom to know the difference."

Recently this prayer has become very popular, so much so that you can even get it on a refrigerator magnet! This is very significant because whenever you can get what you believe on a refrigerator magnet, it means the culture has really accepted it as true. There is one problem, however. I believe that we may be looking at the serenity prayer much like we view the concept of relaxation. For example, we may be thinking of the prayer like this,

If God would give me the wisdom to know the difference between what I can change and what I can't, well then, I would change all the things I can, and I guess I would accept the rest, and then I would get serenity. Notice anything strange about this interpretation? . . . *It's backwards!*

You see, it's not called the wisdom prayer, or the change prayer, or the "get it all done" prayer. It's called the *Serenity* Prayer! What if that's no accident? What if it's called the Serenity Prayer because the first thing that is asked for is serenity? In other words, what if the prayer describes something other than just a plea for help? What if the prayer describes the process by which all of this occurs? For example, imagine that we are able to read between the lines. Can you see how the prayer might begin like this, "God (first) grant me the serenity to accept the things I cannot change"?

Let me ask you this, how much of the stress, strain, grief and/or anxiety in your life would disappear if you could "accept the things you cannot change"? Look again at the *cycle of stress.*

STRESSORS
TRAFFIC
DEADLINES
DEADBEATS
KIDS
PARENTS
TIME
TAXES, ETC.

REACTIONS
ANGER
FRUSTRATION
OVERWHELMED
SMOKE/DRINK
OVEREAT
STRIKE/OUT
WITHDRAW

THE CYCLE OF STRESS

Notice the "stressors" on the left side. How many of these are things that we just can't change? That is, how much of our stress is caused by our continuing to struggle with these people or situations, trying to get them to change but, instead, they seem to get worse? *To what degree would your life be richer, and more meaningful if you could stop this frustrating struggle and accept the things you cannot change?* If you are like most of us, this would make quite a difference. Well, what if the serenity prayer shows us how to do this? In other words, if acceptance (the ability to accept what we can't change) is what we want, *what if serenity is a precursor to this acceptance?*

Again, imagine that the prayer is a description of a process versus a cry for help. What if the prayer describes this process by first asking for serenity which leads to acceptance, and then asking for the courage to change the things we can? Look at the right side of the cycle of stress, our reactions. The truth is, if we make it a priority, we can change the way we react to stress . . . *and* it will take courage for us to see these reactions as habitual, and choose to change them versus blaming them on the situation.

Can you imagine how the quality of your life would improve if you had the courage to change your reactions to life to ones that are congruent with your highest purpose? Well, *what if serenity and acceptance are the precursors to this courage and change?* Further, as we continue to practice serenity and accept-ance, and courage and change, over and over, can you see how we might become wiser in the process? That is, what if wisdom isn't so much what we need in order to make the process work, but instead is the result of following the purposeful process of serenity, acceptance, courage and change?

Make sense? If so, can you see how important serenity is to the success of this process? It is the precursor to acceptance, courage and change and, therefore, *it's the foundation on which everything else is built!*

So, given that we have just made serenity a very important component in our quality of life, let me ask you a question. About how many minutes a day would you say you spend creating serenity in your life ?. . . If you're like most of us, *zero*! Most of us wake up in the morning to an alarm clock, which we turn off repeatedly until we absolutely *have* to get out of bed. This means we are already late and so we rush through the routine of getting ready (and, if we have kids, getting *them* ready). While doing this, we are often worrying about what excuse we are going to use for being late this time. We then get in traffic, which we resent, and fight in a vain attempt to make up for the time we overslept, and when we get to the office (or wherever) we rush to get as much done in as little time as possible.

When lunchtime comes, we take 30 minutes for lunch, struggling to eat as much as we can in the smallest amount of time. Then, we are back doing whatever we consider to be our job (which we're really not *that* crazy about) again with the goal being to get as much done in as little time as possible. Finally, it's time to go home and so we get back in traffic, resenting the fact that we are "forced" to spend so much time sitting in our car. Eventually, we get home, and if we are parents, the "second shift" starts, where we are trying to get our kids to eat more of the "right stuff" (or at all), and then we are trying to get them to go to bed, so we can finally have some time to ourselves. They don't want to go to bed, however, so we get angry and say and do all the things our parents did to us (that we swore we would never do to our kids) until they either become exhausted, or we become intimidating enough to make them go to bed. Then, finally, we are sitting on the couch, it's about 10:30 p.m. and we are watching re-runs of sitcoms, thinking, *at last, I have found serenity.* No! That's not serenity, that's exhaustion!

This is unfortunately an all too familiar description of life for many of us today, and it is built on the belief that we have no choice but to live this way. One question... how is this belief working for you, or to put it another way:

Is this belief, or this experience congruent with your highest purpose?

Isn't it nice to have a question that will give us an immediate answer when we are looking to determine which beliefs we would like to hold on to, and which to change? Still, just asking this question, while valuable, doesn't make the change happen, and again, the purpose of this part of the book is to give you a way to be more powerful or influential in your experience of life.

So, how can we make these changes? Well, we have already seen how becoming clear about our highest purpose in each present moment, can be helpful in creating this more positive life experience. In addition, we have become aware of how our past influences our experience of life, and how this awareness can help us be more purposeful in choosing which beliefs to keep, and which to change. Now we can add the wisdom of serenity as a precursor to the process of acceptance and change, so necessary to achieving our goals. Let's not stop here, however. Let's move on to the rest of the model, so that you can have all the tools at your disposal as you shape your experience of life.

Chapter 7

Choosing The Energy

The next "tool" I want to offer to you is somewhat abstract, however, it's also one of the most powerful components of the model, so please bear with me as I try to make it more tangible. What I'm speaking of is the energy that we choose to drive or motivate our choices and decisions.

Remember when we were discussing our past tendency to worry about doing poorly on tests in school as a motivation to study and succeed? Similarly, we noticed that, in general, we have been taught to worry (or imagine bad things happening to us) as a way to motivate ourselves to take whatever steps are necessary to keep these imaginary concerns from becoming a reality. Initially, I referred to this learned perspective as a kind of a map, or manual that we created to avoid getting hurt. Let me tell you how I came across this concept.

In my travels as a speaker and author, I have had the pleasure of meeting and talking with many fascinating people. One of them was Dr. Martha Serpas, a poet and journalist from Louisiana. She described this childhood tendency of becoming very skilled at knowing what to do or what not to do to avoid getting hurt as a "map of avoidance."

I like this description because it seems to really capture the experience of being a child where we can neither leave, nor change many of the situations in which we find ourselves (especially our families). Therefore, we must become very good at survival, which often means avoiding getting hurt. We create our "map of avoidance," and to some degree, it works (which means we survive). Because it works, however, we continue to refer to it whenever we are afraid. And, as you know, the more we do anything over and over, the more it becomes a habit, and eventually, we may even forget that we are "referring to the map" at all. We just think that this is what to do to avoid problems and pain.

The Map of Avoidance

Don't: Give me that look, Get so excited, Keep secrets, Tell anyone, Rock the boat, Make waves, Upset your Father, Mother, Sister, Brother, Start crying or I'll give you something to cry about, Talk back, Waste your food, Say a word,

Or Else!

Again, it's like growing up in New York City, creating a map of avoidance, and then moving to Chicago, but continuing to refer to the old map. It doesn't work because it no longer accurately reflects where (and who) we really are. Dr. Serpas says that in order to put ourselves in a position to make our lives work as adults, we must be willing to trade our "map of avoidance" for the "map of authenticity." That is, stop being who we had to be, and/or doing what we had to do to survive, and become who we really are. The truth is, as adults, we have more choices and abilities to influence our lives than we did as children. However, if we are unaware that these choices exist, and/or if we are afraid to use them, we will continue to refer to our "map of avoidance" using our fear of being hurt to keep ourselves safe.

For example, have you ever been hurt in a relationship? Most of us have at one time or another. We may even find ourselves replaying the part of the relationship that "hurt" us over and over in our mind, so that we never allow this to happen again. It's almost as if we are hanging on to the pain of the experience (or continuing to refer to our "map of avoidance") as a protective reminder to avoid situations such as this in the future.

In my workshops, I generally illustrate this point by having the group imagine that I've been in a relationship with one of the members of the audience, and they hurt me! At this point I will walk up to one of the participants and ask them to stand. As they do, I will pick up their chair as a representation of the pain that they "caused me" and drape it over my shoulder. Because, hey! I want them to know how much they hurt me. I don't want them to think that it was no big deal, and I certainly don't want them to think that they got away with it, or that they could do this to me again. I've got to protect myself somehow! So I'm going to carry this pain around (their chair) as a symbol of what they did to me, and as a way of keeping it from happening again.

So, now I am looking for somebody very different from that last person to have a relationship with so that I won't be hurt like I was before. At this point (still carrying the chair), I will walk up to another person, and speak of how nice they are, and how I'm convinced that they won't hurt me. But guess what? They do!

Here, I ask them to stand and again take their chair as a representation of the pain that they caused, and as a reminder to not let this happen to me again. I continue this with two or three more people until I have chairs (my "protective" pain), draped all over me. I then turn to the audience and ask, *Who wants to be in a relationship with me now?*

Unfortunately, nobody can even get close to me because of all the pain I am carrying around. Further, rather than protecting me, what the pain is really doing is sapping my strength (it takes a lot of energy to continue to carry all this pain), and keeping me separate from others who might be nurturing and helpful (such as friends).

The energy behind this tendency to hold on to pain in order to avoid being hurt again is fear. Fear of what this means about me. Fear of being taken advantage of. Fear that they will think what they did was "no big deal" and that they "got away with it," and finally, fear that they (or someone like them), will do this to me again. While it's understandable that we might hold on to this fear to try to stay safe, it's my belief that it doesn't serve us. That is, I believe that fear is not the energy that will help us create a life of fulfillment, success, and happiness. It is, unfortunately, the energy that most of us have learned to use to avoid being hurt, however, and "learn the lessons of life."

There is a phrase that I have found valuable in becoming aware of how fear and stress are tied together. It says:

Stress is an indicator of our belief in the value and validity of our worries and fears!

What this phrase tells us is that the more we hold on to the belief that our worries and fears are both valuable and valid, the more we will experience stress. What can we do instead? We can change our view of stress from the problem to the solution! We can choose to see it as a valuable indicator that we may be using worry and fear as a guide for our thoughts and behaviors. We can then choose a more purposeful energy.

What should this new energy be? Well, there are actually several good choices. One might be the energy of awareness. This differs from fear in that awareness feels good while fear generally feels frightening or bad. In awareness, we are wanting to know as much as possible about a situation so that we might make the best choice. We understand, of course, that we can't always be aware of everything, and thus we acknowledge that there will be times when we will want to choose again based upon what didn't work. If awareness is our goal, however, this "choosing again" isn't really a problem because it is the result of increased awareness... "good information," so to speak.

Another choice could be optimism. Optimism is really only the belief (or expectation) that whatever comes our way, we can handle. Pessimism, on the hand is the belief or fear that we won't be able to handle what comes our way, which of course leads to worry and stress. Martin Seligman, the psychologist that we alluded to earlier in our discussion of learned helplessness, has actually done quite a bit of research on the topic of optimism and even written a book on the subject called "Learned Optimism". In his book, Dr. Seligman speaks to the value of this perspective in terms of our ability to succeed in our career, our relationships and even how optimism effects our health.

I call this more purposeful energy "love". However, what we call it isn't important. What is important is that we make a conscious choice between our tendency to use fear and worry (our map of avoidance) as a guide for our life, versus an energy that is more congruent with our highest purpose. Think back to your purpose, or how you would define yourself (characteristics and qualities) if you were living "on purpose." Can you see how the energy of love (or whatever you want to call it), would be a more supportive and congruent guide or foundation for this vision?

Now, some of you may be saying, *Yes, that energy would be more congruent with my purpose or life vision, however, I'm not so sure that I can trust this "love" energy to protect me. In fact, as I look back over my life, it seems as if "love" has almost always been associated with pain!* I can understand this concern. However, when I am speaking of using love as a guide to stay safe and create a fulfilling life, I'm not referring to what was done to us in the name of "love" by others. Nor am I speaking of love as the energy of attraction, or as what we feel when we "fall in love." Instead, I am referring to a positive, truthful, joyful, clear, and complete energy that celebrates who you are versus frightening you, or insisting that you become who others want you to be.

Notice the adjectives I used to describe this type of "love". As you look back over your life, can you see how the energy that caused you pain was neither positive, truthful, joyful, or clear? In fact, wouldn't you say that these painful experiences were really more congruent with the energy of fear? Fear that you weren't being an obedient child, fear that your mistakes reflected negatively on your parents, fear that your natural tendencies would lead to an unsuccessful life, fear that on some level you were unlovable. In general, fear that you weren't a good enough child, student, date, lover, spouse, parent, co-worker, friend, whatever. Feel familiar? This has nothing to do with what I'm referring to as love, and I believe that becoming clear about this distinction (between love and fear) is a crucial element in our ability to create a positive experience of life.

Now, for most of us, this distinction is hardest to make when we are "falling in love," so let's look at how we can use this powerful energy even in this scenario, and still stay safe.

First, let's look at how we tend to think and behave in these "falling in love" situations. Most of us will do at least three things: (1) We will make sure that the person to which we are attracted only sees our "good side," hoping that we can slip the rest in after they're hooked and maybe they won't notice, (2) We become an expert at discovering who they want us to be, and try desperately to be this person, even if this bears little resemblance to who we really are, (3) We become very restricted in our ability to accurately sense who "they" really are. Why? Because just like us, they're hiding all the parts of them they don't want us to see, and we want so desperately for them to be who we "need" them to be, that we will project these qualities on to them while, at the same time ignoring any signs and signals to the contrary. By the way, this is why when we are looking back at a "failed" relationship, almost all of us say something like, *I can't believe it! All the signs were there, why didn't I see them?* to which our friends just roll their eyes.

Incidentally, can you see how fear is the underlying energy for each of these deceptions? First we deceive ourselves by ignoring any signs or clues that the person to which we are attracted may not be who we think they are. Then we continue the deception by trying to hide our dark side from them.

It's true. When creating relationships, most of us will find ourselves holding on to some form of these three fears: (1) We are afraid that if they see "who we really are," they will reject us, (2) We are afraid that if we don't become who (we think) they want us to be, they will reject us, and (3) We are afraid that if this relationship doesn't work, then that means there is something wrong with us, and we will spend the rest of our life alone. So you see, it isn't "love" but actually "fear" that creates these painful situations.

Okay, you might say, *But how can this love you talk about keep me safe?* Well, remember, I described this love as a "positive, truthful, joyful, clear, and complete energy that celebrates who you are, right? My contention is that if this is the energy that we consult as we create a relationship (or any experience of life for that matter), we will be forever and infinitely safe. How? Well, let's imagine that instead of using fear as a guide, we decided to be ourselves and allow the truth (about us and them) to be the criteria for the relationship going forward. This would mean that we would not only be who we are (showing both our strengths and weaknesses), but we would allow (and even insist) that they be who they are (versus who we want them to be). As a result, one of several things will happen: (1) They will not like who we are which means in order to be in this relationship we will have to be somebody we're not. This would be very valuable information and it would mean that the relationship would not go forward. While disappointing in some way, this would actually be the good news, because why would we want to be in a relationship where we can't be ourselves? or (2) They love us for who we are, which again is very valuable information. This would probably result in the relationship going forward, but based upon love and truth, versus fear.

As long as we continue to make love and authenticity the energy with which we create our relationships, we will be safe because no relationship will go forward that isn't based upon truth and love. Now, this doesn't mean that problems won't come up (in fact, this is guaranteed). It just means that they can be healed with the same "real love" (not just the energy of attraction) that created the relationship.

My hope is that you are beginning to see how choosing the energy of love versus fear as a guide can support you in creating your vision of life. Let me give you another illustration of the value of this energy. Have you noticed how wise you are when you're giving advice to your best friend? I mean, really! Have you noticed how clearly you can see what they need to do? Get out of the relationship, get in the relationship, change jobs, take a rest, stand up to the people in their lives, whatever it is, you know exactly what they need to do to take care of themselves. Do you think that your ability to tap into this wisdom might have something to do with the energy you're using as a guide?

The truth is, when most of us think of how we feel about our best friend, what comes to mind is love (or some similar energy). Therefore, because we come from this perspective, we are able to clearly see what is needed.

By the way, have you also noticed that, while it seems to be easy to give wise and valuable advice to our best friend, we don't seem to be able to follow this advice ourselves? Why do you think this is? Could it be that we have been taught to "love others", but when we are trying to make decisions about our life, we have a tendency to worry about negative things happening (or use fear) as a guide or motivation for our decisions? *Could it be that we have been taught to love one another, but not ourselves?* If so, then I believe that this awareness can become good information about which energy would serve us best as we create this more purposeful life.

Now remember, it's important to recognize that we may have some habits, or tendencies from our past that may be more congruent with the energy of fear than love. So, this "choosing of energy" isn't about never having a fearful thought. It's about becoming more aware of which energy we want to use as a guide, and then periodically asking ourselves the question, *Is this thought, belief, emotion, behavior, coming from love or fear?* I have never had an instance when I asked myself this question, and didn't receive a crystal clear answer. Moreover, the answer is always very valuable information.

Now, I'm not saying that I am always able to act on this good information (what we're talking about here is purposefulness, not perfection). For myself, however, once I am able to become clear about the energy (love or fear) that is underlying my thoughts, emotions, and behavior, I am able to also see the ramifications of my choices. I am then in a better position to choose what to do next.

In fact, this is where anxiety, fear, stress, and our physical or emotional pain can become the valuable signals we have alluded to earlier. For example, if we were able to use the signals of stress (anxiety, frustration, fatigue, body pains, etc.) as a reminder to ask ourselves the magic question, *At this moment, am I coming from love or fear?* or *Am I responding to this signal with love or fear?*, we could begin to take steps to align ourselves with an energy more congruent with our highest purpose. In other words, if we discovered that we were reacting out of fear, we could ask ourselves a second question, *What would I be thinking, feeling, or doing if I were coming from love?* Now, this is not a test to see if we are "good enough" to change, or if we can "do it the right way" (which is really about the fear that we can't). It is an opportunity to raise our awareness of how our choice of energy affects our experience of life.

Once we have this awareness, we can then practice becoming more purposeful in this choice, just as we would want for our best friend or someone we loved. In fact, as we have discussed earlier, I have found that one way to tap into the energy of love as a guide for my choices and decisions is to ask myself, *If my best friend were in this situation, what would I want for them, or suggest they do?* or *If this were my grown child, what would I want for them?* I have found that because we are so connected with the energy of love when we imagine what we would want for our child or our best friend, we can often use these questions, or this connection, when we want to tap into the energy of love as a guide for ourselves. In other words, when I suggest that you become purposeful about the energy you choose to guide your experience of life, I am also saying *be willing to treat yourself like you would treat someone you loved.*

In keeping with this goal, I would like to introduce another component of this model which I see as very congruent with the energy of love, and that is *spirituality.* I know that this is a uniquely personal choice and, therefore, I encourage you to honor your own beliefs and apply them here in whatever way works for you.

For me, spirituality is a deep awareness of our connection to each other, to all of life, and to a loving higher power, or life force. Whether we refer to this force as God, Goddess, Buddha, Yahweh, Allah, Jehovah, your inner consciousness, or simply the universal energy of love, isn't important. What is important is how this energy affects our experience of life. If you have determined that love is congruent with your highest purpose and that you want to use this energy as a guide in your life, then, it's my belief that the concept of spirituality can be supportive in this process.

Let me give you an example of how someone could bring this perspective of spirituality to their life. Have you ever had the experience of watching a small child learn to build something out of blocks, or tinker toys, or Lincoln Logs?

Generally, in the beginning, they make some mistakes and often, they then become very frustrated with their inability to put together whatever it is they are trying to build. In other words, they're struggling with their inability to "do it right," and a part of them may even be fearing that they will never be able to make it work. Have you noticed, however, that as we watch their struggle, *we* aren't feeling frustrated and afraid? Instead, we know that they will get it sooner or later because we see their struggle as part of the learning experience. That is because we are able to see the child through love versus fear, we are also able to see them as a work-in-progress, and therefore, we may even see their struggle as kind of "cute." I wonder if, as God watches *our* struggles to "get it right" and the fears that arise around our mistakes and failures, he or she also looks at us and says, "Aren't they cute!" In other words, this energy of love knows that we will get it sooner or later. Therefore, this loving being is able to see us as a work-in-progress, and love us despite our mistakes.

For me, this is one of the ways the concept of spirituality is congruent with the energy of love. Because, if I can see myself as a work-in-progress and loved, even if I make mistakes, then I can free myself to be what I am, an imperfect human being here to learn about life. In fact, couldn't you say that this is our job description for being on the planet? We are imperfect. We make mistakes. It's inevitable, and yet, have you noticed how we seem to measure our worth against the very "un-human" condition of perfection? Or, use the fact that we make mistakes as an evaluation of our lack of worth? It is my belief that this tendency to judge ourselves as "worth less" (or worthless) when we make mistakes isn't working for us. The truth is, it's impossible to not make mistakes, and it may not even be a good idea. In fact, many of the inventions that make our life easier (like Teflon and post-it-notes) come from mistakes. Moreover, have you noticed that sometimes the only way to get the information we need is to take a risk and see what happens? Sometimes it works and sometimes it doesn't. However, we always get good information.

The problem for many of us, however, is that often we don't learn from our mistakes. We are so busy beating ourselves up because we made the mistake in the first place that we miss the lesson, or the information to be gained. Why do we do that? Could it be that we have been taught that the way to avoid making mistakes is to be punished (or experience pain) for our "wrongdoings," and then use the memory of the pain to keep us from making the mistake in the future? Sound familiar? Does this feel like part of our "map of avoidance"? Can you see how this principle was based upon fear versus love? Does it feel congruent with your relationship with God, or your sense of spirituality?

Now, I know most of us were told that the reason we were being punished was "for our own good," and that those who punished us were only doing this because they loved us (which I'm sure many of them believed). However, the problem is if we were taught that we must experience pain in order to learn from our mistakes, what happens when our parents are no longer around to punish us? Can you see how this sets us up to punish ourselves? Further, can you see how this might have us coming from the fear that there is something wrong with us for making the mistake, and that we need to experience pain in order to avoid making this mistake in the future? As I said, I don't believe this perspective is, working for us, or helping us create our lives in a way that is congruent with our highest purpose. Instead of viewing our mistakes as evidence of our failure, or lack of worth, I would encourage us to see our mistakes as actions that we took, or "takes," that missed.

Mis/Takes

In the movies, what do they do when they have a "take" that misses, or a mis/take? They do the scene or the "take" again! In other words, rather than beat themselves up for what didn't work, they take what they learned from the "mis/take" and apply that learning to the next attempt. Have you ever seen out-takes from the movies where they're saying "Take thirty-four"? That means that they have tried this scene thirty-four times! Can you imagine how problematic it would be if they called themselves names, or beat themselves up after each mis/take? They would never get past the first few takes. In fact, have you noticed what they are doing when they make a mis/take? They're laughing!

It's my belief that because they are focusing on the humor of the situation and what they want to produce rather than on what isn't working, they are able to do one scene as many times as necessary until they get what they want. We, on the other hand, are so afraid to make a mistake that often we paralyze ourselves and produce nothing but more fear.

Now, I'm not saying that some of us don't make some pretty awful mistakes, or that at times, remorse or regret couldn't be an appropriate reaction. What I am saying is that beating ourselves up (which is really beating ourselves down) is not the most effective way to learn from (and therefore, avoid repeating) these transgressions, and isn't that the ultimate goal... to make a different choice in the future?

Back to the concept of spirituality. I know that some individuals may have a hard time trusting this concept because they have been taught to fear a jealous and vindictive God. It's my belief, however, that jealousy and vindictiveness are based on fear, and that fear is the sign of a frightened being. It's my belief that

God is love, and the energy of love contains no fear. Therefore, rather than see ourselves as worthless because of our "sins," we can learn from our mistakes and move on, especially when we are using love as a guide. By the way, did you know that the original meaning of the word "sin" was an archery term? It meant to "*miss the mark.*"

Another reason that I believe the concept of spirituality can be a valuable resource as we create a more purposeful life is illustrated in the song, "From a Distance," written by Nancy Griffith, and made popular by Bette Midler. The gist of the song was that as we view our struggles, conflicts, and worries from a distance, they seem less overwhelming and/or problematic. In other words, from a distance, we can see truth and love with greater clarity. This is evident from our earlier discussion of how we can give such wise advice to our best friend, and yet have difficulty applying this wisdom to ourselves.

The chorus of the song alludes to how "God is watching us, from a distance" which speaks to a view of the greatest clarity, from the ultimate distance. When I am caught in my dramas of mistakes and injustice and I am having trouble connecting with the clarity of love and truth, it is congruent with my purpose to believe that there is a loving being (or energy) that sees me as a work-in-progress, has faith in my ultimate success, and loves me in spite of my "mis/takes." That way I get to be authentic, or who I am, an imperfect human being whose mission on earth is to learn to trust in the power of love.

Some of you may be saying, *Okay, I can see how I have learned to use fear as a guide, and I can also see how the energy of love (and spirituality) is much more congruent with my highest purpose. However, we live in a world of fear. How can I change my life when everywhere I turn, people are worried or afraid?* That's an understandable concern because many people do seem to be caught up in fear as a motivation for life. In fact, fear is used to sell newspapers, magazines, deodorant, alarm systems, guns, toothpaste, insurance, and even feminine hygiene. You name it, and someone has spent time and money trying to make you afraid of not having it. Even "The News" we watch each evening isn't really about what's new. It's about what you "should be" afraid of. It's not really "The News," it's "The Fears!"

As a culture, we seem to have a fascination with fear. For example, have you noticed how we (and the media) react to the threat of bad weather, like tornadoes and/or hurricanes? There seems to be a "charge" or energy (the fear of what could happen) around the problems that could result from these experiences. Based on this, the TV and radio stations send crews to the area to get "live footage" of all the "storm's fury," ostensibly to "keep us informed," or motivate us to take whatever steps necessary to be safe. However, have you also noticed that, when the situation doesn't materialize, or when the storm isn't as bad as originally "feared," there is almost a sense of disappointment? As if, because there's no more "danger" (which one would think would be the good news), those who were just wanting to keep us "informed" seem somewhat disappointed.

In fact, rather than relay their happiness at the advantageous turn of events, they may even try to "hang on" to the energy of fear, and make the situation seem worse than it is. It's almost as if they believe that if we aren't frightened, we won't pay attention. Now, this isn't about whether or not we should take the necessary safety measures in bad weather. It's about how we, as a culture, seem to gravitate to fear, and how this attraction is used by media and advertising to motivate our choices. So, again, what can we do? Great question, because it leads me to the final aspect of this model for creating a more purposeful life, and that is the concept of responsibility.

Taking Responsibility

I used to think responsibility was a bad word, because to me, it meant that if I was "responsible" and something went wrong, it was my fault! For instance, as an only child, I would make a mess of my room on a regular basis (because that was my job, and I did it well). My parents would come in and, upon noticing the state of my room, would ask me, *Who's responsible for this mess?* I would answer *Beats me* (only child, right?), *maybe the monsters did it. We really have got to call someone about these messy monsters!* You see, I didn't want to be "responsible," because I didn't want to be blamed if anything went wrong. Even during my early adulthood when I was a professional musician, I would always back away from anybody complaining about the band by saying, *Hey. . . not my fault. I'm only the drummer. I don't make these high corporate-level decisions.* I thought the best way to never be blamed for anything, was to never take responsibility for anything.

After a while (somewhere in my late twenties), however, I noticed a fatal flaw in my philosophy. As long as I abdicated responsibility for my life, I also gave up any power to influence or change my experience of life. In fact, I noticed that if I continued to follow my old way of dealing with life, I would have to change everybody around me before I could find peace of mind, because I had made *them* responsible for my happiness! I was smart enough to know that this wasn't working, and so I began to look at changing the meaning of the word "responsibility." After a long search, I found the answer. I changed the meaning of "responsibility" from "who's to blame" (a fear-based interpretation), to "having the ability to respond," or the ability to purposefully influence my response in ways that are congruent with my highest purpose.

Response ability: The ability to respond

I like this new definition, and I would like to offer it to you as the last component in this model. In fact, I would encourage you to take 100% responsibility for your ability to respond to life (or the quality of your responses to people and situations). What does this mean? Well, it doesn't mean that you have to do it all by yourself, and it certainly doesn't mean that you are responsible for the happiness of everyone around you. Taking 100% responsibility for your "ability to respond" just means that you aren't going to wait for some situation or person to change before you begin to define yourself and your responses in a way that is congruent with your highest purpose.

Taking 100% responsibility for your "ability to respond" also means that you are willing to acknowledge that, of all the people on the planet, you are the expert at knowing what you need, and how to best meet these needs. Now, on the surface this sounds somewhat self-evident. However, have you noticed how many of us will not tell others what we need (or ask for what we need) out of fear of being seen as pushy, or demanding, or selfish? In fact, some of us are so entrenched in this "don't ask, don't tell" philosophy that we will even evaluate how much someone loves us by the degree to which he/she is able to guess what we need, and meet those needs without our saying a word. Further, if we have to tell them what we need, then whatever they do doesn't count. Sound familiar?

Why do we do that? Could it be that we have learned that we aren't supposed to take care of ourselves, especially before we take care of others? In fact, isn't it true that most of us have been taught that we are supposed to take care of everyone else first and if there is any left over, then we can have this for ourselves? Or if we take care of others first, then they will take care of us? How's that working for you?

The fact is, most of us have learned to see our interactions with others much like a pitcher of water, with the water representing our life energy.

We have been taught to give some over here, and some over there, until we find ourselves feeling *drained, depleted and empty.* Further, if the people in our life continue asking us to do things that really don't work for us, rather than tell them, we just feel bad (because, hey, they wouldn't listen anyway, right?). Now, at this point, we may try to drop a hint, however, have you noticed they generally don't get it? So what do we do? We drop bigger and bigger hints, which isn't hard since we are becoming more and more frustrated and resentful as our life energy slowly drains away. Finally, we reach our breaking point. We've had it, and we let those in our lives know what jerks or jerkettes they have been, and how (to take a phrase from the movie, *Network*) *We're mad as hell and we're not going to take it anymore, and if you aren't going to take care of me, well, I'll just take care of myself!#@%*!*

In other words, we have finally felt bad enough to justify taking care of ourselves, as if we had to get to the point of pain or anger before taking care of ourselves was an option. Sound familiar? Again, *how's that working for you?* It is my belief that there's a better way.

Rather than think of ourselves as a pitcher of water that must give to others first and just hope that they will give back, I would encourage you to imagine that there is a wellspring coming from deep inside you and this is the source of much of your life's energy. You are the only one who knows the location of this wellspring, and therefore, you are 100% responsible for keeping it clean and free-flowing. As you tend to this spring (which will take much love and attention), you allow this loving energy to fill you up first and then spill over to those around you.

They still get the love and attention, however they now get it from a fulfilled person. Rather than being selfish, what we're really doing is preventing blame and resentment from poisoning the relationship. Therefore, taking care of ourselves first is actually a gift to everyone we interact with (including, of course, ourselves).

Further, as we become clear how taking responsibility for taking care of ourselves (versus waiting for others to read our mind) will be a gift to those with whom we interact, we can frame our intent to change in the form of this gift, and they may be more receptive. For example, we might say something like, *(name of the person),I've noticed that up until now, I may have been doing you and our relationship, a disservice.* This will get their attention. *I've noticed that I have been expecting you to read my mind and meet my needs without me telling you what they were, and then I found myself getting upset with you because you couldn't do it. I'll bet this was frustrating!* I think you will be amazed at how many people will say, *Yes it was. I'm so glad you noticed.* You might then say something like, *Me too! Well, I'm not going to do that any-more. What I'm going to do, instead, is take more responsibility for taking care of myself as much as I can and, in addition, I'm also going to do a better job of letting you know what I want from you so that you no longer have to read my mind. Then, you can decide how you would like to respond based upon what works for you. Okay?*

Now, these are my words, and I encourage you to choose words that best reflect your personality and style of communica-tion. However, can you see how this might have those in your life appreciating your talking to them about this subject?

The main reason people respond positively to a communi-cation like this is because they don't feel they are being blamed for the past, or pressured to read your mind and meet all of your needs in the future. In fact, by taking more responsibility for your con-tribution to the relationship (i.e. not feeling resentful and blaming them), you are also inviting them to take more responsibility for the quality of *their* participation in your experience together. Who knows what could happen?

Now, some of you might be afraid that if you "allow" those in your life to respond to you only when they want, they will never respond. Well, it's my belief that this is exactly what is going on now, except that your pressure may be making it worse. In other words, what's probably happening is that they are either resisting your pressure to get them to be how you want them to be (which means they're also resentful of you for implying that they are wrong), or they're responding as best they can, and that's all there is. In any case, your decision (to take care of yourself) will either free them to stop resenting you for pressuring them (and maybe even allow them to do more) or give you good information about who they are.

If you find that "who they are" is someone who has no motivation to do anything for another out of love, then you might want to reconsider whether being in a relationship with such a person works for you. I would, however, encourage you to be *absolutely* sure that your assessment of their motivation (or lack thereof) is accurate. My experience is that when people are not nurturing their relationship, most of them are frightened or confused in some way, rather than having no desire to be in a loving, nurturing relationship.

Remember, our purpose here is not getting others to take better care of us, but to see the advantages of taking better care of ourselves. Then, as we are able to communicate this to another in love, how they respond can be valuable information about them and the relationship.

Now, as I mentioned earlier, this doesn't mean that somebody else shouldn't meet your needs. Often, it feels very nice to have someone do something for us because they want to. Taking care of *yourself* just means that you are not going to wait for, or depend on them to do so, and then resent them for not doing it, or not doing it "right."

The result of this more "responsible" way of being is that the experience of giving will feel better to you, and the quality of your giving will increase because you will no longer feel drained, depleted, resentful and angry. In addition, you will no longer be blaming those in your life for not keeping you full (or fulfilled).

In other words, taking care of ourselves can be a gift to all concerned because we actually become better at taking care of, and/or interacting with others, meaning that we become better husbands, wives, parents, lovers, friends, etc.

Can you see how our willingness to become more responsible for our "ability to respond" could effect our experience of life in a very positive way? *Okay, okay,* you might be saying, *I can see how becoming more responsible for my happiness could have a positive impact on my life, but this is a pretty tall order. How can I make this happen, especially since my habitual reactions to life seem to be so entrenched?* Again, great question! Let's look at everything we have been talking about during this second part of the book, and see if we can discover the answer.

First, it's important to find an overriding purpose or reason for everything we do and create a vision of what our "living on purpose" would look like. The questions: *What is my highest purpose here?* and *What qualities would I be expressing if I were living on purpose?* could help in this endeavor.

Highest Purpose?

Next, imagine a specific situation in which you would like to become more influential, responsible, or purposeful. You might look at some situation that you know isn't working for you, and therefore, one to which you would like to change your response. Now, ask yourself this question, *If I were living "on purpose" (or defining myself in ways that are congruent with my highest purpose), how would I be responding differently?* Then, create a mini-movie of what this more purposeful experience/response would look like.

Next, you want to become aware of what might get in the way of this purposeful creation. Of course, what I am referring to here is *our past*, or our habits, tendencies, old beliefs, or old ways of reacting that are incongruent with this highest purpose. Becoming aware of these old habitual reactions is important because:

"What we are unaware of controls us, What we become aware of, we can change."

Now we know what we *want*, and which habitual aspects of our past might (if left unchecked) sabotage our creating this experience. Our next step is to look for opportunities to practice. In other words, because we always become more skilled at whatever we practice, the next step is to look for situations where we can practice responding and/or, creating our experience of life "on purpose".

Purpose (Highest)
Our past

It's been my experience that if we look for them (and even if we don't), life will always give us plenty of opportunities to practice. As a matter of fact, some people think this is what life is, a series of situations designed for us to practice living "on purpose". I tend to agree, however, whether or not this is true, what is clear is that we never seem to run out of situations that give us a chance to become more purposeful.

The bottom line is that we are always practicing something. We will either find practicing our old habitual responses and behavior patterns, or we will look for opportunities to practice responding in ways that are congruent with our highest purpose. Our choice. Since you're reading this book, chances are good that you're wanting to be more purposeful, so let's look at how the wisdom of serenity can be supportive in this process.

Purpose
Our Past
Wisdom of Serenity

The problem, of course, is that most of us find ourselves caught up in, and then overwhelmed by, situations before we have a chance to practice being purposeful.

This is where the "Wisdom of Serenity" can be helpful. For example, what if we were doing such a good job of creating serenity in our lives, that we were able to enter these challenging situations more serenely, and, therefore, more intentionally? In other words, because we were creating a sense of centeredness and balance on a daily basis, we were able to enter each situation with more clarity and purpose.

If this were the case, our more serene foundation could help us accomplish several things. First, we would be more likely to recognize which aspects of the situation are beyond our ability to influence and stop trying to change them. Second, we might become more aware of the aspects of the situation we can influence (most of which are our thoughts, emotions, and behavior), and courageously take responsibility for bringing these in line with our highest purpose, or the quality of life we wish to create.

As we practiced this serenity, acceptance, courage, and change on a regular basis, my sense is that we would also gain more wisdom, and become more skilled in our ability to discern the difference between what we can and can't change. This would likely make us even more effective in the future. In fact, we could even use the words of "serenity" and "courage" to help us find the wisdom to know the difference between what we can change and what we can't. For example, we could say:

> "You know, it's going to take a lot of serenity for me
> to accept the fact that . . . . ."

This sentence will help us become aware of what to practice accepting. Additionally, we could also say:

> "You know, it's going to take a lot of courage for me
> to change the fact that . . . ."

This sentence could be helpful in giving us the wisdom to know what we might want to practice changing.

In addition, we could become more purposeful about the energy we choose to guide our behaviors and decisions (love versus fear), and tap into our sense of spirituality as a support. If we believe that God is love, and see our relationship with God as a source of our connection to this energy, we could ask: "What thought, belief, interpretation, expectation, emotion and or behavior could I choose here that would be congruent with my relationship with God?

Purpose
Our Past
Wisdom of Serenity
Energy

Finally, rather than waiting for some person or situation to change so that we will feel better, we could accept 100% responsibility for our continued ability to respond in this more purposeful manner. Part of this ability would be taking care of ourselves as if we are someone we loved. Can you see how employing these concepts would help us create a more fulfilling, joyous, powerful and quality-filled, experience of life?

Let me give you an example of someone living life in this purposeful, powerful way. You see, I believe that there are "master teachers" who live among us and, often, we miss their wisdom because we don't recognize them for the brilliant beings they are. These master teachers that I am referring to are our children (or children, in general). For instance, have you ever watched small children learning to walk?

They are very clear about their purpose, and they are completely immersed in living that purpose in the present moment. Often, as they take their first step, you can see in their eyes how they're marveling at what they've accomplished. Then, because they have yet to master the art of balance, they generally fall down. However, because they are so focused on their purpose, they don't see this as their failure. That is, they don't lay there and think, *I'm so embarrassed. People are looking at me. I'm a failure at walking. I guess I will just worm around on the floor for the rest of my life. Oh, poor, pitiful me.* No, because they are focused on their purpose (what they want, versus what's wrong with them, they are able to see their "mis/takes" as good information, and even look forward to trying again, which they will generally do very quickly.

They might even be thinking, *Great! Now I know that*

when I take a step and lean too far in that direction, I fall over! Great information! Whatever they're thinking, however, they generally pull themselves up again and, knowing that leaning in one direction doesn't work, they might lean the other way, which of course has them falling again, this time in another direction. However, these teachers are very wise. They don't lay there and blame the environment. They don't think, *It's this floor! That's why I can't walk. Who's in charge of this floor? It's their fault!* No. Again, because they are so focused on what they want to learn and are caught up in their love of learning, they see their "failures" as valuable information.

In addition, they seem to accept the fact that this is a learning process, and that it will take some time. Moreover, they are courageously and continuously attempting to influence this process as, time and time again, they pull themselves up, try to walk, and fall down. Eventually, however, due to their desire to walk, love of learning, and willingness to take 100% responsibility for their progress, *they **will** learn to walk.*

In other words, their ability to apply what they learn by risking and making "mis/takes," results in their ability to find the balance they need to move forward on their own two feet in a more natural, effective way. Pretty impressive, don't you think? Can you see how this process might be worth learning? If so, you might thank those wise teachers you find yourself interacting with for their wisdom, and look to see what else they can teach you (I understand they love hugs).

As you may have noticed, I like to turn the concepts that I use and recommend into acronyms. My hope is that they become more memorable in this form. The first model spelled BRAIN and this one spells POWER.

Purpose
Our Past
Wisdom of Serenity
Energy
Responsibility

Put this together with the BRAIN model, and you have BRAIN POWER, which represents both our ability to become more effective when we find ourselves in the middle of stressful situations . . . and how to create our life so that we find ourselves in fewer and fewer stressful situations in the first place. How do these models work together? That's what Part III is designed to address.

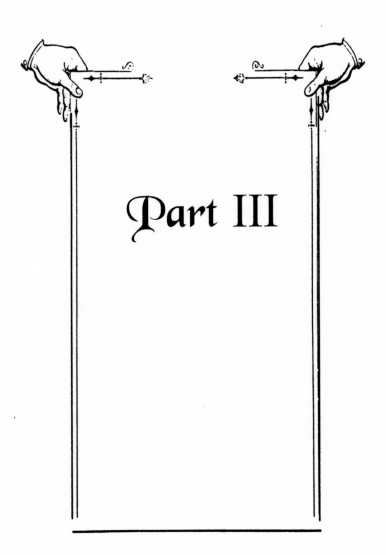

Part III

Chapter 9

Putting It All Together

U p to this point, we have only discussed the BRAIN and POWER models separately and, if you wish, you may continue to think of them that way. However, because both models offer ways of becoming more influential in our lives, I believe that they can be used together to become even more powerful. For example, the BRAIN model doesn't have to be limited to what can be done when we find ourselves in the middle of a stressful situation. It can be used as a precursor to dealing with situations (much like the concept of the wisdom of serenity in the POWER model).

Let's imagine you are about to go through a challenging situation. You can become more influential in terms of how you define yourself by going through the BRAIN model first. You might take some time prior to entering the situation to focus on your breathing, saying the word "relax" to yourself as you exhale. This ensures that your neo-cortex is in control versus the emotional and/or fight-or-flight parts of your brain. You can then ask yourself how would you like to be feeling and imagine a time in the past when you felt, and/or, responded this way. Then you can create a vision of how you would be responding if you were able to bring these feelings into this upcoming situation. If you have never responded the way you want to respond this time, you can still create a vision of how you would like to be, and then use this situation as an opportunity to practice. This is the value of purposeful serenity.

In fact, the more you create a sense of purposeful serenity as a precursor to life, in general, the more influential you are likely to become in all aspects of your life. For example, you could practice the BRAIN model each morning. Before you get out of bed, you could pause, take a few deep breaths saying the word "relax" to yourself as you exhale. Then, ask yourself how you would like to feel this morning and vividly imagine a time when you felt this way. You could then picture going through your morning feeling (being) the way you have just imagined. Can you see how this might have a positive impact on the quality of your experience? You will actually be defining who you are/want to be and then practicing bringing this purposeful self-definition to life!

How about during the day? Can you see how pausing to breathe, relax, and become clear about how you want to "be" (how you want to think, feel, act, etc.) several times during the day might be supportive? Remember, habits are habitual and old patterns can become ruts. This is all about becoming aware of what your experience of life would look like if you were living "on purpose," and then practicing these new ways of being until they become habits.

By the same token, the BRAIN model can be very effective when your purpose is sleep. Almost all of us have trouble going to sleep now and then, and I believe that the reason is that we have never been taught how. When it is time to go to sleep, most of us just lie down and impatiently wait for sleep to "happen." When it doesn't, or as we are waiting, many of us use this "spare time" to begin worrying about what we did, or didn't do today, and/or what we have to do tomorrow. This is often unproductive because, (a) what we really need at this time of the night is sleep, and (b) we are worrying about situations that aren't happening, and therefore there's nothing we can do about them. Plus, as we have discussed, when we worry our brain produces fight-or-flight chemicals (adrenaline, nor-adrenaline, and cortisol). These hormones are actually designed to wake us up!

Instead of actively worrying, and passively waiting to "fall asleep" (even the phrase implies that we can't influence the process), what if we began to focus on our purpose or the experience of life we want to create, . . . sleep? We could do this by breathing deeply three to five times and saying the word "relax" to ourselves on the exhale. We could then ask ourselves how would we like to be feeling? My guess is words like "sleepy "and "drowsy" would come to mind. Then, we could remember a time in our past when we were actually feeling sleepy and drowsy which would trigger our brain to release the same hormones and/or chemicals that it has released in the past and, most likely, we would "fall" asleep. However, this time we would be purposefully influencing the chemicals in our brain to produce the "fall".

The main point here is that the BRAIN model doesn't have to be reserved just for dealing with stressful situations. You can use this process in as many ways as you can imagine, and . . .the more you use the model, or the more you practice this process, the more skillful you will become, and the more influential you can be in creating your experience of life.

In fact, given that one aspect of the BRAIN model is about asking more purposeful questions (i.e. *How would I rather be feel-*

ing? versus *What's wrong with these people?*), we could use this opportunity to incorporate the POWER model into the process. For example, after breathing and relaxing, we could begin to ask ourselves the question *How would I be feeling if I were living "on purpose?"* or *How do I want to define myself in this situation?* We could then become aware of what aspects of our past (habits, etc.) were incongruent with this purpose so that we don't find ourselves falling into these old patterns of thought and behavior.

We would already be creating serenity (by breathing and relaxing), and so we could add to this by becoming clear about what aspects of the situation we wanted to practice accepting, and what aspects we wanted to change. Further, we could decide what energy we wanted to use to guide our thoughts, emotions, and behaviors during this process (love versus fear), and what we would be doing if we were coming from love (generally, what we would recommend to our best friend and what is congruent with our relationship with God). Finally, we could decide to take 100% responsibility for implementing this process versus waiting for the situation, or some person in the situation to change. This would give us very valuable information about how we wanted to create our experience of life, and we could begin to practice this creative process, noticing what worked and what didn't, doing more of what works and less of what doesn't.

Again, what we are talking about is being as influential and purposeful as possible in creating our experience of life and our definition of who we are. We have already discovered that what we believe (and think, and imagine), affects the chemical make-up of our body (remember the lemon and our sexual fantasies?). Further, this chemical change happens whether the experience we are imagining is actually happening at that moment or not. Therefore, as we are able to imagine more positive ways of being, we generally create a corresponding positive effect on our body (serenity), which then allows us to accept more of what we can't change, and change what we can.

In some sense, what we are talking about is bringing more love to our life. However, in order for this to happen, we must learn to let go of fear, because fear can't create love. Can you see how paradoxical this is? In order to regain control (or influence) in our lives, we must be willing to let go of the energy that we have used in the past to maintain control - fear. If love is what we want, we must be willing to trust (which means use, or consult) that energy as a guide. It's somewhat like snow-skiing. In order to ski smoothly (and enjoy the experience), we must first overcome the fear of pointing our skis downhill. In one sense, our challenge is to lose control (to gravity) in order to gain control or ski.

This reminds me of an experience I had when I was getting my master's degree. The opportunity came up for some of us in the program to go through what is known as a ROPES course. ROPES stands for Reality Oriented Physical Experience Services, which is really a fancy name for an obstacle course designed to build self-confidence and team cohesion.

The purpose of going through the course (which I would highly recommend) is to learn how to work with others, and overcome your individual fears. The final "challenge" on this course came at the end of the second day. The element was affectionately referred to as the "pamper pole" (so called because often we need pampers when we find ourselves at the top). The "pamper pole" was a forty-five foot telephone pole, and the object was to climb the pole, and then jump off.

Now, of course, no one was allowed off the ground without a helmet and a safety harness, so that even if we fell, we would be perfectly safe. However, as I climbed the pole, even though I wasn't someone who was generally afraid of heights, I felt anything but safe. I remember at that time of my life, I had heard a song by a composer named Kate Wolf called, "Give Yourself to Love." The chorus of the song went, *Give yourself to love, if love is what you're after. Open up your heart to the tears and laughter, and just give yourself to love - Give yourself to love*

I really liked the song because it spoke of what I believe we must do if, indeed, we want to create a more loving life; we must trust in, or give ourselves to that energy. I also remember that during that time in my life, whenever I was frightened, I would think of that song to remind myself of what was important and it seemed to help. As it happened, the group that I was in was running late that second day, and instead of ending at around 6 p.m. we were beginning to do the "pamper pole" at around 8. It was evening, and the scene was lit only by the moon and stars.

So, here I am, climbing a forty-five foot telephone pole *in the dark* and, as you might imagine, I was singing, "Give Yourself to Love" to myself as, convincingly as possible. When I got to the top, I recognized that my next challenge was to stand up on the top of the pole. If you can't imagine what the top of a telephone pole looks like, it's about the size of an eight-inch round saucer. Now remember, I was fully protected by a safety harness which was being anchored by my teammates and a certified, experienced "ROPES" instructor, so I was never in any danger. However, just as we are rarely in any real danger when we are worrying about all the things that we imagine might happen to us in life, our mind reacts to our fear, not necessarily to what is real.

Once I was able to stand up on top of this (now swaying) telephone pole, the *real* "challenge" became apparent. About six feet out and six feet up was a trapeze bar. My mission (if I decided to accept it) was to leap from the top of the pole and catch the trapeze. It was truly to be a leap of faith. Faith that my team wouldn't let me fall. Faith that the harnesses were secure and the ropes were strong enough to hold me. But most of all, faith in some energy other than fear. Fear was saying *Are you crazy? Get your-self back down that pole the same way you came up, and let this be a lesson to you to never try anything stupid like this again!#@%!*

There comes a time in many of our lives when we have to choose what we are going to trust as a guide for our decisions, what we are afraid of, or what we know; the voice of truth or fear. If you haven't had the chance to make this decision prior to an event such as the "pamper pole," this experience is designed to give you the opportunity to choose.

The truth was, I was safe and I knew it. In fact, I was more likely to get hurt climbing back down the pole than jumping, and being lowered to the ground by my teammates. My choices were clear: trust in fear or truth, self-confidence, or self-doubt. I remember very consciously making that choice. I decided to take the leap of faith. I crouched down, and with every bit of strength my trembling legs could muster, I pushed myself off the pole and toward the trapeze.

As I left the pole, I wasn't sure if I had jumped far enough to catch the trapeze. To my amazement, however, I recognized that it didn't matter. Whether I caught the bar or not, I now knew I was safe because I had not listened to fear. I had pushed through the belief that fear would keep me safe, and trusted truth and those around me. *I was free.*

Now, this isn't about whether you should go jump off a telephone pole. Remember, I had chosen to do the ROPES course for very specific reasons. I wanted to be there. In fact, the experience was very congruent with my purpose (as a psychologist), which was learning to help others push through their fears. The "pamper pole" was the culmination of two days of learning about myself and my teammates, and going through many other experiences and many hours of training which prepared me to make that jump.

I have told you this story because, to me, this represents our choice and our challenge. Do we cling to the energy of fear to stay safe or take the leap of faith necessary to recreate our lives more purposefully? Do we continue to trust the energy that we have used to survive, and therefore, continue to refer to our "map of avoidance" for guidance, or are we willing to "lose control"(let go of fear) and courageously be who we are (create our map of authenticity) in order to gain control of our lives?

It's as if many of us have spent the majority of our existence in a canoe, furiously paddling against the current of a very powerful river. We are afraid that if we "lose control," we will be swept away by the current and crashed against the rocks. We may even have a very convincing movie continuously playing in our minds to remind us of this horrible fate.

The problem is, however, that if we spend our lives fighting the current, we will only know struggle and eventually we will die exhausted, having never moved from one spot. However, if instead, we are willing to turn our canoe into the current and yes, momentarily, lose control, we can then take the paddle we have been using to fight the current and use it as a rudder to purposefully navigate around the rocks. We might even begin to enjoy the journey, allowing the current to take us downstream while we choose which side of the river we wish to experience. From my perspective, the current is love, and we can either spend our lives fighting it, or joining it and use its power to define who we are and take us where we want to go.

Now, the good news is that to accomplish this transfer of

power from fear to love (or whatever you would like to call it), we don't really have to "get rid of" anything. In fact, to see fear as the enemy, and begin to fight it or plot its assassination is only fearing fear (which just reinforces its influence and importance). The truth is that, as a natural response, fear is very valuable in any fight-or-flight situation. Moreover, even when we find ourselves feeling afraid in situations where no real threat exists, we can use fear in the service of purpose, serenity, and love. Just as we have learned to use the sensation of stress as a valuable signal that something needs to change, we can use the experience of fear to signal a return to love as a guide for what to do next.

I say "return" because I believe that this energy (love) is our essence, or "who we are" when we are born. Some of us have been fortunate enough to grow up in environments where this natural essence could evolve and be nurtured and nourished and, therefore, we may have an easier time using love as a guide. For those people, the "map of authenticity" is easier to create, because they have been allowed to be who they are (or live authentically) all along. Many of us, however, learned to distrust love and truth (and, therefore, distrust who we really are) and instead, learned to trust fear.

We did this because in our past, to trust in what was called love, or to say the truth may have been dangerous. Therefore, we became very good at using our fear of being hurt (physically or emotionally) to create our "map of avoidance," and we have been referring to this map in some form or another ever since. It's as if we are born as pure love, and then we learn that shining our light of love and truth (which means being who children naturally are, spontaneous, playful, inquisitive, honest, etc.) may not have been welcomed by everyone in our environment. In fact, early in our lives, most of us are given the message to hide who we are and become who others want us to be. Because this admonition or edict is linked to our getting the love we so desperately want and need, we are often willing participants in this process.

It's almost as if our light is too bright or incongruent with the environment in which we find ourselves. Therefore, as we grow up, we are given a costume to hide those parts of us that they (parents, guardians, society, etc.) don't like, so that we can appear to become who they want or need us to be. This costume may even have a mask frozen in the expression they want or need us to wear.

Now, for a while, this seems to work fairly well, and we even may participate in weaving our map of avoidance into this costume, because it's designed to help us fit into (or survive, as the case may be), our family. In other words, we might even come to see those parts of us that seem to "cause problems" (such as our playfulness and frankness) as "problematic," and begin to distrust, or even fear these parts, because they seem to keep us from getting what we want.

Eventually, however, because the wearing of this costume (hiding who we are out of fear) becomes such an integral part of our learning about life and the world, we may forget that we are hiding anything, and begin to believe that *we are the costume.*

The problem here is that the disguise is designed to fit a child, (just like our map of avoidance is about childhood) and therefore, as we grow into adults, it starts to become ill-fitting, constraining and restrictive. Unfortunately, because we have forgotten that we are even wearing a costume, we are confused as to why our lives don't seem to be working.

Now, in my opinion, this is the good news because our discomfort with being other than who we really are can be a valuable signal that something needs to change. That is, we can begin to let go of this costume, or map of avoidance and begin to construct a map of authenticity, where we re-discover and celebrate those parts of us that we may have had to hide in our past. . . those parts that are more about love than fear . . . those parts that are congruent with who we really are.

This has been my reason for writing this book, not to tell you what to do or how to think, but to help you respond and thus define yourself more purposefully, lovingly, and authentically

. My hope is that you have read some things here that made sense to you. For example, did the *Cycle of Stress* seem somewhat familiar? If so, can you imagine how we might find ourselves feeling out of control, tense and asking questions like, "What's wrong with them or me?" as a result of that cycle? Can you also imagine how, as we continue this cycle, we might find ourselves worrying more about life in general, and as a result, begin to feel even more out of control, tense etc.? If so, does the idea of breathing purposefully and saying "relax" (or some other meaningful phrase) as you exhale (allowing our neo-cortex to regain control) seem like a good way to begin to break this cycle? Further, can you see how asking ourselves questions that we really do want the answer to could be supportive of us in creating the experience of life we desire?

Questions like:
- How would I *rather* be feeling?
- Is what I'm worrying about happening now?
- Is how I am responding to this situation congruent with who I really am and/or how I want to define myself?
- What is my highest purpose in this situation? Or what are the qualities, characteristics, and/or behaviors I would be practicing if I were living "on purpose"?
- What aspects of my past (habits, learned beliefs, etc.) are incongruent with my purpose?

- How can creating more serenity in my life be supportive of living my life "on purpose"?
- What would be valuable for me to practice accepting during this process?
- What will I need courage to change in order to become who I want to be?
- What is the energy (love or fear) that I want to use as a guide for my thoughts, emotions, and behaviors?
- How would tapping into my spirituality be supportive of this vision?
- How is my choice of what to trust or how to be, congruent with my relationship with God?
- How can I take 100% responsibility for my *ability to respond* to life during this process?
- What would I recommend to my best friend to support him or her in living "on purpose?"

You may have noticed that much of the material presented throughout this book has been in the form of questions, such as those listed above. My frequent use of questions is purposeful, because I believe that we each have the answers within ourselves, and that if we ask ourselves purposeful questions, we can create an authentic life that we will love.

Living the answers to these questions then has us living "on purpose" or practicing the qualities that we believe would be most congruent with how we want to define ourselves and the quality of life we wish to create. Regardless of whether you choose some of these questions or create your own, there is one that I would definitely encourage you to continue asking, *"Do I wish to use love or fear as a guide in creating this moment, and in creating my life?"*

As you know by now, I am a big proponent of the energy of

love. I don't believe that fear is a valuable guide unless it is a biological response, triggered by our autonomic nervous system to a situation in which we must either fight or escape (fight or flight). Fear in any other form is like a shadow on the wall.

If we cup our hand into the right shape and cast this shadow on a wall, it will look very frightening (like fear). Further, if we try to run away, it will follow, and even get bigger (like fear). However, if we were to take a light (such as love) and shine it on the shadow, the shadow will disappear. Because all along, the shadow has never been more than a blockage of the light.

What if love is like light? A force that when focused upon a fear makes it disappear, because the fear is only an absence, or blockage of love? What if one of the reasons we find ourselves feeling less afraid when we are around truly loving people is that these multiple sources of love (and light) make our shadows, or fears disappear?

Funny thing about light. It only becomes visible when it encounters some form of matter. For example, light can travel through space for millions of miles, however, unless it encounters something to reflect this energy, it will remain unseen. Almost as if both the light *and* whatever it encounters are necessary to produce the experience of illumination.

I wonder if this mirrors the relationship between us and love, that we are partners and both necessary to each other? Perhaps our reason for being on the planet is to allow the energy of love to shine on all our fears, on all of our shadows cast by our costumes and disguises. We could even take responsibility for bringing these fears into the light and have them disempowered and disappear. In addition, we could practice living authentically, being truly who we are, congruent with our purpose, taking care of ourselves as we would take care of someone we love.

As we do this, we become beacons of light and love, and we begin to see through the disguises of others, seeing them (and ourselves) as the brilliant beings that we all are. I wonder if all of this is what it means to become . . . enlightened? What do you think?

Epilogue

fter this book was written, but before I sent it to the printer, I had lunch with my ex-spouse, Sharon Crawford. Sharon had been digging in the attic of her parents' home in a small town in northeast Texas where we both grew up, and had found several old suitcases that belonged to my parents. She was kind enough to call me and ask if I wanted them, and, of course, I said yes.

After I got the suitcases home, my wife Georgia and I were enjoying looking at all the old pictures and newspaper clippings from before I was born, through the year, 1972, when my parents died. In one of those suitcases was a yellowed newspaper clipping from a small town in northeast Texas. It was an article written by my father, Burton Crawford entitled, *Alcoholics Anonymous Is Force In Molding Lives.* As we read the yellowed print, both Georgia and I were moved, touched, impressed, and astonished by what we saw. I think you will see why when you read Dad's words.

The clipping didn't have a date on it, but it had to be written sometime after 1947 because that's when Dad joined AA. Still, keep in mind that, even if this was written sometime in the early 1950's, much of what we speak of today in terms of the mind-body connection, and the degree to which we create our own reality, was not part of that culture.

One thing this article does demonstrate is the degree to which our lives can be influenced by the environments we grow up in, and how fortunate I was to have grown up in an AA home. I have added the words in parentheses to give you some idea of how closely my father's thoughts about AA mirror my philosophy of life.

Alcoholics Anonymous Is Force In Molding Lives. Editor's note: This is the last of brief daily articles written by a local member of Alcoholics Anonymous, Burton Crawford, who will speak at the Loyal Men's Bible class, at the First Christian Church, Sunday at 9:45 a.m.

One of the most important lessons we learn in Alcoholics Anonymous (and life) is that whatever comes to us in the way of happiness or unhappiness, health or sickness, abundance or lack, we attract by our own consciousness. When things go wrong the human tendency is to place the blame on circumstances or luck, (or ourselves), but the real truth is that we have "gone wrong" somewhere in our thinking about life (choosing fear over love as a guide).

With most of us the transformation of our thoughts about ourselves and life is not an immediate but a gradual process, for the habits of years are not easy to change in the twinkling of an eye. This apparently slow process brings discouragement and the inclination to give up to many beginners in AA, for appearance rarely changes overnight. But each victory gained, however small, is a step towards the goal of a richer, happier, more satisfying life.

Each time we replace an unloving thought with a loving one we are building a consciousness of love into our life. Each time we replace a thought of fear and doubt with one of faith and confi-

dence we are changing the pattern of our life. Each time we affirm health and abundance instead of talking sickness and lack we are becoming firmly established in the consciousness of life and richness.

A heart that is filled with love and expresses this love in kindness, consideration, and tolerance toward all attracts loving and happy experiences. A consciousness that is filled with thoughts of life and strength and vitality brings into manifestation a strong healthy body. A mind that acknowledges the everywhere presence of God (love) establishes prosperity and order in outer affairs.

The purpose of our 24-hour program in Alcoholics Anonymous (and this book) is to give us at least one constructive thought upon which to construct each day. Every time we manage to replace one negative thought with an affirmative one we make an important advance in spiritual growth. To build constructive, uplifting ideas into our consciousness is like mastering a subject by daily study. Attainment may seem far away at first, but each day's application brings its reward, and sometimes gradually, sometimes suddenly, we realize that we have achieved our goal.

The power to transform our lives lies within us. The Spirit of God (Love) is with us to uphold us and sustain us, and as we work with Him, the way is made clear and easy for us. We are assured of continual growth and life is transformed and blessed.

I have always been aware, even as a small child, how important my father was to the AA community. In fact, I have many vivid memories of people relating stories of their lives and how they owe whatever success they might have achieved, to him. I was always touched by their stories and, at the same time, somewhat saddened because I couldn't say the same thing. As I read and re-read these words, however, I am beginning to realize just how much my life has been influenced by my dad's work and ideas.

I still wish he had been home more, hugged me more, not waited until he was dying to tell me he loved me, and, in general, given Mom and me more of that powerful love and energy he so effortlessly gave to those in AA. Yet, as I hold the written pieces of his life, I find the compass that confirms my direction. My father, in his quest to touch others, has also left me his love. Thanks, Dad.

Appendix

Recommended Reading List

Bach, Richard, *One*. New York:
William Morrow & Co.,1988.

Bach, Richard, *Bridge Across
Forever*. New York: William
Morrow & Co., 1984

Bach, Richard, *Illusions*. New
York: Dell Publishing Co.,
1977.

Bach, Richard, *Jonathan
Livingston Seagull*. New
York: Avon Books, 1970

Bach, Richard, *Running From
Safety.* New York: William
Morrow & Co., 1994.

Benson, Herbert, M.D., *Timeless
Healing: The Power & Biology
of Belief.* New York, NY: Scribner,
1996.

Covey, Stephen R., *The 7 Habits of Highly
Effective People.* New York, NY:
Fireside, 1990.

Goleman, Daniel, Ph.D., *Emotional
Intelligence: Why It Can
Matter More Than I.Q..*
New York: Bantam Books,
1995.

Jampolsky, Gerald, M.D., *Love
Is Letting Go Of Fear.* Berkeley,
CA: Celestial Arts, 1979.

Jampolsky, Gerald, M.D., *Teach
Only Love.* New York:
Bantam Books, 1983.

Rodegast, Pat and Stanton,
Judith, *Emmanuel's Book.*
New York: Bantam Books,
1985.

Walsch, Neale Donald, *Conversations With God.* Charlottesville, VA: Hampton Roads Inc., 1996

Seligman, Martin, Ph.D., *Learned Optimism.* New York: Simon & Schuster, Inc. , 1990.

Questions to Keep In Mind

- How would I rather be feeling?
- Is what I'm worrying about happening now?
- Is how I am responding to this situation congruent with who I really am and/or how I want to define myself?
- What is my highest purpose in this situation? Or what are the qualities, characteristics, and/or behaviors I would be practicing if I were living "on purpose"?
- What aspects of my past (habits, learned beliefs, etc.) are incongruent with my purpose?
- How can creating more serenity in my life be supportive of living my life "on purpose"?
- What would be valuable for me to practice accepting during this process?
- What will I need courage to change in order to become who I want to be?

- What is the energy (love or fear) that I want to use as a guide for my thoughts, emotions, and behaviors?
- How would tapping into my spirituality be supportive of this vision? And/or, how is my choice of what to trust or how to be, congruent with my relationship with God?
- How can I take 100% responsibility for my ability to respond to life during this process?
- What would I recommend to my best friend to support him or her in living "on purpose?"

About the Author

Bill Crawford, Ph.D. is a psychologist, organizational consultant, corporate trainer, and professional speaker currently residing with his wife and two children in Houston, Texas. His corporate clients include many of the Fortune 500, as well as professional associations and a variety of other organizations nationwide. He holds a Bachelors degree in Music Education, and both Masters and Doctoral degrees in Counseling Psychology from the University of Houston. In addition to being quoted in such diverse publications as *The New York Times*, *Investor's Business Daily* and *Cosmopolitan*, Dr. Crawford is also the creator and host of two PBS specials entitled *All Stressed Up & Nowhere To Go!* and *From Chaos to Calm: Dealing with Difficult People*. Known for his dynamic, entertaining, and yet practical presentations, Bill blends humor with concrete, "real world" suggestions to support individuals and organizations in reaching their personal and professional goals.

If you enjoyed the material in this book and believe that it would be valuable for others in your organization, Dr. Crawford is also known for his ability to impact audience on many other topics as well. The most popular are: Change • Conflict Resolution • Stress • Leadership • Creativity • Customer Service • Diversity • Dealing with Difficult People • Decision-Making • Team Building • Job Satisfaction • Negotiating • Problem-Solving • Effective Listening • Motivation • Setting Priorities • Self Esteem • Health/Wellness • Time Management • Activity-Based Learning with or w/o the ROPES • Personality Types • Building Consensus • Ethics • Spirituality • Parenting • Presentation/Speaking Skills • Living and Working "On Purpose." For descriptions of these presentations, please visit *www.billcphd.com* or call *888-530-8550*

Other Titles from
Bill Crawford, Ph.D.
and Humanics

COMING SOON

FROM CHAOS TO CALM: **Dealing with Difficult People**
ISBN 0-89334-356-0

HOW TO GET KIDS TO DO WHAT YOU WANT: **The Power and**
Promise of Solution-Focused Parenting
ISBN 0-89334-362-5

Order online at:

www.humanicspub.com

Printed in the United States
6053